OUT OF RANGE

Published by
S.S.T.S. Press
Currabinny, Carrigaline, Co. Cork
www.sstspress.com

A catalogue record of this book is available
from the British Library.

ISBN 978-0-9557738-0-8

Printed in Ireland by KWP Print & Design

This book is respectfully dedicated to the men and women of the Irish Naval Service, the Irish Air Corps and the Irish Coast Guard Helicopter Service, people whose honour ensures that they will always operate at the 'cutting edge' when something goes wrong.
And we know they will do it again and again ...

We make men without chests and expect of them virtue and enterprise.
We laugh at honour and are surprised to find traitors in our midst.

C.S. Lewis

To Finbarr and Nora

Acknowledgements

My principal advisor for this, my first novel, was Commander Mark Mellett, DSM, Irish Naval Service. Words cannot adequately describe my gratitude for the mountain of help he so generously and enthusiastically provided. Several other members of the Irish Naval Service also helped me greatly, especially in the technical aspects of the work and in facilitating the huge amount of research needed: Commander Hugh Tully, Lieutenant Commander Declan Power, Lieutenant Commander Martin Brett, Lieutenant Commander Jim Shalloo and the crew of LE *Niamh*, Lieutenant Commander Pearse O'Donnell and the crew of LE *Roisin*, Lieutenant Commander Charlie Lawn, Chief Petty Officer Muiris Mahon, Chief Petty Officer Nial Dunne, Petty Officer Joey Morrison, Leading Seaman Ross Gernon, Leading Seaman Colin Mulligan, Leading Seaman Stephen Deegan, Leading Seaman Derek Nagle, Leading Seaman Jerome McCarthy, Able Seaman David Jones.

To the crew of LE *Eithne* I would like to say a special 'thank you' for all your help.
I am grateful to Commodore Frank Lynch, Flag Officer Commanding Irish Naval Service (FOCNS), for his blessing in this project.

In fact, I would like to salute the Irish navy as a whole, for the courteous and professional way that they helped me gather the monumental amount of research needed for this book.

Special thanks to Colonel Paul Fry of the Irish Air Corps, also Commandant Brian Moynihan, Commandant Ron Verling, Corporal Jemma O'Donovan, Corporal Finbarr Cotter and Airman Willie Galligan (the crew of 'Casa 253')

I would like to pay tribute to the huge patience of Captain Jim Kirwan, the senior training captain of CHC Ireland, who time and again gladly fielded long technical phone calls and introduced me to the operation of large helicopters.
Lorna Siggins was right when she said: 'The people who do this work are not cut from the average cloth!'

In the Irish Coast Guard I would like to sincerely thank Chris Reynolds, who provided a great overview of the ICG and its crucial role.

It would be difficult to describe the enormous amount of help I received from Judy Welland, the long hours and the enduring patience. Thank you.

I am also indebted to the following people: Lorna Siggins (the *Irish Times*), Senator Eoghan Harris (*Sunday Independent*), Dave Flanagan (for his graphic design and jacket cover), Evelyn Wilson, Diarmuid Ó Drisceoil (who helped me navigate the literary world), Donal Ó Drisceoil, Catherine Foley, Breda Lymer, Ty Francis, Aonghus Meaney (copy editor), Ed Drennan, Richard Neill, Captain Simon Pearson (cruise liner skipper, SA), Commander John O'Driscoll, MBE (Royal Navy, ret.), Lieutenant Colonel John Hanlon (Irish Army), Captain Conor O'Donovan (helicopter pilot, Cork).

And finally to Eileen, Bobby, Ray, Lynda and Gary, whose love and support I could not be without.

Cast of principal characters

Irish Navy
Commodore Tom Garrett (Flag Officer Commanding Irish Naval Service (FOCNS)
Captain Alan Parle (CO Naval Base & Dockyard)
Commander Joe Lyden (Naval Intelligence)
Warrant Officer Ray Moran (Senior NCO Naval Base)
Lt Cdr Clare Collins (Personal Staff Officer to FOCNS)

LE *Eithne*
Commander Mike Ford (Commanding Officer)
Lt Cdr Jamie Morrisson (Executive Officer)
Lt Cdr Jimmy Casey (Engineering Officer)
Fl Lt Jim Angland (Helicopter Pilot)
Fl Lt Matt Connolly (Helicopter Pilot)
Lt Gerry Stewart (Gunnery Officer)
Sub Lt Neil Kennedy (Nav Officer)
Sub Lt Angela Hogan (Supplies Officer)
Lt John Kana (Royal New Zealand Navy)
Senior Chief John Morgan (Coxwain)
Chief Mulligan (Supplies Chief)
Chief Stephen Mackey (ERA)
Petty Officer John Ryan (Comms)
Petty Officer Mark Power (Bosun)
Petty Officer Tom Dunne (Supplies)
Leading Seaman Dan Kearney (Radar Operator)
Leading Seaman Denis O'Callaghan (Jaguar One Coxwain)
Leading Seaman David Moynihan (Jaguar Two Coxwain)
Leading Seaman Stephen Jones (Clearance Diver)
Able Seaman Tom Whelan (Lookout)
Able Seaman Bill Deasy

LE *Niamh*
Lt Cdr Charlie Keane (Commanding Officer)
Lt Michael Long (Executive Officer)
Petty Officer Gerry Stapleton (Clearance Diver/ex ARW)

Irish Air Corps
Commandant Brian Gould (Captain Casa 'Charlie 253')
Commandant Aidan Vallely (First Officer 'Charlie 253')

LE *Roisin*
Lt Cdr Joe Sorensen (Captain)
Lt Tony Kelly (Boarding Officer)
Chief Ray O'Donnell (2ic Armed Boarding Crew)
LS Peter Delaney (Rib Coxwain)

Irish Coast Guard MRCC
Colin Dowling (Duty Officer)

Irish Coast Guard Search and Rescue (SAR) Helicopter crews

Helicopter 'Romeo 22' Shannon
Captain Paul O'Sullivan (Captain 'Romeo 22)
First Officer Anne O'Donnell (First Officer 'Romeo 22')
Winch Operator Jim Carroll ('Romeo 22')
Winch Man John O'Donovan ('Romeo 22')

Helicopter 'Romeo 25' Sligo
Captain Cathal Langton (Captain 'Romeo 25')
First Officer David Horgan (First Officer 'Romeo 25')
Winch Operator Henry Leach ('Romeo 25')
Winch Man Finn Lawson ('Romeo 25')

The White House
The President
Admiral James Fischer (Director, National Security Agency)
General John Kowolski (Chairman of Joint Chiefs of Staff)
Admiral Frank Hughes (Chief of Naval Operations CNO)
Admiral Tom Kane (Commander in Chief, Atlantic Fleet)

USS *Samuel B. Roberts*
Commander Tom Turner (Commanding Officer)
Lt Lorraine Ellis (Weapons Officer)

Cruise Liner *American Princess*
Captain John Whiteman (Captain)
Scott Jablonsky (Passenger)
Marie Jablonsky (Passenger)
Doug Chambers (Passenger)
Loretta Chambers (Passenger)

Tug *Swiftsure*
Frank Blokland (Captain)
Piet Stam (First Officer)
Frans de Vries (Engineer)
Jan (Ship's Cook)
Johann (Deck Hand)

Al Qaida Operatives
Khalid (Intelligence Officer, Co-ordinator)
Mohammed (Sleeper agent, Amsterdam)
Abu (Bomb Maker)
Tarka
Jabir

Secret Intelligence Services (SIS) London
John Winthrop (Senior Agent)
James Calthorne (Agent)
Jeremy Aldridge (Agent)

Commander Mike Ford's Family
Cathy 'Cas' Ford (Mike's Wife)
Emma (Daughter)
James (Son)
Cormac (Son)
Tom Ford (Father)
Gretta Ford (Mother)
Cormac (Brother)
Bernie (Sister)

Smit Tak
Captain Johann Naaler (Senior Captain/Operations)

Amsterdam
Carla Blokland
Amy Blokland

Gardai
Chief Superintendent Barney Fitzgerald (Cork)
Chief Superintendent John Madigan (Galway)

New London
Joe Ellis
Marian Ellis

OUT OF
RANGE
SCOTLAND
NORTHERN
IRELAND
Sligo
REPUBLIC OF
IRELAND
IRISH SEA
Dublin
Galway
Porcupine
Bank
Shannon
ENGLAND
WALES
Cork
ATLANTIC
OCEAN

PROLOGUE

March 1977

It was savagely cold. Freezing north easterly weather brought almost arctic conditions down from the north. The imposing edifice of the Britannia Royal Naval College, high on a hill overlooking the river Dart, stood in silent testimony to one of the world's greatest naval powers, its red and grey stonework almost like a bulwark against the weather outside in the early morning frost. Here was the ultimate university in the world for naval officers, matched only in stature by the United States Naval Academy in Annapolis.

Mike Ford stood inside the main entrance of HMS *Britannia* pondering how he happened to be there ... how a boy from Rossaveal, a small harbour in County Galway in the west of Ireland, had made it to the hallowed halls of Britain's highest naval academy. He was here to learn, he knew that, but Mike Ford never considered anything to do with ships and the sea as a learning chore. He couldn't get enough of it. Born into a family whose past generations had worked the sea, he had it in his blood – and not just any old sea; his was the Atlantic. The ocean off the west coast of Ireland, which is rightly regarded as one of the most inhospitable places in the world, especially in winter. The Irish Navy, who patrol it, had offered him an officer cadetship, which was why he was standing where he was.

His midshipman training had begun five months previously. Having reported to the naval base at Haulbowline Island in Cork harbour, the first part of his course in military training began, and then it was off to the UK where he would join Britain's future finest, along with students from other selected navies of the world, to study the serious business of one day commanding a ship of his own. For the most part he liked studying in the college; the culture of the Royal Navy and its global reach contrasted sharply with his own navy, which was quite small at that time. He also liked mixing with the students from other countries, and his easy-going friendly manner made him popular in his class group.

But today Mike Ford had other things on his mind. Her name was Cathy, and to the nineteen-year-old navy cadet, she was beauty personified, although he still wondered, even after eleven months of knowing her, how he could be going out with someone who knew so little about the sea.

Cathy O'Donoghue was a land person. Her family were farmers from near the small village of Caherlistrane in County Galway, but Mike saw in her a sort of inner something that he was not able to fully understand. She was a trainee nurse in St Finbarr's hospital in Cork at the time they met. She had been celebrating her birthday with a group of work friends in Rearden's pub in Washington Street when Mike, along with two of his navy classmates, walked in. Inevitably, the two groups merged and Mike was taken, not just by her beauty, but also by the fact that she was from Galway. He had gone out with other girls before he met Cathy, but this was different. He knew that she was the one for him. It's just that, at nineteen, he wondered if he should even be having those sorts of feelings. Never mind, he told himself, he could work that one out some other day; today was going to be special.

Cathy had phoned him on the previous Wednesday evening to surprise him. She was coming over for the weekend to see him and luckily he was not rostered for duty. He planned to take her to the harbour area of Plymouth and show her an aircraft carrier and maybe even a submarine. Then, later in the evening, he would take her for a nice meal in a Chinese restaurant.

As he thought about the weekend, his mind went back to the telephone call. Although she had sounded enthusiastic, as she always did, he thought he detected that something was not right with her ... ah, maybe it was him. Still, he couldn't have been happier. Mike's taxi eventually arrived and whisked him the short distance into Dartmouth where he got on a bus to Plymouth airport. He had three full days off and to get this much time with Cathy was rare in this part of his training, and so he relished every minute of it. In his mind life was just about as perfect as it could be right now. His long-held dream of being accepted as a cadet into the Irish naval service had, to his great joy, come true, but also, unlike the four others in his cadet class, he had Cathy. He was sure she would be his lifelong partner, but, at nineteen, he imagined that people thought like that anyway.

At 1355 the British Airways Saab 340 turboprop from Cork entered the downwind leg of the pattern for Plymouth's short uphill runway 'one three'. Mike watched as the plane turned finals and landed. It seemed like forever until the shutdown was completed and the cabin door opened and there she was, the third passenger down the steps. Almost immediately, she saw Mike behind the glass front of the terminal building waving frantically. He could not wait to hug and kiss her, and he didn't care what other people thought. It took about ten minutes for the suitcases to be brought into the terminal before Cathy could make her way out into the arrivals hall.

'Hey Cas,' Mike called when she was in earshot of him, using his pet nickname for her. 'I've been up since six this morning, I couldn't sleep knowing you were coming.'

Cas hugged him tightly, almost tighter than ever before, he noticed … and longer. Then he felt it. The warm wet trickling of tears, which had landed on the side of his head, and now flowed down the side of his face.

'Its okay, babe,' he said, still holding her firmly. 'You know how much I love you Cas.'

'Mike … I have something to tell you.'

A cold shiver went through Mike Ford's sturdy frame. In the pause that ensued, Mike was sure he was about to hear Cathy say that she had a crippling or terminal illness, or maybe that she wanted to finish the relationship.

'Jesus Cas, what's wrong?' he asked, loosening his grip on her. He put his left arm around her and they moved to the almost empty airport cafeteria.

'Mike, there's only one way to say this to you.'

'What is it Cas, what's wrong?'

'I'm pregnant … I'm sorry Mike, I'm just …'

At that point Cathy O'Donoghue burst into uncontrollable floods of tears. There was an almost palpable silence for a few moments while both came to terms with the new reality of their relationship and also its implications. In his own mind Mike was, at that moment, somewhere between huge relief at not hearing what he himself was thinking and a massive feeling of responsibility at the overwhelming enormity of what he just heard. What would it mean? What should he do? Cas had obviously known about it for some period of time. God knows how long!

'Oh Jesus, what has she been feeling?' he thought.

Mike held Cas for what seemed like an age, still aware of the tears running down her face. His mind was racing uncontrollably. 'God, what am I going to do?'

In that moment his mind was frozen in a wasteland of uncertainty.

The number one engine in the Saab 340 spooled up again causing a din in the poorly insulated terminal. When the second one started Mike gently suggested to Cas that they should get a taxi into town. He had rented a room for the weekend in the Adelphi hotel in the Hoe area of Plymouth.

'Cas, what are we going to do? I mean, your family … my family, what are we going to tell them?'

'Whatever about your family Mike, there is no way on God's earth we could tell mine, the shame would be just too great for them. You have to understand, Mike, this would be the worst thing that could ever happen to my parents. The notion of having people talking about the O'Donoghue family whose daughter had just got pregnant would be a situation that they would never recover from.'

Mike, who had twice visited his girlfriend's parents' house outside Caherlistrane, could not figure it out. On the one hand, they seemed like very nice people, and yet, to him it was like Cas would be disowned or maybe cast out.

'Anyway,' said Cas, 'I have had plenty of time to think about this, and I think I can cover it up until seven months, and then a change of job will take me away for the rest of the time. My parents would not suspect anything if, after starting a new job, I didn't come home for two months.'

'Yeah, but what are we going to do then?'

Tears came to Cathy's eyes again.

'We don't have a choice Mike, we'll have to put the baby up for adoption.'

Mike sat there stunned, a sort of suspended animation sweeping over him.

'You have this all worked out, haven't you?' he said, looking at her.

'It's for the best Mike. I know it is. I went to a counsellor last week. She talked about all the possibilities, including the notion of me … us keeping the child. She said the most important consideration is the child, we have to do what is best for the baby.'

'I feel so helpless in this whole thing, Cas, and you seem so strong. What about us? Surely there is something we can do. I mean … I want to be with you always, I love you so much.'

'I feel the same as you Mike, and I have thought a lot about it. You need to look after your career, and so do I; otherwise we may resent each other in the future, and anyway, what would we do, give up our jobs and get married? How would we both feel in ten years' time? Would that be fair on the baby?'

Mike watched as the Saab gathered speed on the runway and noted the time, 1323, when the plane disappeared into the low overcast surrounding Plymouth. At that moment he resolved that, no matter what, he was going to marry Cathy O'Donoghue.

Seven months later, on a bright October day, Cathy gave birth to a beautiful baby girl. She immediately christened her with the name Marian, which was her mother's name. Two weeks after that, she asked Mike to come home, on a particular Friday, to sign the final adoption papers with her, and then it was all over. The adoption agency had found a couple 'from somewhere up the country' they told her, and they assured her that her beautiful baby daughter Marian would be well looked after.

For the rest of that fateful weekend, Cathy could not stop crying. The deep, searing and lonely pain of losing her baby was beyond the scope of rational understanding by anyone other than those who had had a similar experience. Along with that there was the interminable knowing, that her own mother and father and her brothers and sisters were blissfully unaware of any of these events. At some deep level of being, perversely, Cathy knew that she had to bear this terrible pain out of some sense of belonging.

Mike, on the other hand, was somewhat relieved that the process had come to an end, but at the same time he wondered whether or not they had made the right decision, when he saw the abject loss and pain etched on the face of the girl he loved. Maybe out of a sense of loving her, or never wanting her to suffer a loss like that again, he made up his mind in that moment that he would stand by her forever.

As the young midshipman flew back to the Royal Naval College in Dartmouth, he became aware of an almost primal feeling welling up in him, that somehow or other he had crossed a subconscious threshold into manhood. On the bus back to Dartmouth he began to realise the full import of the situation in terms of himself. His concern for Cas's awful pain had somehow clouded his own feelings, which were now flooding into sharp relief. 'This was his daughter also, his father and mother's granddaughter, his brothers' and sisters' niece … and now she's gone, never to be seen again! As he unpacked his bag in his room in the college he could feel tears begin to roll down his face.

Two years later, on a beautiful mid November morning, Mike, dressed in the uniform of an Irish Navy sub lieutenant, waited anxiously at the altar of St Joseph and Mary Immaculate Church in Caherlistrane, in the county of Galway, for his beautiful bride, Catherine O'Donoghue, to walk down the aisle on the arm of her father. As was the practice in many Irish villages at that time, quite a few of the local women had gathered outside the gates of the small church, ostensibly to wish the bride and groom well, but also to see the style, as it were. Just as the ceremony was about to end they saw eight men dressed in the smart uniform of the Irish Naval Service, armed with naval swords, coming out the main door of the church and promptly forming into two lines opposing each other. As Mike and Catherine appeared at the door, the officers of the guard of honour drew their swords in perfect synchronicity and elevated them so that the tips of each almost touched.

'Well now,' said one of the local women to the small group she was with, 'ya wouldn't see that too often round here.'

Plotting, Planning and People

2005

Amsterdam

The tray of food arrived at their table promptly. Khalid noticed the miniskirt on the waitress and came to the conclusion that it would definitely qualify for one of the shortest he had ever seen.

'You must live happily in this city, my brother?'

'Amsterdam has lots of sights and the people here are very friendly,' replied Mohammed. 'There are benefits to be had from living among the unbelievers,' he added.

'How are operations progressing elsewhere?' he asked.
Mohammed knew that the choice of location for this meeting was one of the safest in Holland. Dam Square was always full of tourists of all shades and colours and the constant noise would camouflage most conversations, if one were careful.

'Our brothers in Iraq do well, if only in small measure, but each time they exploit a weakness in our enemy, he closes the gap ruthlessly.'

'I have read the reports in the media,' replied Mohammed.
Khalid had been an intelligence officer for nearly seven years, moving from country to country. At this point in his life there was nowhere he could call home. He knew that he could never again stay in one place for longer than a few days, lest his cover be compromised. He also knew that he would not be happy doing anything else ... and that was okay. Was that not his path in life? Was Allah Himself not the great protector of all believers? No, he had no fear, just a strong desire to be professional in his service to the great prophet.

He was not naïve, he knew exactly who he was up against. America would lethally punish any carelessness on his part, like it had done to his fellow brethren who were not as careful as he was.

He had travelled by train from Hamburg to Amsterdam to meet with Mohammed, his German passport and drivers licence a virtual guarantee of safe passage anywhere in mainland Europe, as long as he did not call attention unnecessarily upon himself. One wrong move, one careless word, could spell disaster. He had received a coded e-mail from Mohammed a week and a half ago to meet.

Mohammed had been a sleeper agent in Holland for three years and was well trusted by Khalid. One of a growing number of such agents scattered around the world, his main objective was not just to watch out for the potential for a 'spectacular' against the Great Satan, but also to keep his eyes open for seemingly routine or even useless information, which maybe could be used elsewhere.

'So what news do you have for me, my friend?'

Naval Base, Haulbowline Island, Cork

Lt Cdr Jamie Morrisson approached the gangway to board the LE *Eithne*, the flagship of the Irish Navy, which was alongside the oil wharf in the Haulbowline Island naval base. This was to be his first patrol as executive officer, or XO in navy speak. His appointment as second-in-command of the ship had come through from naval headquarters only two weeks before, but to Jamie it was not before time. He had been deskbound in a shore appointment for the last eighteen months, and he was really looking forward to going back to sea. Especially in *Eithne!* ... he had been her gunnery officer three years ago.

'Morning sir, welcome back.'

'Good morning senior chief,' replied the new XO. 'It's good to be back, how is this lady behaving?'

'Pretty good sir, we got a partial comms upgrade before our last Canadian patrol, and as you can see our new caley davit launch and recovery systems are finally operational.'

The caley single point davit system had been fitted to the navy's two new *Roisin* class offshore patrol vessels and were so successful that it was decided to retro fit them on *Eithne* also. For a navy whose number of boardings per annum ranked among the highest in the world, this was an excellent addition to any of the ships. Its secret was its simplicity.

'I think the skipper is planning some launch and recovery exercises, together with boarding evaluation, next week to get the crew up to speed.'

'What are those welders doing, senior chief, they seem to be working dangerously close to the JP 5 fuel tanks?' asked *Eithne's* new XO, referring to the aviation fuel tanks aboard *Eithne* for her Dauphin helicopter.

'They are sir, the tanks have been drained and those welders are increasing the capacity. Skyfuel are coming down on Monday to top them up again,' replied Senior Chief John Morgan, *Eithne's* coxswain.

'Okay senior chief. By the way, when is Cdr Ford due back aboard?'

'Monday sir, 1300,' replied the highest ranking non commissioned officer aboard.

Mike Ford sat at the kitchen table at home drinking tea while reading the morning paper. He was on four days' leave, which ended at 0700 on Monday morning. But today was Saturday, and he had plans to take Cas out to dinner that evening. Their twenty-eighth wedding anniversary was due to occur the following Friday, at which time Mike would be somewhere out in the Atlantic ocean on patrol, and so dinner and a little celebration before he left on Monday seemed like a good idea.

'Well good morning sleepy head,' he uttered to his very sleepy looking wife with a half smile on his face. Cas had appeared in the kitchen in her dressing gown rubbing her eyes and looking a little the worse for wear.

'You look like you had a good night with your work colleagues?'

'Yeah, I did, but the girls I work with are mad, or else I must be getting old. I wanted to leave at two thirty but by the time I was in the taxi it was three thirty.'

'I never even felt you get into bed, not to mind come in the door, and I was in bed quite early,' said Mike, pulling back the chair a little so that his wife could sit on his knees. 'I played Monopoly with Emma and Dave, and when the game ended early I decided to leave the lovebirds a bit of space.' Mike's daughter had decided to bring her new boyfriend home and a board game seemed like a good idea. They were both attending college in Dublin and Emma usually came home every second weekend.

'So tell me, what is he like?' inquired Cas while kissing her husband. 'He seems to be a nice guy. He comes from Waterford and he is one year ahead of Emma in college.'

'Hmmm,' uttered Cas and then continued, 'so were you enjoying the peace, reading the paper and drinking your tea all by yourself?'

'Yeah but you are now in my direct line of vision so I guess I can't read anymore. Anyway, I was finished and you're much nicer looking than the paper.'

'Anything interesting in it?'

'Yes, in fact there is,' replied Mike, opening the middle pages of the paper. 'It seems the government have finally decided to go ahead with the procurement of that ocean-going tug which the navy will operate … sometime early next year. In the meantime they are going to lease one temporarily from a Dutch company, complete with crew who will operate it themselves for the duration.'

'That must be good news for the navy?'

'Good news for the country more like it,' replied Mike. 'If a 250,000 ton oil tanker gets into difficulty near any of our coasts we must have the capability to tow it offshore, otherwise we risk having a similar fate as France and Portugal. It's a good thing the *Kowloon Bridge* was carrying iron ore and not crude oil.'

Mike was referring to recent oil spillages from tankers, which had caused huge damage to the beaches of these very tourism-dependent countries. The Irish coast also had its share of spillages, although much smaller by comparison. However, it was when the iron ore carrier, the *Kowloon Bridge,* was sunk in November 1986 that the Irish government began to seriously acknowledge the possibility of a devastating spillage destroying the coast, which was such a vital component of the country's tourism industry. The ship was en route from Quebec to the River Clyde in Scotland, loaded with 160,000 tons of iron ore consigned to the British Steel Corporation. She put in to Bantry Bay to carry out repairs to cracks that had appeared in her deck. These were sustained during heavy Atlantic weather. While there she lost her main anchor and it was decided to sail her out of the bay, but then she lost her steerage and began to drift in continuing heavy seas. A decision was taken to abandon ship and the twenty-eight crew members were winched off. The now completely helpless ship was then driven aground, by gale force winds, on to the Staggs Rock, a couple of miles east of Baltimore on the County Cork coast. She subsequently broke her back on the rocks and started to leak her 1,200 tons of bunker fuel, which itself caused a serious enough pollution problem in the area. However, had the Kowloon Bridge been an oil tanker the consequences were almost unthinkable. And it was this realisation which had exercised minds.

'Where will the tug be based?' asked Cas.

'Almost certainly, Cork,' replied her husband.

'I see,' said Cas. 'By the way, what time have you booked the table for tonight?'

'For you, my darling, eight thirty.'

Amsterdam

'As you know, Khalid, the Americans have all but stopped coming to the Middle East and Mediterranean areas. They are not fools. They know that our potential to mount a large 'spectacular' against them is far greater in those areas than it would be in their accursed homeland, where their security level has increased to the point where it is very difficult for us to even consider a strike. For example, Americans are very fond of cruising in big ocean liners. For years one of their most favoured destinations for this activity has been the Med. This is no longer the case. This market suffered a big knock down and would have collapsed completely had the tour operators not offered Europeans heavily discounted cruises to make up for the absence of the Americans.'

'That is true my brother – and a pity,' replied Khalid. 'Some of those ships carry 1,500 passengers, a nice target by any standards. Alas, we have had to look at other ways to silence the infidel. Our intelligence also indicates that the culture of security is not just apparent in airports around the world but is also spreading to seaports everywhere in the wake of September 11th. Special port security firms have been set up with an expertise in assessing the existing threat level in a harbour anywhere in the world, and recommending the necessary measures needed to achieve a standard that will satisfy the American government. Otherwise they will not allow their ships enter that harbour. This makes it even more dangerous for us to conduct operations in this area.'

'Unless of course there is something that I am unaware of, Mohammed?'

'Well, yes there might be,' replied Mohammed, taking out a small map of Europe from his inside pocket.

'Six months ago, presumably as a response to this situation, an American cruise company set up a new route for a cruising holiday. They called it the 'Cold-to-Warm' cruise! It works likes this. Planeloads of Americans are flown into Prestwick in Scotland. They board the liner in the port of Leith, which is in the Firth of Forth on the east coast. The ship then sails north around the top of Scotland passing close inshore to the Orkney Islands where there is a lot of marine wildlife to be seen. It then turns south along the west coast of Scotland staying between the Hebrides and the mainland and then turns southwest en route to the Azores where it stops for two days. After that the ship visits Bermuda before the cruise finishes in Florida.'

'Mohammed, even with the great prophet Allah beside us, I cannot see how we could strike at such a target. Of all our mortal enemies, none has a better security apparatus than the British. Their intelligence agencies have confounded our efforts many times in the past. Long before the great Satan himself felt his vulnerability at the hands of our warriors, the British have strongly secured their borders. From what you say, after the ship leaves British waters it would appear to spend most of the rest of the cruise in open ocean. It would be impossible for us to attack such a target.' Mohammed opened a new packet of cigarettes and slowly lit one while taking in the streetscape that is Dam Square.

'Yes Khalid, it would be impossible, except for two small details ... two small little details!'

Cork

Mike chose a nice restaurant in the small coastal town of Kinsale, which was just seventeen miles down the coast from where he lived. Not quite the most expensive, but then any eating house in Kinsale had to be way above what would commonly be called 'good'. Kinsale has for years been regarded as the gourmet capital of Ireland, winning many international awards, and Mike liked the maritime ambience of the town. The journey down took approximately twenty minutes and soon after, Mike and Cathy were escorted to their candlelit table.

'How long will this patrol be, Mike?' Cathy asked after they were seated.

'Actually, this one is shorter than normal because we are running some launch and recovery exercises with the ships' new RIBs (rigid inflatable boats), and also some RAS (replenishment at sea) exercises with *Niamh,* so I guess about two weeks.'

To Cathy Ford this was just part of life, ever since she had married Mike. Every so often there would be a break when he would be posted to a shore appointment, which could last up to two years, but just like most naval officers' wives anywhere in the world, she accepted the fact that a sailor's life was to go to sea and that's what Mike had to do. She had married an officer from the Irish Naval Service and that was that. Not that she would be bored or anything like it. On the contrary, she was, she thought, busier now than ever before. Cathy worked as a nurse in the Cork University hospital, in a position as theatre sister which she 'job shared' with another girl. This meant that she only worked three days one week and two the next and so on. She had returned to work seven years earlier on a part time basis, on the suggestion of a friend, as their three children had at that stage moved into the secondary school system, and accordingly were gone from eight in the morning until after five in the evening, which suited her job perfectly. She tried to get to Galway once every two or three weeks to see her mother and also Mike's parents, who were both still alive. Now, all of their three children were in college. Emma, their eldest daughter was in Dublin, but James and Cormac attended University College Cork, which meant that they both still lived at home.

The drive to the naval base took just fifteen minutes. Mike turned on the radio at two minutes to seven to listen to the Radio One news. Some flights originating from British airports had been either delayed or cancelled that morning due to a suspected terrorist threat at Heathrow airport. As a commander and senior ships captain in the Irish Naval Service, Mike was a member of the Defence Security Committee (DSC) which consisted of members from the navy, air corps and army, together with the Gardai and various secretary level civil servants. His first meeting on the base this morning was with the flag officer commanding naval service (FOCNS) in the naval headquarters building at seven thirty.

'Good morning Mike, how are you keeping?'

'Very good sir.'

Commodore Tom Garrett was a tall, powerfully built man. As the professional head of the Irish Naval Service, he elicited a respect amongst lesser ranks which manifested in rigid salutes, sometimes accompanied by 'sir'. The reality was that, professional head or not, his mere physical presence could induce enough fear in any other mere mortal to earn a similar sort of respect.

As a former inter services boxing champion he had spent fourteen months seconded to the army ranger wing (ARW), the elite 'special forces' division of the Irish Army. Here, he had proved how tough a man he really was, when on a course in Fort Benning in the USA, he was invited to train with the US Navy Seals at their base in Coronado, San Diego. At fifty-two years of age he was regarded as a tough but fair naval officer, and he was always concerned about the well being of his ships' captains. He was affectionately known in the navy as 'golfer Garrett', a nickname he picked up seven years earlier when he took up golf. Very few meetings with him occurred without the subject of golf coming up at some stage.

'How's Cas?'

'She's keeping very well, sir.'

'Good, good, very glad to hear that. Tell me, Mike, have you bought yourself a set of golf clubs yet?'

'No, sir. Now that our children are less demanding in terms of time, I don't think that I would be on Cas's favourite list if I suddenly announced that I was taking up golf!'

'Yeah ... I suppose I'm lucky Marie plays golf too. Anyway, the reason I called you in here this morning is a bit vague in one sense but we gotta be aware of it nevertheless. We received some very non-specific intel from the Brits, more a case of just keep our eyes and ears open. It seems that one of their intercepts showed up something to do with the south of Ireland. It's that vague that they don't have a clue what it is, and I certainly don't either.'

'Sir, is there any particular reason that the intel is coming to us rather than to the army or Gardai?'

'That's a good question, Mike. As far as I know, it went to all the agencies; the only reason I can see that it came to us also is that it apparently originated out of Rotterdam and maybe there is something in that, it being the biggest seaport in Europe. Beyond that, however, I really don't know.'

'Well, sir, I heard on the news this morning that a couple of flights from the UK to here were cancelled. I wonder if these two things are connected?'

'Who knows?' replied the commodore. 'The way the terrorist threat is at the moment, anything is possible. By the way, what time are you sailing, Mike?'

'We'll be clearing the base at 1200, sir.'

The *Eithne* and her crew were essentially going on a two week patrol, at the end of which the ship would dock in Galway harbour for three days. After that the ship would go on patrol in the Atlantic for a week and a half, before returning to the base in Haulbowline Island.

'Talk to Joe Lyden in the mess before you sail,' said the commodore, referring to the commander of naval intelligence in the base.

'He could probably shed a little more light on it than I can at this point.'

As Mike walked back towards the officers' mess on the base, he thought about what the commodore had said. For sure all intelligence is important, but what could he do? What do you do with totally non-specific intel? Not a lot, it seemed. He reflected that a lot of patrols conducted by Irish naval vessels concentrated on fishery protection duties, boarding and checking trawlers, as well as search and rescue/recovery (SAR) in all weathers.

But no Irish naval officer ever lost sight of the fact that the navy's primary duty was the protection of the state against any and all forms of external aggression, and that meant covert as well as overt threats. He knew that, although his navy was one of the smaller ones in the world, it nevertheless had a supremely professional attitude around operations (ops) of any kind.

Small navy or not, no other navy in the world conducted as many boardings as his one ... moreover, in the Atlantic in winter. He also knew that his navy had, as a result, developed niche capabilities that few others had in the area of armed boarding and takeover of a vessel in atrocious conditions.

As he approached the steps of the mess he more or less concluded that the rules of the game had changed now. The enemy was not as obvious any more and terrorist activity worldwide blurred the natural boundaries of where incidents were planned, arranged and executed.

As Mike Ford picked up his cup of strong coffee in the officers' mess he scanned the room looking for Cdr Joe Lydon and immediately made his way towards him.

'Hi Joe. Good weekend?'

'Yeah, Mike,' said Joe, smiling, 'United beat Arsenal 3-1 on Saturday. I'd call that a good weekend, wouldn't you?'

'Well I have to say, that second goal was a beauty,' said Mike, who had watched highlights of the match later that evening.

'Hey listen, I was talking to the boss earlier, he was on about some intel that came in. Said to talk to you about it.'

'I saw that,' replied the navy's intelligence officer.

'The truth is, Mike, I haven't got clue what it is at this time. If it develops any further I'll send you a signal.'

Amsterdam

'The first detail is that the important part of that cruise for us is an area approximately two hundred nautical miles off the west coast of Ireland. It is known as the Porcupine Bank. The Irish have discovered the existence of rare and beautiful coral banks there, apparently on a par with those in the Great Barrier Reef, but of more significance is the profusion of whales and dolphins and other as yet unheard of marine life. One of the attractions of the cruise is that the ship slows right down for several hours to facilitate the viewing of these animals.'

Khalid's face contorted with indignation. 'My dear brother, are you suggesting that we enlist the support of the whales and dolphins to attack this ship?'

Mohammed laughed at the thought of Khalid's suggestion, which caused a slight softening of his superior's incredulous facial expression.

'Of course not. Let me take you to the second little detail, specifically to the eastern Med, where the connection will become clearer.'

Mohammed then started to talk about the new oil pipeline which was being built in that region. It started from the port city of Baku on the eastern shore of the Caspian sea and ended on Turkey's Mediterranean coast. The pipeline, which is 1,094 miles long, passes through Azerbaijan for 277 miles, and then on through Georgia for 152 miles. The final part passes through Turkey for 665 miles. It is known as the capital BTC (Baku–Tblisi–Ceyhan) pipeline and its purpose is to provide an alternative to the reliance on the immense oil reserves of Saudi Arabia.

'Since our attacks on September 11, 2001 in the US, concern over the West's dependence on Persian Gulf oil has intensified. This project was developed by British Petroleum (BP) and cost nearly four billion euro. The oil can flow through the forty two inch diameter pipeline at a speed of two metres per second, which is three quarters of a mile per hour. It finally delivers this oil to the Turkish coast in the Mediterranean right next to the accursed American air base at Incirlik in Turkey.'

Khalid's trust in Mohammed curbed his building impatience at the slow development of the plan. He knew that Mohammed was leading to something significant and that it was important to let him develop the scenario as he saw it. Mohammed worked for a ship supply company in Amsterdam, and Khalid knew that this provided him with an uncommon access to all sorts of maritime information.

'This pipeline project is nearly completed now, and there are two Dutch ocean-going tugs which have been working on it due to return from a one-year contract there. They depart in three weeks time. The thing is, one of them is coming back to Rotterdam, but the other is going directly to Ireland from the Mediterranean. The Irish government have contracted it for six months together with its crew.'

'For what purpose?' asked Khalid.

'The Irish are very concerned about the possibility of an oil tanker getting into difficulties off their coast, and accordingly they wish to acquire a similar suitable tug for their navy, so that they can tow it away from their coast should it be threatened. A major oil spill on their coast would represent a disaster in terms of tourism, which is one of their main sources of revenue.'

Mohammed continued: 'the purpose of the six month contract is to conduct trials and an evaluation, to establish the suitability of such a vessel, especially with regard to the Atlantic ocean on their south and west coasts. This area has some of the worst weather conditions in the world in the winter.'

Mohammed paused for a few moments ... 'It is the coincidence of these two events which I believe provides us with a possible opportunity.'

Khalid thought about the possibilities of what he had heard. In his mind two things stuck out. The first was the fact that the idea was so far-fetched that it probably would never even occur to anyone else, and by 'anyone else' he meant the anti-terrorist agencies of the world, especially the Americans and the British. The second was the fact that the tug had to steam through the Mediterranean sea en route to Ireland, which presented an opportunity to somehow or other take control of it. In Khalid's mind there were a lot of details to work out, but he instinctively knew that if Mohammed had worked out the plan to this point, then he had also worked out a rough draft of the finer details.

'My brother, this plan is so crazy, it might just work.'

Mohammed then continued with the other minute details of the plan, which he had carefully worked on over the previous two weeks. Khalid was indeed impressed.

Naval Base, Cork

Fore and aft line parties close up. The unmistakable order emanating from the bridge of *Eithne* signalled the imminent departure of the ship on patrol. On the oil wharf, where *Eithne* was berthed, line parties also took up station in readiness to let go the ship's lines. At this stage her engines were fully on line with personnel in the engine room standing by to receive the intricate set of orders that facilitated the careful manoeuvring of the ship away from the dock, together with the safe recovery and storage of the lines. *Eithne* then moved gently towards the centre of the river, where with the assistance of the tide and alternate engines, she slowly turned through 180 degrees.

She slid forward in the relative calm of the harbour, passing the historic town of Cobh (once known as Queenstown) on her port side, and onwards towards the big right hand turn she would have to make around the Spit Bank shallows. Passing the Whitegate oil refinery to port, and a fleet of Optimist sailing dinghies to starboard, between Spike Island and Currabinny wood, Captain Ford ordered an increase in speed. *Eithne's* crew felt the slight increase in engine revolutions. Then she passed through the narrow part of the channel between Fort Meagher and Fort Davis, which, perched high up on both sides, constituted two of the three forts (the third being Spike Island) built by the British in the eighteenth century for the defence of Cork harbour.

Ever since his days as a midshipman, moving towards the mouth of the harbour outbound always reminded him of coming out of the school gates on the day of the summer holidays. The freedom to manoeuvre had a sort of relief quality about it. He watched as the forward jackstaff was lowered and horizontally secured to the inside of the bow, as if signalling that the ship was now ready to take on the ocean ahead.
As *Eithne* surged past Roches Point, right at the mouth of the harbour, a few members of the crew could be seen making last minute phone calls on the flight deck from their cell phones, before the ship got out of range of the land-based cell network.

Mike Ford's patrol plan determined that the ship took up a southeasterly heading to an area of sea known in the Irish navy as the

'Gaza Strip'. Basically, it is a long narrow triangular area of sea where the Irish territorial limits overlap with the British. This is known as the South East Grey Area or SEGA. In short, although disputed by both, each navy patrols it, and nobody takes too much notice anyway. In fact, trawlers in the area have reported being boarded by both navies, sometimes in the one day.

Eithne was now steaming at sixteen knots towards the Gaza Strip even though her radar operators would still monitor all fishing activity en route. All contacts would be reported to the captain as they appeared on the radar, and the name of the trawler, together with details of previous boardings and findings, would also be logged. Captain Ford then announced to the officer of the watch (OOW), Sub Lt Gerry Stewart, that he would be working in his day cabin until lunchtime. The Sub Lt's main responsibility, apart from the operation of the ship, was to make sure that *Eithne* was not brought within one and a half nautical miles of any surface contact. As Mike Ford left the bridge he turned to the OOW and said, 'In fact Gerry, close any fishing contact with a view to boarding.'

Officers started to come in to *Eithne's* wardroom at ten minutes to one. The wardroom's table had been neatly set for lunch by the duty steward who occupied a small kitchen off the wardroom, into which meals arrived through a lift system from the ship's galleys. The informality of the wardroom usually gave rise to discussions on all sorts of topics, but today there was only room for one; Munster's superb win over their arch rivals Castres in the Heineken European Cup.

Eastern Mediterranean

Frank Blokland sat in the elevated captain's seat on the bridge of the ocean tug *Swiftsure,* noting the forecasted high pressure and its pleasant effect of flattening the sometimes lumpy Mediterranean sea. He was glad to be leaving Turkey after a one-year stint as master of one of Smit Tak's finest tugs, which had been working in the terminal area of the Baku–Tbilisi–Ceyhan pipeline.

As *Swiftsure* eased through the calm Mediterranean with fourteen knots showing on the log, Frank thought about being based back in Amsterdam again. It didn't have the fabulously tropical weather that was almost a constant off the coast of Turkey, but it was home and home meant being near his wife Carla and his very precocious four-year-old daughter Lisa who had started school two months earlier.

Piet Stam, *Swiftsure's* able first officer, ambled out to the bridge from the radio room.

'Hey skipper, we just got that confirmation signal regarding the refuel in Algiers.'

'Good,' replied Frank, it'll be great to stroll around the markets for a few hours and pick up a few presents.'

The *Swiftsure* had recently been contracted by the Irish government, and Frank Blokland's job at this time was to sail it from Ceyhan in Turkey to Bantry in the southwest of Ireland. Within one week of arriving there, he and two other members of the five-man crew would fly back to Holland after handing the ship over to a new crew. At that point, *Swiftsure*, in conjunction with personnel from the Irish navy, would start a six-month trial period to evaluate the operational feasibility of the vessel in Irish waters.

'Anyone for coffee?' asked Piet Stam.

Two 'yeah's signalled the almost lazy response from the captain and Frans de Vries, the tug's amiable engineer, who were totally immersed in what was displayed on the ship's radar screen. Nothing bad or anything like that; in fact, what had caught their attention was the unusual configuration of other vessels in the general area, as the tug was still in Turkish waters.

First Officer Stam called up the galley where Jan, the ship's cook, was busy preparing the vegetables for that evening's meal.

'Hey Jan, how about a pot of coffee and some of those lovely biscuits we picked up in Turkey?'

'Okay Piet, gimme five minutes.'

Captain Blokland was first to pour himself a cup of coffee while simultaneously picking up three of the very nice biscuits. He was quite relaxed, now that the *Swiftsure* was properly settled into the rhythm of her long voyage to Ireland, in terms of crew watches and waypoints and all of the other tasks, big or small, that were the responsibility of any ship's captain. However, as important as this was, it did not require quite the same focus as when the tug was involved in towing or ship manoeuvring operations, especially in harbours, which did not have a lot of manoeuvring space.

LE *Eithne*

As lunch ended in the wardroom, most of the officers returned to their various posts aboard the ship. The officer of the watch was relieved by Sub Lt Angela Hogan so that he could have lunch. This procedure was formally carried out between the two officers.

'Sub Lt Stewart, OOW reports ship's course "one nine zero", speed sixteen knots, no contacts to report.' The new OOW reiterated what he had heard as he took over control of the bridge. At this stage of a patrol, things generally start to settle down. It was as if the crew started to let go of land-based thoughts around things like family, mortgages, the pub and so on. The ship and its crew started to get into a rhythm and somehow or other things begin to feel a little easier.

Leith, Scotland

The two aircraft left the United States from Newark airport in New York within ninety minutes of each other, both bound for Prestwick on the west coast of Scotland. Each was a Boeing 747, one of which had 340 passengers, the other 312. The cruise company's costings were based on the flight to Scotland originating in Newark, which meant that the 652

Americans had to position to that airport from various points around the US at their own expense, unless of course they lived close to New York. For the passengers, quite a few of whom were veterans, this was the most tiresome part of the journey, and most just looked forward to boarding the *American Princess* in Leith, on the other side of Scotland. That was when their holiday of a lifetime could really begin.

Modern cruise packages did not skimp on ensuring passenger satisfaction, and the *American Princess* was no exception. Almost all the ship's cabins were luxurious and all had 'sea views'. Passengers could eat till they dropped, at any time of day or night. At seven different locations on the ship, the huge variety of food served aboard was comparable with the best restaurants in the world. A vast array of entertainment was provided to suit all tastes. On deck, three swimming pools, together with what was essentially a running (or walking) track right around the ship, catered for the healthier and health conscious, not to mention the gymnasiums for those inclined.

The ninety minute spacing between the two 747s' departure out of Newark made it easier for the ship's reception crew to comfortably board the passengers and in turn maintain the good name the cruise company enjoyed. Most cruise operators never lost sight of the fact that a substantial amount of their business emanated from the referrals of previous passengers, and their positive experience in the hands of the ship's crew, which contributed greatly to the company's revenue.

The second 747 touched down in Prestwick at 9.30 in the morning, and within forty five minutes a small fleet of coaches with the passengers and all their luggage was making its way along the coast road towards Glasgow, affording all aboard a great view of the entrance to the mighty Clyde estuary. For a small number of the ex-navy veterans aboard it was a return to the place where they had in fact served or visited in the course of their duties during the Cold War. One or two could be seen pointing across the estuary to Holy Loch, where the United States maintained a significant submarine base. The 'base', which was in fact a large ship alongside which submarines would tie up, either for maintenance or rest and recuperation for their crews, was positioned there so that submarines could effectively patrol the 'GI UK Gap'. During the Cold War, the only way that Soviet submarines could break out into the Atlantic from their bases in Poljarny and Severomorsk on the Kola peninsula was to pass through the freezing cold sea area between Greenland and Iceland and also Iceland and the United Kingdom, hence the GI UK Gap.

Across these not inconsiderable sea areas NATO had stretched underwater sosus warning nets, which listened out for passing soviet submarines. Essentially they were a series of fixed passive sonar arrays to provide an early warning of Soviet submarine deployments into the vastness of the north Atlantic. The policy of NATO at the time was to catch them going through, and then monitor their tracks or shadow them wherever they went. The seabed hydrophones simply locate a passing submarine and the information is immediately flashed to the nearest NATO flag commander, and to this day they are still used to great effect.

The coaches would bypass Glasgow and proceed on to the cultural city of Edinburgh, on whose outskirts the port town of Leith is situated. As the coaches pulled up alongside the huge cruise liner to facilitate an easy boarding for its new guests, a man stood one and a half miles down the road, his arms resting between the opened door and the body of his hired car. When the last of the passengers had boarded the cruise liner he pressed the 'send' button on his mobile cell phone, allowing a message he had typed in two and a half hours earlier to travel nearly 1,500 miles and one time zone, almost instantly. Two rings on the receiver's mobile phone were enough to get him to open the message.

It read: '*Strawberries and Blackberries are now in the basket.*'

Rotterdam

Another meeting was arranged between Khalid and Mohammed, except this time it was in Rotterdam. Part of Mohammed's job was to travel on the same day once a month to oversee business on behalf of his company in this famous seaport. This was significant from a security point of view, as this day and the arrival time of the train he took was already known to Khalid.

As such, a permanent arrangement existed whereby, on arrival, Mohammed would check a particular area for Khalid's presence, thus obviating the need to make any prior arrangements, using communication modes like e-mails or texts, which would always leave a record that is the life blood of Security agencies worldwide.

Somehow or other Mohammed intuitively knew that Khalid would be in the station in Rotterdam today. As he stepped off the train and walked with hundreds of other passengers along the station platform, he considered in his mind that time was now becoming a factor in their plans, and crucial pieces of information needed to be exchanged. Sure enough, Khalid was sitting at a table sipping coffee and dressed in a three piece suit, with an expensive briefcase at his side. Mohammed walked up to him and both men shook hands and smiled in the manner westerners would adopt for a business meeting.

Algiers

The two RIBs had been bought in Spain. They had been specifically selected for their deep vee hull and their legendary stability. In fact, the Avon 5.4 metre 'Searider' up to recently had been the RIB of choice for many of the world's navies. Each had been purchased with a roller coaster trailer, and fitted with a Yamaha 90 horsepower engine. They were now parked in a small warehouse in the south of the city. Khalid had carefully selected this location, but had even more carefully selected the man who was now working on them.

Abu was a relatively slight man in his mid thirties, sporting a seven-inch long beard. He was particularly excited about this job; he never usually saw the fruits of his labour, but on this occasion Khalid wanted him as part of the crew in case any last minute adjustments needed to be made en route. His skills as a bomb maker were usually deployed teaching others on a training camp somewhere deep inland and away from prying eyes. But this one was different; firstly, it was an altogether different kind of bomb, and secondly, there was a huge challenge for him to make sure that the bomb could be accurately sent to its intended target.

Abu figured that the bomb part of the whole assembly was relatively easy. For him, the real challenge was the radio control devices that would steer the RIBs accurately through the water for a distance of two kilometres. Khalid had insisted on this as a minimum distance to maintain control, and Abu knew that ultimately the only way to make sure of this, prior to the mission, was to conduct trials when he was finished. He also had to consider the long sea journey that the RIBs would undertake to the target area, having regard to proper sealing of the RIBs batteries and making sure that the electronics at all times remained dry. He was thankful for the rib covers that came with each boat, which stretched right over the sponsons. These would be invaluable for protection against rain and spray.

Abu thought about the design required for both building the bomb and delivering it to its target. He was aware of the fact that when the USS *Cole* was hit in Yemen harbour, the explosion blew a large hole in her side but did not sink her. One of the reasons for this was that the explosion occurred just above the waterline of the ship, which meant that the prompt action of her crew in sealing off the affected area, together with getting pumps going, saved the ship from settling in the harbour mud. The other reason why the *Cole* didn't sink was that the explosion took the line of least resistance. Although a hole nearly thirty feet wide was blown in the side of the ship, her hull plates took the worst of the damage, instead of the inside of the ship.

In Abu's mind, he needed to come up with something that would strike the cruise liner approximately six feet below the waterline. He also needed a mechanism that would drive the projectile into the ship as it exploded, so that maximum damage was caused inside the hull, hopefully compromising a few watertight hatches or even bulkhead sections. Yes, yes, that would render the infidels' attempts to save their ship close to useless; especially when his plan was to deliver two of these projectiles to different parts of the ship. In the end, he decided that simplicity was the best course of action. He manufactured two ten-foot cylindrical metal tubes big enough for each to carry just under half a ton of plastic explosive. At the forward end of these he configured a simple detonating system, which would be activated by a one-foot plunger at the front. When he had finished the second missile-like cylinder, he proudly smiled to himself: 'Maybe I should go into manufacturing torpedoes.'

The reality was, however, that for a man with Abu's skills this was the easy part. At this stage in his life he had built hundreds of bombs and so to him this was just another – an underwater-friendly torpedo-like bomb, but nevertheless just another bomb. His real task was to figure out how he was going to deliver this weapon to its target below the surface at a speed above ten knots with, as he called it, a hard-bottomed inflatable boat.
In the end, he once again relied on complete simplicity.

Firstly, he got some four by four box section steel and cut it into two five-foot lengths. Then he made a 'V' plate that could be bolted on to the underside of the deep vee hulls of the RIBs, through a corresponding 'V' plate inside the hull of the RIB. When he was finished he welded this 'V' plate in a line through diagonal corners of the box section, which ensured that the vertical box sections would flow through the water in a more bow-like attitude. To connect these five-foot box section lengths to the projectile he simply welded a similar plate onto both the projectile and the top of the five-foot cylinders, and drilled four nineteen-millimetre matching holes in each, so that the whole assembly would be simple enough to put together when the tug was within range of the cruise liner. All that was required was to first of all connect the five-foot sections to the projectiles on the deck, and then bolt the whole assembly onto the RIBs.
The positioning of these joining plates on both the RIB and the projectile were such that over two foot of the projectile extended forward underwater beyond the bow of the RIB. Abu's idea was to drive the RIB at the side of the ship, so that the projectile hit the ship six feet under the suface first and, with a fraction of a delay in the detonation, the still forward-moving RIB would drive the explosive a little bit further inside the ship, thus maximising the damage. Everything worked out fine until he floated the combined assembly. The RIB, together with the cylinder section suspended six feet under its keel and two feet forward of its bow, caused the front of the RIB to have a slightly hull down attitude in the water. He fixed this quite simply by adding enough ballast in the RIB's stern to counteract it, and when he conducted final trials with the remote control he was delighted to see that the RIB, with its underwater assembly bolted on, could easily achieve nine knots.

It was in fact crucial that he got it right, because now the clock was ticking. He had exactly eight days before the tug arrived.

A fishing boat was enlisted from sympathetic sources to conduct the remote controlled RIB trials. The fishing boat's crew were amazed at the two rigid inflatable boats being towed behind, so many wires and lever-like devices connected to the steering mechanisms of the two ninety-horsepower engines. Abu wanted an area of water with a sea state or swell that would test the directional stability of the RIBs; moreover, RIBs controlled by a radio. Wave height and wind direction would be a factor in handling the boats in rough water and, after all, the whole mission depended entirely on his ability to make them connect with a very large target approximately one and a half miles away, in a very different ocean which was terrifyingly different to where Abu was going now. Nevertheless, he had read about the north Atlantic and although knowing that his proving ground for assessing the remote control system was hopelessly inadequate by comparison, he took some measures to create a degree of sea state that might test the remote control's performance. First of all, despite the protestations of the fishing boat's crew, he insisted that the trial be carried out at 3.30 in the afternoon.

At this time the strong offshore breeze would whip up a nice chop. Also, when the crew realised that he needed rough water, they steered the boat to the windward side of a particular headland where, as waves crashed into it, a return echo of the waves made the sea state even more confused. Abu decided that this would do just fine. It didn't matter whether the RIBs hit the cruise ship fully bows on. The detonating plunger at the front of the bomb would work inside an arc of fifty degrees. Abu had cleverly fitted a studded rubber pad at the front of the plunger, the better to grip the side of the ship at a less than optimal angle, thus ensuring detonation.

He also considered the transportation to the north Atlantic of his home-made 'torpedo assembly parts'. Each part of the assembly was designed to fit into the hull of each RIB during the voyage, so that it wouldn't attract any unwanted attention, and also to keep it dry under the RIB's covers.

Rotterdam

'My dear brother, how are you and how goes our plan?' asked Mohammed.

As always, Mohammed's eyes were constantly scanning the area around where they were talking. In fact, he had a great skill in using his peripheral vision to make sure that other eyes and ears were not picking up any part of the discussion that he was engaged in.

'The answer to that will be much clearer in a few days,' replied Khalid.

'Then I will be in Algiers and I will know a lot more than I do now. I can tell you that most of our preparations are being completed; however I would like to see this for myself.'

In Mohammed's mind Khalid had always been the epitome of thoroughness. In fact, he had learned a lot since he had met Khalid from just observing his legendary attention to detail. Khalid had told him when they met that a lack of attention to detail was the fastest way to die when you are dealing with the unbelievers, especially the Americans and the British.

'I have something that may be very helpful to you when the tug comes into the harbour in Algiers,' said Mohammed.

He took an envelope from his briefcase and handed it to Khalid, who immediately put it in the inside pocket of his very smart suit, not daring to open it. Once again, it was okay to talk as the surrounding noise of both trains and people made sure that their conversation would not be heard if they were careful.

'There are three photographs in the envelope. One is a photograph of apartment F, number 26 Ferdinand Bolstraat in Amsterdam, the second one is a photograph of Carla Blokland and her four-year-old daughter Lisa coming out of their apartment, and the third shows Carla collecting Lisa from the junior school she attends which is three blocks away from the apartment.'

'And who is Carla Blokland and her daughter?' asked Kahlid.

'They are the wife and daughter of Captain Frank Blokland, who as you know is the master of the *Swiftsure,*' replied Mohammed, with a tone of satisfaction.

'Hmmm,' intoned Khalid. 'You have done well, my brother.'

Mohammed was beaming.

'I am sure that Captain Blokland, how shall we say, will be more compliant to our wishes, when he sees these photographs,' said Mohammed smugly. He then added: 'There are two copies of each in the envelope, should you feel like handing the good captain one set to remind him throughout the voyage of the futility of any heroism. Also, the photographs are dated and timed so that he will be in no doubt as to their complete authenticity.'

Mohammed felt like a schoolboy who had put up his hand and got the right answer to the question that the teacher asked!

Khalid considered this. The photographs would indeed be helpful in controlling the captain, and perhaps his crew, on the long sea journey from Algiers to the seas off the west coast of Ireland. However, he realised that this phase of the mission had other vulnerabilities.

'Mohammed, it is quite possible, in fact almost a certainty, that Captain Blokland will need to talk to both his lovely wife and his employers. He will, almost certainly, have a requirement to update them on the tug's progress. We cannot reasonably force him to speak English on the radio to people with whom he would naturally converse in Dutch, without arousing suspicion. You, my brother, speak fluent Dutch.'

The conversation continued over a second cup of coffee. Khalid told Mohammed that he was travelling to Schiphol airport in Amsterdam by train in an hour, and then catching a flight to Rome where he would board another taking him onwards to the north African city of Algiers.

'Khalid, I can take holidays at any time. I will see you in three days in Algiers.'

Swiftsure

At 0800 first officer Piet Stam had operational control of the tug as she passed longitudinally abeam of the most southern point of Italy. In fact this was the southern tip of the island of Sicily. *Swiftsure* was passing through a line that joined the islands of Malta and Sicily. It would be another two hundred nautical miles or fourteen and a half hours before the tug came abeam Bizerte in Tunisia, and a further 270 nautical miles, or twenty hours, before it reached the port of Algiers.

His captain had gone to his cabin at 0700 for a well earned sleep, having been on duty on the bridge from 2130 the previous evening. For the most part, the voyage stayed monotonous as the *Swiftsure* ploughed on through the still very becalmed Mediterranean sea at fourteen knots. Just about the only thing that bothered Piet at this time was the fact that his beloved Turkish biscuits were gone, so he had to make do with toast with his coffee. Still, he reasoned, this was probably a good thing for his not inconsiderable waistline. And anyway, he was sure he would find more when the *Swiftsure* arrived in Algiers.

Sitting as he was in the skipper's high chair on the bridge, he contemplated the utter calmness of the Med and wondered what it would be like when the tug entered the Atlantic ocean, and then turned right at Cape St Vincent. That would be a different sea. The captain, he knew, would position *Swiftsure* well offshore on its journey northwards along the Portuguese coast, which acts like a wall for the Atlantic and her prevailing winds to slam into. This, of course, has the effect of creating short, steep and uncomfortable seas inshore when the incoming waves collide with the outgoing ones. Piet knew that most skippers would happily avoid this situation by staying offshore.

But right now, that was not his concern. He figured that today would be a good day to get some essential maintenance done on the tug's machinery, especially the exposed parts of the gearing on the after deck. The salty atmosphere played havoc with the intricate parts of the towing mechanism on the tug. Moreover, in the Med ... which is regarded as one of the saltiest seas in the world. Regular greasing was needed to make sure that the tug was at all times ready for any challenge that might come her way. Piet figured that two hours in the morning before the heat of the day became too severe would do nicely. The captain had asked to be called at 1400 if he hadn't already woken before that time.

LE *Eithne*

As *Eithne* continued on a southerly heading throughout the afternoon and early evening, there wasn't much activity on the radars in terms of fishing contacts. A number of large cargo and container ships and an oil tanker were sighted, but in this particular area that would be normal. A large volume of traffic coming into or out of the western approaches would be en route to ports north of the Isles of Scilly, like Liverpool and the ports of south Wales. Although not important to *Eithne*'s executive function, these contacts concentrated the minds of the lookouts and the officer of the watch. In fact anyone who was on the bridge automatically scanned the horizon.

As the light began to fade, the visibility was further reduced by a frontal depression, which was coming in from the Atlantic. Depressions in this part of the world would usually bring with them cloud, wind and rain, due to the temperature and humidity differences across the fronts. In short, Sub Lt Stewart, *Eithne*'s amiable gunnery officer, noted that visibility for the night was going to be, in his words, 'shit'.

As the ship was steaming steadily south, LS Kearney reported two contacts at twenty-one nautical miles' range on his radar screen. At that moment Commander Ford walked onto the bridge from his day cabin, and on hearing this announced to everyone that this would be a perfect opportunity to conduct an exercise in 'over the horizon' night boarding. Lt Commander Jamie Morrisson then ordered the duty PO to announce 'Boarding stations, fifteen minutes'.

As soon as this message went out on the ship's PA system, twelve people started moving towards *Eithne*'s diving stores area, where they immediately kitted up in black drysuits, together with life jackets, GPS and radios. Another four sailors moved towards the port and starboard RIB stations, taking up positions on the controls of the new caley davit systems. When the boarding party, led by Sub Lt Neil Kennedy, were fully ready they reported to the bridge for the briefing, which tonight was going to be given by Commander Ford himself.

'Okay, gentlemen, range to contact is now eighteen nautical miles; we are conducting a surprise night, over the horizon boarding. None of these contacts have the faintest idea that we are here, and the first they will know about it is when you guys appear on their deck. After that, you revert to standard procedures in terms of compliance, log books etc. For the purposes of the exercise, use comms only in an emergency. We'll launch the port RIB first, then we'll turn the ship and launch the other. We'll be monitoring your progress on the RIB tracker, so be safe. Any questions?'

'No, sir,' replied Sub Lt Kennedy.

As the crew made their way to where the RIBs were sitting in their cradles, Commander Ford turned to the coxwain.

'Cox, bring her around to one seven zero at four knots.'

'Course one seven zero, speed four knots, aye sir.'

Senior Chief John Morgan brought *Eithne* on to a heading of one seven zero degrees.

'Steady one seven zero speed four knots sir, helm's amidships'.

The ship was now positioned so that she provided shelter for the launching of the first RIB from both the sea state and the strong wind, which was hammering into the starboard side of *Eithne* at this time. This of course was one of the best things about the Caley system. The entire launching operation could be carried out with the ship providing a perfect lee.

A ten-foot steel boom which was located approximately twenty-five feet forward of the caley davit position was lowered to the horizontal. It had a strong rope attached to the end of the boom. This rope was connected directly to the bow of the RIB about to be launched.

Petty Officer Mark Power, *Eithne*'s bosun, then eased forward one of the levers on the Caley control console. This caused the crane-like structure to lift the RIB, complete with crew, clear of the steel cradle that it sat in, and eased it out over the side of the ship. Another lever then allowed the steel hawser to gently lower it down towards the water, while all the time the rope connecting the bow to the steel boom twenty-five feet forward maintained the parallel aspect between the RIB and the mother ship. Approximately one metre above the water the RIB's coxwain, Leading Seaman Denis O'Callaghan, started the powerful diesel engines. The moment the RIB hit

the water the steel hawser was released, and the RIB, attached now only to the horizontal boom rope, was being towed in perfect station with the ship. LS O'Callaghan then advanced the throttles, which took the strain off the boom rope enabling his bowman, Able Seaman Bill Deasy, to let go. Once free, LS O'Callaghan steered Jaguar One slowly around *Eithne*'s stern, the RIB falling into fifteen foot valleys of water and then climbing back up the next wave in the constant swell in total blackness and driving rain.
The second RIB, Jaguar Two, was then launched. LS David Moynihan, her coxwain, expertly steered her to a position about twenty-five metres abeam Jaguar One. The throttles of both RIBs were then slammed open and both took off like scalded cats.

All the while up on the bridge, Sub Lt Hogan watched the three flashing indicators on the RIB tracking screen. Almost as soon as the RIBs had cleared *Eithne*'s bows, two of the flashing lights began to separate from the other, the gap getting wider with each nautical mile that the RIBs travelled. With no lights showing and very poor visibility, they were out of visual range from the ship within a minute.

All of the ship's crew knew that it wasn't necessary, especially at this time of night, to travel such a long distance in a RIB in a worsening sea state and very poor visibility to board a trawler. However, they also knew that it was constant exercises of this sort that maintained their edge. Every time the ship went to sea it was subject to a patrol plan which was prepared in advance by Naval Operations. However, nobody knew what challenges would be thrown at the ship – perhaps a rescue operation or a drugs interdiction, or indeed any other emergency that it may be called to assist with. The navy had to be ready every time, no matter what. They never stopped operating at the cutting edge.

'Sir, Jaguar One and Jaguar Two are three miles from the target,' reported Sub Lt Hogan, whose eyes were glued to the RIB tracker screen.

Swiftsure

At 1310, Frank Blokland woke to the low frequency throbbing sound of *Swiftsure*'s powerful diesel engines. Not that this would interrupt his sleep or anything … his years at sea meant that, where sleep was concerned, noises like this never really affected him. However, he did notice a slight increase in the sea state when he hopped out of his bunk. As he showered, his mind wandered towards the beautiful port city of Algiers, which was now twenty-eight and a half hours distant. For the most part formalities there had been taken care of by his head office in Rotterdam. The tug itself wouldn't take long to refuel, perhaps two hours, but Frank had decided that they were going to have a twenty-four hour stopover. In his mind, Algiers was not a place you visited for just two hours. On the other hand, he had a strong desire to complete the voyage to Ireland, and fly back to his beloved wife and daughter; but, stepping out of the shower, he concluded that it was a win–win situation anyway, by doing both. Hunger then forced him to pick up the telephone in his cabin.

'Jan, I haven't eaten since yesterday afternoon.'

'Well, skipper, if you give me twenty minutes I can rustle up a very nice steak with fries and onions.'

'The day is starting to look good already, Jan. Give me a call on the bridge when it is ready.'

'How is she going, Piet?' asked the skipper as he entered the bridge.

'We're just about here,' he said, pointing to a position on the electronic plotter.

'It's amazing, we're still in 2,800 metres of water, but the 2,000 metre contour is only about four miles off our port beam.'

It often amazed the two mariners that such a small sea could be so deep, particularly within such a short distance from the coast, coming as they did from northwest Europe, where depths of fifteen to twenty metres would often be the norm at this distance from the coast. The conversation then came to a rather abrupt end, as Captain Blokland picked up the ringing telephone on the bridge.

'On my way,' said the skipper, and then turned to Piet.

'Back in twenty minutes; steak, fries and onions await me in the mess.'

The first officer looked at his skipper, and uttered an envious groan.

LE *Eithne*

The trawler's skipper was sitting in his high chair in the pilothouse, as his boat moved along at four knots. While two of the crew were actually sleeping in their bunks, two others were catching the last quarter of an hour of a football match on Sky Sports, also in the pilothouse. They had been seine trawling now for approximately two hours, and none of them had even the faintest idea that two sleek black rigid inflatable boats, which were showing no lights, and each carrying six members of the Irish navy, were screaming towards them at thirty-two knots. It wouldn't have mattered anyway, as the night was so dark, and the visibility so poor, and they wouldn't have heard them either over the trawler's noisy diesel engine and machinery. LS Moynihan, Jaguar Two's coxwain, expertly glided the RIB along the starboard side of the trawler, making certain that he kept in close enough so as not to get entangled in the hawsers that were streamed out either side of the trawler booms, dragging the massive nets and their contents.

With the sea state present at the time, the RIB, once it was alongside, was rising and falling through five feet from the trawler's rails. This made life difficult for the boarding party, as they had to choose their moment to leap over the side and into the trawler. Each was acutely aware that falling overboard during this phase of the boarding was definitely not an option, as it could result in being sucked straight in to the churning propellers of the trawler. However, two things were on their side; the first was their expert training and professionalism, the second was the RIB coxwain's ability to keep the inflated sponson right against the trawler's hull.

The boarding itself was, for the most part, routine. For sure, there was absolutely no reason to travel eighteen nautical miles over the horizon in rough seas at night to board a trawler. A normal boarding would usually involve the ship heaving to within sight of the trawler, and then launching its RIB and boarding crew to make the short journey to the trawler. The exception to this, of course, was if the navy suspected that either the trawler's records or fish stocks could be quickly tampered with on sight of the approaching naval vessel. However, when Mike Ford saw the sea conditions, together with the total blackness of this particular night, he decided that the circumstances were perfect to use this boarding as a training exercise also.

Each member of the two black drysuit-clad boarding crews waited for the opportune moment, where the level of the RIB's sponson and the trawler's railing were close enough. One by one they leapt aboard, three of them immediately making their way across to the port side of the trawler, being careful to stay out of sight of the trawler's crew in the shadows under the pilothouse. On most trawlers this would be difficult because not only were the decks lit up, but most skippers, for health and safety reasons, had all deck areas of their trawlers monitored by CCTV, which they could view from the pilothouse. When the boarding crews were safely aboard, the coxwains simply allowed the RIBs to slip back into the wake of the trawler until a radio message would signal them to return alongside and recover the boarding crew.

Their ultimate objective in the exercise was to arrive undetected at the doors on each side of the bridge. Once that was achieved they naturally reverted back to normal inspection procedures.

For the most part, trawlers' skippers, especially in this part of the world, would be conditioned to regular boardings, day or night, by either the Irish navy or fishery protection vessels of the Royal Navy. One of the trawler's crew, whose eyes were concentrated on the football game on the small television in the bridge, suddenly dropped the half full mug of coffee he was drinking as the corner of his eye looked out the bridge windows and saw three blackened faces peering in at him.

'Oh Jesus Christ,' he blurted, almost fainting from the shock, which was made slightly worse by the fact that the boarding officer, together with the other blackened faces, simultaneously knocked on the door on the opposite side of the bridge. The trawler's skipper had in fact experienced one of these boardings three years previously, and so was not quite so perplexed. In fact, he promptly turned around to Sub Lt Kennedy and said,

'Good evening, gentlemen, you shouldn't have gone to so much trouble. We've already been boarded today by your esteemed colleagues in Her Majesty's navy. And I have to say, they came aboard in a much more civilised manner than your good selves,' smugly handing the officer the appropriate and completed paperwork on catches.

'Thank you very much, sir,' said Sub Lt Kennedy, handing the documentation to PO Tom Dunne for inspection. 'So you were visited by our erstwhile friends from across the pond?'

'Yeah,' grinned the trawler skipper 'but at least they had the good manners to announce their arrival both visually and on the airwaves.'

Even though, at one level, both of these seamen were on opposite sides of a maritime fence, especially from a compliance and a rule of law point of view, there was, nevertheless, a mutual respect for the job each had to do, particularly given their difficult working environment. Notwithstanding the fact that the navy, as far as fishermen were concerned, were the policemen of the sea, many trawler skippers were acutely aware of the fact that this same navy would go to any lengths, in any sea, to rescue the crew of a fishing boat that got into difficulties or was sinking.

'Captain – AIS, Jaguar Two indicating return to *Eithne*.'

Mike moved over to the console that Sub Lt Hogan was sitting at. He saw the two blue lights slowly making their way back to the ship on the electronic track. *Eithne*, still blacked out to preserve the integrity of the exercise, slid forward now at twelve knots to close the distance to the recovery point for the incoming RIBs. Twenty minutes later, *Eithne*'s Caley recovery crew peered out into the pitch blackness of the ocean, and noticed Jaguar Two with her blue flashing light punching through *Eithne*'s wash and the now worsening sea state. The Jaguar Two's bowman was searching the water directly in front of the slowed RIB for the illuminated rope being towed along by the deployed boom on *Eithne*. Once he saw it, he waved the coxwain forward and picked up the rope attaching it to the bow ring on the RIB. The RIB coxwain then put the engines into neutral and Jaguar Two momentarily drifted backwards until the rope snatched, positioning the RIB perfectly below, where the lifting hawser would connect with her upper steel frame. When this was connected, both RIB and crew were simultaneously lifted twenty-five feet up the side of the ship into the jaw-like structure of the caley davit system. The XO then ordered the towing boom to be tilted up and secured to a vertical position against the side of the ship and, five minutes later, the whole process was repeated on the ship's other side.

Algiers

Khalid's plane descended in a westerly direction out over the sea, affording him an excellent view of the bowl shaped bay in which the city of Algiers was situated. He was hoping that Abu had everything ready in terms of both the remote control system and the explosives. He needed all his energies and the energies of the others to focus on the planning and execution of the take-over of the tug, and he had just three days to accomplish that.

Nobody met him at the airport, exactly as per Khalid's doctrine: 'don't introduce risk or suspicion where and when there is no need to'. One hour later, he was sipping coffee in an apartment with Abu, who to his great relief assured him that all was ready with the RIBs and their lethal cargo of explosives. Abu also told him that the inflatable boats were safely parked up in the warehouse. At that moment, Kahlid received a text which read '*the tulips will be in the sun tomorrow at two*'.

'Excellent,' responded Khalid to his mobile phone. This was the final part of the logistics in place. The plan would now go ahead.

Swiftsure

As the *Swiftsure* entered the bay, the crew marvelled at the stunning vista of the Atlas mountains to the south. Even though their visit was to be for only twenty-four hours, they nevertheless relished and looked forward to being ashore for a while, sampling the delights of this great Algerian city. Frank Blokland told the crew that he would be quite happy to have just a few hours' shopping in the fabulous markets, followed by a nice meal in one of Algiers' many restaurants, at which time he would return to the ship at 1800, enabling the others to enjoy a night out on the town. He figured that as well as maintaining a presence on the ship, thus freeing the others to go out for the night, he would be quite happy to relax aboard and have a nice long conversation with Carla and his daughter.

Piet Stam spoke up first.

'Skipper, are you sure? Look, I'd be quite happy to come back early and allow you to go out for the night.'

Frank Blokland just waved his hand.

'No, no, I'm quite happy. You guys carry on, and don't get too drunk! The plan is that we get refuelled at 0900, and after that we don't have too much to do because of the maintenance we were able to get done en route, so I reckon the ship should be ready to sail at about midday. After that, some of you can go ashore for a few hours and then someone needs to come back and relieve me until 1800, and then you can all go out tonight. Just make absolutely certain that everyone is aboard before 0600 tomorrow morning, when we sail.'

The port of Algiers is not so much a harbour in the normal sense of the word. It is more a collection of strategic breakwaters attached onto the coast which enclose a series of docks that are created by several piers, which jut out from the land. These docks are, for the most part, adjacent to the city. Captain Blokland, together with the harbour pilot, who had come aboard an hour earlier, expertly manoeuvred *Swiftsure* through the northern entrance formed by the breakwaters. Within minutes the ship slid alongside the refuelling pier where she would be secured for the next twenty-four hours. Two pairs of eyes had watched the entire event, taking note of several details that would be discussed at length later.

Khalid, together with Mohammed, Abu and Jabir, sat around a table which was located in an almost decrepit back office behind the warehouse that housed the two Avon RIBs. Jabir was a trusted associate of Abu, and had helped him on many missions previously. They were waiting for the arrival of Tarka, the final member of the assault team. Tarka was different to all the rest in that he was literally the muscle in the team. Although the brawn rather than the brains, Khalid was happy that he was coming along, simply because he cut a very intimidating figure, with a physique that few would be prepared to tangle with. In Khalid's mind, apart from the weapons that they had, Tarka would make certain that the *Swiftsure*'s crew were compliant to their every wish.

With all five now seated and drinking tea, Khalid proceeded to outline the plan.

'My brothers, there are two pieces of information that we know for certain at this time. One is that the crew of the *Swiftsure* number five, including the captain; the second is that she sails at six in the morning. We have seen three of the infidels leaving the tug one hour ago, presumably to go shopping or walk the markets. As we speak, the tug is being watched, specifically to notice who else leaves the ship and who comes back, and when. It is my feeling that tonight there will be only one, perhaps two at the most, left on the ship.'

Khalid continued: 'At the hour of midnight, myself, along with Tarka and Jabir, will take over the ship. We will covertly await the arrival of the rest of the crew, which we know has to be before six in the morning. In my opinion, it will be more like one thirty or two, we will then take measures to ensure that the ship sails on time without anybody knowing that we are aboard.'

Jabir then asked: 'Khalid, my brother, how will we get the inflatable boats aboard the tug, and what about the harbour pilot?'

Khalid replied: 'Well, firstly the *Swiftsure* will not need a pilot in the morning; in fact, it did not need a pilot coming in either. Although an ocean-going tug, it is still a relatively small ship. We know that Captain Blokland requested one on arrival, perhaps just to be extra careful and to show him any potential dangers; he did not request a pilot for his departure. Secondly, Abu and Mohammed will drive the RIBs at about eight knots, so as not to make too much noise, out to a position approximately fifteen miles from the harbour, in two hours' time. There they will await the rendezvous with the tug. Abu has fitted strong webbing slings to the RIBs, all connected to a single eye; it should be easy for the tug's crane to lift them on board. He has also made wooden 'V' sections, which the RIB hulls can fit into on the after deck of the tug prior to being lashed down for the journey north. Each of the RIBs has two spare Kalashnikovs and two hundred rounds of ammunition. My dear brothers …' Khalid paused. 'Once we have the tug's crew under our control, and sufficiently compliant to our wishes, we should not have any more problems until we get to the north Atlantic.'

Frank Blokland trawled the markets for just about two hours, trying to find nice presents for his wife and daughter. In his mind, the easy part of that equation was his wife. An avid art lover, she had a great appreciation for water colours, so Frank picked what he thought would look well in their apartment, a landscape which embraced Algiers harbour and the Atlas mountains set into the background.

For his daughter, it was a little trickier, but eventually he settled on an enormous stuffed camel. Happy with his purchases, he decided to have a meal of spicy lamb and rice, much to the amusement of his fellow restaurant patrons, who were amazed at how he managed the painting and the camel around the table. He got so much food that he physically couldn't finish it. Having left the restaurant, leaving a nice tip, he then, together with his camel and painting, in an expression of experience over hope, hailed a taxi and returned to the ship. As he was about to walk up the gangway, he heard a voice from the bridge which turned out to be Jan, the ship's cook.

'Hey, skipper, do you want me to prepare an extra cabin for the camel?'

Thirty minutes later the two sets of eyes again watched four of *Swiftsure*'s crew leaving the ship, setting out for a night on the town, leaving only the captain aboard. At 23.50, two figures walked along the pier, towards the stern of the *Swiftsure*. Both had Kalashnikov rifles under their coats, and the bigger of the two had a large, extremely sharp knife in a scabbard at his side. They easily boarded the tug, and jumped onto the afterdeck. Each was wearing soft-soled shoes, so virtually no noise was made. The semi automatics were kept tightly to their bodies, to make sure that they didn't bang off railings or the tug's superstructure. They climbed one flight of stairs to where Khalid had noticed a light coming from a porthole. He eased slowly up to it, and saw Captain Blokland sitting on one of the large armchairs in the wardroom, sound asleep. Khalid and Tarka moved on to the next door on that deck level. Once inside, Khalid's spatial orientation led him easily and quietly to the door of the wardroom, which was half open. He signalled behind him for Tarka to move forward. When Tarka arrived on the other side of the wardroom door, he quietly withdrew his knife from its scabbard. Khalid was amazed that the two men were in fact able to enter the mess without waking the captain. Khalid then signalled to Tarka, who tapped loudly the tip of his knife off a nearby metal chair. Frank Blokland woke, though not with any sense of anxiety, and took a second or two to take in what was in front of him, a menacing man of about six feet in height aiming a semi automatic weapon straight at him from a distance of seven feet, and another who looked like a guerrilla, wielding what appeared to be a long, sharp knife.

'Who the hell are you?' asked Captain Blokland.

Khalid looked at him straight in the eye.

'My dear captain, I have no wish to harm you, but I must tell you that if you move any muscle in your body, you will say hello to Allah in the following moment.'

After a pause that seemed to last forever, Khalid continued.

'Can I now expect your full co-operation?'

Frank Blokland was a practical man, 'Right now,' he said, 'I am in no position to answer anything but yes. However, I would like to know who you are and what you want.'

Khalid replied: 'All in good time, captain, all in good time.'

'Listen,' said Frank Blokland, 'my crew will be coming aboard shortly …'

'I know,' replied Khalid, cutting him off, 'and you will make certain that they come aboard quietly. And just in case you decide that some heroics might be in order, apart from Tarka here, may I also ask you to look at the contents of this envelope.'

He then threw the envelope onto Frank Blokland's lap. The photographs were arranged in a certain order, so when the captain looked at them, the first thing he saw was the front door of his apartment in Ferdinand Bolstraat in Amsterdam. Moving to the second, he saw a picture of his wife returning to his apartment, and a third was a picture of his wife collecting his daughter from school. Frank went white and roared at his tormentor.

'What are you trying to do?'

Khalid waited for him to settle, and then in a very quiet voice replied:

'My dear captain, if you try anything – and I mean anything – you and your family will not live to see the next sunset.'

He then took his mobile phone from his pocket and held it up in front of the now shocked tug skipper.

'A one-word text is all it would take to seal the fate of your family.'

There was a quietness in the cabin which seemed to last a few moments, after which Khalid said softly:

'Can I now expect your full compliance with our wishes, captain?'
Frank Blokland looked at him and said quietly 'Yes'.

Five minutes later Jan arrived aboard and, having seen the light on in the mess, presumed his captain was watching television. Khalid stood behind the door, while Tarka moved into the shadows. They heard a voice coming down the companion way.

'Hey, skipper, you watching telly?'
Frank looked at the muzzle of Khalid's weapon, which was aimed at his chest, and then replied:

'Yes, Jan, I'm here.'
The diminutive ship's cook walked straight in to the mess and sat on the arm of the settee next to his skipper, and immediately saw Khalid move out from behind the door.

'Jan, sit down and stay sitting.'
Jan looked at his skipper with an air of disbelief.

'Skipper, what the hell is going on?' he asked, looking at Khalid.
Out of his peripheral vision, he detected a movement to his left, and nearly had a heart attack when he saw Tarka move towards him with the long knife in his hand.

'Do exactly as they say,' repeated his captain.

Tarka moved towards the chef and literally picked him up by the scruff of the neck, and dragged him towards a chair at the dining table. He put down the knife under one of his feet, and pulled the small frame of the chef onto the chair. He then tied him to it with a length of polypropylene rope, so tightly that Jan had difficulty breathing. Tarka then picked up the knife and roughly grabbed the now petrified cook by the hair, pulling his head backwards, and exposing the full extent of his neck. He brought the blade of the knife to where it touched his windpipe.
There was a loud roar from the tug's skipper.

'No, no, you can't do that.'
Khalid looked at Captain Blokland.

'If there is even the slightest difficulty in ensuring the total compliance of your other three crew members when they arrive, this man will be without a head.'

Jan, who at this stage was almost mortally shocked and on the point of fainting, allowed a tiny sigh of relief. He was absolutely certain that he was living the last minutes of his thirty-nine-year-old life. He looked at his captain and became slightly embarrassed at the fact that tears were falling down his face. Forty minutes later, a taxi arrived at the bottom of the ship's gangway, disgorging three very happy and slightly drunk crew members. Frank Blokland could hear them laughing and joking as they noisily made their way up the gangway. It was customary for all the crew of the *Swiftsure* to give a look into the mess when they came in after a night out, just to check if anybody else was up, at which point experiences would be exchanged and maybe someone would make tea. This night was no different; the mate, the engineer and the deck hand trooped in, still laughing and joking, and had actually sat down on the armchairs before they realised the deadly presence in the room. As each of them went through the process of their brain believing what their eyes were seeing, they became paralysed with fear and disbelief.

Piet Stam slowly looked at his skipper, his eyes begging for an explanation. His captain responded immediately.

'None of you are to make even the smallest movement of defiance. You will do exactly as these people say, and that is an order, is that clear?' Frank looked sternly at each one of them, and each of them could only nod their head in the affirmative.

'You have spoken wisely, captain. This tug will sail on schedule at six a.m. As for the rest of you, you will be at your posts as usual. Let me remind you all that if any of you enters the radio room or attempts to compromise our plans, you will watch your colleague being beheaded, and you will personally throw his body over the side. Your captain has some photographs which he might like you to look at.'

At this stage pure terror had enveloped all of the crew, with the exception of Frank Blokland.

Abu and Mohammed had made final preparations to the RIBs before bringing them to a quiet slipway. They had, on the orders of Khalid, bought several bags of food, including rice, meats, and fruit, which were stowed in the small space that was left in the back of the RIB after the torpedo assembly parts had been put in. Because of the darkness, nobody could see the RIBs as they made their way quietly out from the slip, towards the open sea, which was a good thing, because they resembled a horse-drawn wagon loaded with all manner of things. When they were approximately three miles out, each of them opened the throttles slightly, bringing their speed up to eight knots, which is an uncomfortably slow speed for a RIB to drive at, as they are designed to plane along at thirty knots.

The tug slipped her lines at 0547, and gently turned left towards the entrance in the breakwaters.

Having cleared the nub of the northern breakwater, Frank Blokland turned the *Swiftsure* through ninety degrees, onto a northerly heading. At this point, even though he had a good idea that the people who now controlled his ship were terrorists of one sort or another, he had no idea what they had planned. Right now his greatest concern was Jan, who was still trussed up in the wardroom with Tarka and his blade hovering close by. He was certain that the rest of the crew, even if presented with an opportunity, would not do anything stupid, but at the same time he knew that terrorists 'terrorise' and, accordingly, Khalid may be looking for the slightest reason to absolutely terrorise his crew into total compliance to whatever their plan was.

Approximately forty minutes later, Piet Stam, who was acting as lookout on the bridge, reported to his skipper.

'Skipper, two contacts dead ahead, they look like RIBs … with some sort of cargo.'

Khalid then quietly spoke to the captain.

'You will rendezvous with the inflatables.'

Frank slowed the ship at first, and then, with the small bit of 'way' under her, allowed it to drift right up to the RIBs. A final short burst of 'astern' revolutions stopped the ship in the water.

Khalid then ordered the skipper to make arrangements for the ship's crane to be manned, telling him that they were going to take the two RIBs aboard, and once again reminding him of the consequences of any wrong moves.

Frans de Vries, the ship's engineer, turned to his skipper.

'I'll operate the crane, skipper.' and then, turning to Khalid, 'what exactly do you want me to do?'

Khalid replied:

'Each of these RIBs is rigged with a central lifting point; you will lift each one of them onto the stern of the ship. As you can now see, both of the RIBs carry wooden 'V' sections, so that they will sit comfortably on the deck. When this is done, they will be lashed down.'

Frans made his way aft towards the ship's crane, his engineering mind trying to figure out what exactly these people were up to. However, at this stage, he simply concluded that, whatever it was, it wasn't good. By the time he had sat himself comfortably into the little enclosed cockpit that housed the crane's controls, he could see that both RIBs were now alongside the tug. When he had the crane's jib right over the first RIB, he advanced the lever that caused the hook to come down towards the RIB. The lifting point of the RIB was then swiftly attached to the crane's hook by what seemed like the only person who was on the RIB. Through the tug's radio system, Frans heard his skipper say:

'Hold it there, Frans.'

Johann, the tug's deckhand, then put a boarding ladder over the side, and almost as soon as it reached the level of the RIB, Abu, with a Kalashnikov slung around his neck and chest, scrambled up onto the tug's deck. Frans then lifted the RIB straight onto the afterdeck on the starboard side, and to his astonishment saw Abu untie the large wooden 'V' sections which the RIBs would sit in. Frank Blokland, who was now looking out the aft bridge windows, and controlling events on his afterdeck, then ordered Johann to lash down securely the RIB. He then ordered Frans to lift the second RIB onto the port side where the same process was repeated. Two minutes later, the still water at the stern of the tug boiled as its twin screws started turning clockwise.

'Would you please tell me exactly what we are supposed to be doing?' asked a slightly impatient Captain Blokland when the second RIB was securely lashed to the deck.

'Captain,' replied Khalid, 'your company has ordered you to sail this fine ship to the south of Ireland, and that is precisely what you will do.'

'Look,' said the captain, 'if that is what we are doing then I ask you to please untie Jan. He is our ship's cook, so if you want to eat on this journey, and more importantly if you want my crew to function on this journey, I urge you to release him. I have given you my assurance that none of my crew will do anything stupid.'

'How fast can you get this tug to the south west of Ireland?' asked Khalid.

'At fifteen knots, I can be there in four days,' came the terse reply.

'In that case, captain, I will release your cook, but let me remind you that in the event of any incident, your wife and child will be the first to die, and I will execute the cook anyway.'

Captain Blokland brought the *Swiftsure* onto a heading of 'two six zero' degrees en route to the Strait of Gibraltar as the tug once again crossed the 2,800 metre depth contour.

LE *Eithne*

Eithne was now moving in a north westerly direction, in the early morning rain. She had conducted four more conventional boardings throughout the night, at which point Mike had given the order to secure from boarding stations and proceed on track to Galway, where the ship was going to be berthed for the weekend. The weather had got progressively worse during the past hour, and *Eithne* was smashing her way through large Atlantic seas with white crests on the waves, the constant rain reducing visibility. Jamie Morrisson, *Eithne*'s capable XO, now had command of the ship.

'Looking at that weather, sir, I think we are going to be punching into it all the way to Galway Bay. If it gets any worse I'll bring her back to one engine.'

'Okay, it certainly looks like it's going to deteriorate,' said Mike.

'I'm going to get some sleep now,' said the ship's commander. 'Call me at 1300 please. Oh, and by the way, Jamie, you can stand down the boarding crews now, and let 'em get some sleep; they've done a good night's work.'

Mike then made his way two decks below the level of the bridge to the wardroom where Sub Lt Gerry Stewart was already eating breakfast.

'Good morning, sir,' said Petty Officer Bill Cashman, *Eithne*'s wardroom steward.

'Good morning, PO,' replied the captain, making his way towards the very neatly laid head of the wardroom table.

'What would you like, sir? I can offer you scrambled eggs on toast, or I could quickly rustle up a fry.'

Mike thought about that, and immediately ruled out the fry, on the basis that when he woke up in the middle of the day he was going to do a workout in the ship's gym. This was in fact one section of the huge hangar deck, where there were six pieces of gym equipment for the general use of the crew.

'Scrambled eggs it is, PO, with some brown bread, please.'

'Yes, sir, two minutes,' replied the PO.

'Tiring night's work, Gerry,' said the captain.

'Yes, sir, looking forward to some shut eye now.'

'Ye must have given that poor trawler crew the fright of their lives,' said Mike, who had personally debriefed the over the horizon boarding crew.

'Yeah,' said the gunnery officer, 'the amazing thing about it was that we were standing outside the bridge windows looking in for quite a few moments before anyone copped on, and then, sir, to be honest, we scared the fucking shit out of them.'

Mike's attention was then drawn to Sky News on the large television in the opposite corner of the wardroom. Having got the main headlines, he then tucked into his breakfast, which had just arrived on the table, after which he made his way to his cabin, where within five minutes he was sound asleep.

Back up on the bridge, Sub Lt Neil Kennedy, *Eithne*'s navigation officer (or 'nav' in navy speak), was talking with Able Seaman Tom Whelan, who was on duty on the bridge as a lookout. Able Seaman Whelan had a great interest in the science of navigation, and the nav officer was quite happy to explain the reasoning behind the course and speed the ship was now on.

'The thing is,' said the nav, 'as you know, we are now en route to Galway. Our speed is fifteen knots and we can't enter Galway docks until there is sufficient water for the tidal locks to be opened. We are now 210 nautical miles from Galway. Divided by fifteen, that gives us an elapsed time of fourteen hours. Fourteen hours takes us to 2300, which is exactly when the tide is high enough, and the locks open. But of course, the ship will start slowing once we close Kilcolgan point in Galway Bay. That process will add another, say, twenty minutes onto the fourteen hours, which in turn will have us going through the gates twenty minutes after they open.'

'I see,' said the able seaman, 'and how long do the locks stay open for, sir?'

'Two hours,' replied the nav.

In fact *Eithne* maintained two separate navigation plots – one was a GPS-based electronic chart plotter, and the other was on Admiralty paper charts which were updated every fifteen minutes. These were housed, together with a myriad of manuals, in the navigation area aft of the bridge. At 1530, Sub Lt Kennedy wrote in the nav log:

'Blasket Islands off starboard beam. Course change 050º.'

The ship was now on a course which would take it past Loop Head and the mouth of the Shannon estuary, and on up past the County Clare coast, where she would pass through the South Sound, a narrow stretch about five miles wide, with Doolin Point to starboard, and the smallest of the Aran Islands, Inis Oirr, to port. Twelve and a half miles from here *Eithne* would enter Galway Bay, on its southern side off Black Head. As the ship made its way north eastwards, she was being hammered by huge Atlantic swells. In the Irish navy, you were either sailing in the Atlantic ocean or the Irish sea. There was, in fact, no comparison.

At 1600, Lt John Kana came onto the bridge to relieve *Eithne*'s executive officer as officer of the watch (OOW).

'G'day, sir. Jees, I thought the southern ocean was bad; this is worse and we are hardly five miles from the shore.'

Lt Kana was Royal New Zealand Navy officer, who was on an officer exchange programme with the Irish navy. One of his tasks while up in the northern hemisphere was to evaluate the effectiveness of the caley davit system, and also the highly efficient method that the Irish navy used for boardings.

'Have you ever been into Galway, John?' asked the XO.

'No, sir, but I have heard a lot about it. I believe the skipper is from around there?'

'Yeah, he is in fact,' said the XO. 'He learned a lot about this particular ocean growing up in this area, long before he came into the navy. I think he's from somewhere around here,' putting his finger on a point on the electronic chart near Rossaveal on the north coast of Galway Bay. 'Anyway, John, this is what is happening in the next hour or so. They'll be rolling out the Dauphin in about a half an hour's time, when we get into the lee of the Aran Islands. There, we'll be turning the ship into wind so that the helicopter can take off before we turn east again towards Galway docks.'

'Where is the helo going, sir?' asked Lt Kana.

'She's due a fifty hour check, which would normally be carried out aboard, but Jim Angland isn't happy about one of the fuel boost pumps, so he is flying her to Baldonnel where hopefully they will sort the whole thing out there tomorrow.'

'And what … does he land back on the flight deck when we're alongside in Galway?'

Jamie Morrisson gave a little smile.

'No, he's got the weekend off and he'll land back on the ship when we're sailing out the bay again. It's not as if the crew couldn't do it. It's well within their capability, but as you'll see, Galway docks is pretty much in the centre of the town. No point in taking unnecessary risks.'

Thirty minutes later, the rotor blades of the Dauphin were brought up to full military power, as *Eithne* steamed in a south-south westerly heading. The flight deck officer (FDO) was now talking to the pilots.

Delta 234, FDO.

Delta 234, go ahead.

Delta 234, wind 210 at 24 knots, ship's speed 12 knots.

Delta 234, roger copy and we're ready to lift.

Delta 234, clear take off, left hand turn out on track Baldonnel, report Shannon control at altitude.

Roger, copy, lifting now, Delta 234.

After the helicopter lifted up into a hover, Fl. Lt Jim Angland's right hand moved the cyclic less than an eighth of an inch to the left, enabling the Dauphin to drift sideways out over the port side of the ship, then easing it forward so that the helicopter could increase speed and climb out to fifteen hundred feet. The minute it came out from the lee of the ship's stern, she was able to take full advantage of the strong wind blowing in from the Atlantic and gain some more free airspeed. She then climbed rapidly before making a left turn in along the south shore of the bay, initially towards Kinvara and then on an easterly heading direct to Baldonnel.

Swiftsure

The steady hum of *Swiftsure*'s twin screws was made all the more constant by the still, very flat Mediterranean sea. Frank Blokland knew, however, that this would change when they went through the narrow strait that separates the tiny British colony of Gibraltar, in the south of Spain, from Morocco. Then the Atlantic would come into play. He was aware of a frontal depression moving in a westerly direction, which was positioned north west of the Azores. In his mind the tug would be coming into contact with that at some stage.

Khalid was standing at the starboard door of the bridge, his eyes taking in the early morning light contrast caused by the sun rising in the east, and the still sheltered western side of the rock, that looked down on the naval base and the town of Gibraltar. In there was danger. A strategic British naval depot, which would unquestionably house, at the very least, a detachment of royal marines complete with helicopters who, if they knew what was going on, Khalid thought, would not be slow about putting a stop to his plans. But all that was academic; most likely, he thought, the same marines were probably scattered around in pubs or nightclubs or, maybe, tucked up in their bunks. He was certain that the Royal Navy knew that the *Swiftsure* was passing through the strait tonight. In fact, he concluded, they probably knew the identity of every ship that passed through it. The important thing was that they had no idea that this tug was no longer being commanded by its captain.

Thirteen hours later, *Swiftsure* was abeam Cape St Vincent, and now feeling the effects of that westerly flowing frontal depression. The motion was no longer like the silky smooth of the Mediterranean, but a sort of low grade pitching and rolling. Piet Stam, who now had the con, wondered if this might start to have an effect on their obviously non seagoing 'guests'. He hoped it wouldn't make them more short tempered or cranky. Mohammed, who was now on the bridge giving his leader a chance to get some sleep, turned to the *Swiftsure*'s mate.

'We will be turning right soon, yes?'

'No,' replied Piet, 'we will initially take up a north westerly heading for approximately four hours, and then we will turn the ship into the north.'

'Why is that?' asked a curious Mohammed, speaking in near perfect Dutch to the mate.

'Because the Portuguese coast is not friendly when you sail too close to it. First of all it is quite shallow out to about forty miles, and it has a transverse effect on the waves, which can create a very confused sea state quite a few miles out.'

Piet thought about the fact that he was having what could be described in any other circumstance as a very normal conversation with someone he regarded as a 'terrorist'.

About an hour later, Frank Blokland was back on the bridge. He noticed that Khalid and Tarka seemed to cope best with the new motion of the sea. Abu looked like death and had been getting sick for about three hours. Trouble was, Frank thought, most people got over that within two to three days at sea. Then again, that could be a good thing; he was still very fearful of the possibility that one of his crew could be executed at the mere whim of these people. He knew that he and his crew had no option but to comply completely with everything Khalid wanted, but at the same time he found it strange how a sort of normality prevailed as the tug put mile after nautical mile behind them heading northwards. At this stage he had guessed that the two RIBs aboard his ship were in fact two large bombs. Why else would somebody want to bring two RIBs, which were virtually full to the brim, onto a_ship which already had a RIB aboard.

The only reason he could imagine was that they intended to use it in some nefarious way or other. After all, he thought, isn't that how these people blew a big hole in the side of the USS *Cole* in Yemen? But what could it be? The north eastern Atlantic wasn't what you would call a target-rich area for a terrorist and, anyway, there wouldn't be any ships tied up alongside out here. Since the tug came abeam Cabo da Roca near Lisbon, Khalid had ordered a course change to 'three five zero' degrees magnetic, which in Frank's mind wasn't going to take them near a port any time soon.

One hundred and thirty miles south of Mizen Head Frank Blokland had noticed that Khalid, Mohammed and Abu were spending a lot of time in his cabin, presumably fine tuning their plans. He still didn't know where his tug was going, but he had a good idea what it was going to be used for. It didn't take a genius to work out that a ship like this, taken over by a group of fanatical terrorists who had brought aboard two RIBs which were obviously full of something or other, was not going to do anything good for humanity.

At that moment Khalid came onto the bridge and smiled at Tarka. He turned to Captain Blokland and said:

'Captain, how long more to the Porcupine Bank?'

'Seven hours.'

'I see,' said Khalid. 'You will take us to the southern end of that bank.'

'Look,' said Frank Blokland, 'I need to ring my wife. When I am at sea, she knows that I will never leave three days pass without contacting her. Whatever you may think, it would be worse for you if I didn't make contact. She would probably contact my employers, who would no doubt then contact me.'

Khalid smiled. He knew that what the captain was saying was correct. Having come this far, he didn't want to alert in any way the owners of the tug. He had come this far confident that nobody outside of this ship had any idea what was going on. The longer he could keep that situation going, the better.

'Yes, captain, you may speak to your wife, but there are two conditions. Firstly, Mohammed, as you know, speaks fluent Dutch; he will listen in on your call to make sure that you say absolutely nothing, even in coded language to your wife, that would compromise us. Secondly, if you do, or if Mohammed even thinks that you might have had, I will personally bring the head of your ship's cook and present it to you on the bridge.'

Frank Blokland exhaled slowly, trying to rid that horrible image from his mind.

'I will do exactly as you say.'

'Good,' said Khalid, 'you may ring her now, but you are not to disclose the position of the ship. You can say that everything is going according to plan – and keep the conversation brief.'

Frank then entered the tiny comms room off the tug's bridge and made the connection, with Mohammed staring into his face, and Khalid standing next to him.

'Carla, how are you?' (Pause) 'Yeah, things are going pretty well, Piet sends his regards. How is Amy?'
(Longer pause) 'Good, good, I'm so looking forward to coming home, I really miss you both. I gotta go now, so take care and I'll ring you in a couple of days.'
(Pause) 'Okay, see you soon and give my regards to your mother. Bye, bye.'
(Click) Frank broke the connection.
Mohammed then turned to Khalid, who could not speak Dutch.

'The cook can keep his head for another while.'

The three men then stepped outside of the comms room, which was promptly locked by Khalid again.

Amsterdam

Carla Blokland put down the phone and stared at a photograph of her mother and father on the wall. Her thoughts seemed to be all over the place; it was like a battle going on in her head. On the one side she had an image of her husband, a very strong, resilient and capable man, who took his job very seriously and, on the other side, the picture in front of her. Her father was killed in a traffic accident ten years ago and her mother died six years ago ... How could Frank possibly say what he said to her when the call was closing? She tried her best to remember the comment literally *See you soon and give my regards to your mother.*

She began to go through the whole gamut of possibilities: Was he tired? Maybe. Was he sick in some way or other? Unlikely. Was it a slip of the tongue? Hardly. She knew that from the comms room of the tug there would always be other people around, so she accepted that these conversations didn't embrace too much intimacy. But nevertheless, she felt that this conversation was different. His phone calls from the ship were always brief anyway, of necessity, but this one was especially short. It was so strange, and then she thought: 'Maybe it's nothing, yeah, probably just a slip of the tongue.'
She had to get ready soon as she had planned to collect her daughter and take her into town for the afternoon.

Secret Intelligence Service (SIS), London

It wasn't so much that they were perturbed by it, but they really wanted to understand the nature of it. What exactly did '*strawberries and blackberries are now in the basket*' mean? The mobile phone text message was intercepted by MI6, Britain's main anti terrorist agency, and the only reason it came on their radar was not so much where it came from, but where it was sent. It had originated from somewhere near Edinburgh in Scotland, and its destination was somewhere in Algiers. James Calthorne and Jeremy Aldridge, the two agents who had already spent about an hour speculating on what it might mean, were about to give up when their boss, John Winthrop, walked into the room.

'Still trying to make sense of that text, are we?' asked the senior agent.

'Well, sir, it's like two entities are now in one. The question is what could those entities be and what could they have gone into?' replied James. Jeremy then added: 'I've been trying to look at it from a terrorist point of view … what would you put in, and what would you be putting it into? Strawberries and blackberries for all we know could be ingredients for a bomb. Where its been put into could be that which is being blown up.' Jeremy couldn't know at that time that he was perhaps half right in his assumption.

John Winthrop then said: 'Well guys, you know the drill, all you can do is keep at it and keep an open mind. Something else will turn up sooner or later; it always does and it will either rule it out as a threat or confirm our suspicions.' Special Agent Winthrop turned as he was going out the door.

'Mightn't be any harm to talk to our Dutch colleagues again.'

LE *Eithne*

Harbour stations, fore and aft line parties close up.

The order went out on the ship's intercom when *Eithne* was about two miles from Mutton Island inbound to Galway docks. Galway docks would test the skills of any captain bringing a ship in, and the LE *Eithne*, a naval vessel with a fully trained crew, was no different. The biggest risk going into these docks was going aground as ships made their way from the leveret's tower between Mutton and Hare Island and the entrance to the docks. There, a dredged channel of about three and a half metres at lowest chart datum, and less than one cable in width, was what concentrated the mind of any skipper. In *Eithne*'s case it wasn't helped either by the strong south westerly wind and driving rain hitting her sideways on, with very little way under her.

As she inched her way to the inner part of the docks, a small tug positioned on her starboard side towards her stern to complete the manoeuvre of bringing her alongside. Once secured, those of the crew who were now off duty made their way towards the myriad of restaurants and bars that were literally a stone's throw from where the ship actually docked. Some of the younger more enthusiastic crew members set their sights on the clubs. Forty-five minutes after the ship docked, a discussion was still going on in the bridge, between Commander Ford, Lt Cdr Jimmy Casey, *Eithne*'s engineering officer and Chief ERA, Stephen Mackey.

'Sir, I have been working on that pump on the number two engine most of the afternoon, and it looks like we're going to have to get a new one,' said the chief.

'Yeah, sir, I concur,' said Jimmy Casey. 'We can't really go to sea without that, so I've sent a signal to the naval base to get one up to us over the weekend. Trouble is, there's nobody in the stores now, at least not anybody who would have the slightest clue what it is, so I'm expecting a signal back in the morning with more information about when we are going to get it.'

Commander Ford thought about this, in terms of his intention to sail again early on Monday morning.

'Okay, Jimmy, let me know what's happening as soon as you get the signal back. I'm going ashore in the morning, I'm heading out to Rossaveal to see my parents, so you can get me on my mobile. The thing is, if that part doesn't come up 'till Monday morning, we won't be able to sail until Tuesday morning.'

'Yeah, sir, I think the lock gates open on Tuesday morning at 0400,' replied the engineering officer.

***American Princess*, Leith, 0900 Monday**

Slowly but surely, a combination of bow thrusters and two tugs eased the massive cruise liner away from the Britannia docks, and turned her towards the North sea. Leaving the tiny island of Inchkeith to port, the *American Princess* slowly gathered speed, and by the time she passed the Isle of May heading towards Fife Ness, she was up to her cruising speed of twenty-two knots.

For most of the passengers, going up the east coast of Scotland just did not compare, from a sightseeing point of view, with the rugged northern coast beyond John O'Groats and the many islands that would be on view as the ship passed through the Inner Hebrides. In fact, the only diversion was when the ship passed Aberdeen, where quite a few of the passengers were amazed at the volume of helicopter traffic heading to and from the oil rigs.

Eleven hours later the captain announced that the ship, having come through the gap between Scotland and the Orkney Islands, was now passing the infamous Cape Wrath. As big as the cruise liner was, passengers could feel the slight pitching as her bows were faced squarely into the Atlantic. However, two hours later, the ship was firmly back in the lee of the Western Isles, as she made her way now more slowly down past the Isles of Skye and Rum. Soon though she would once again be exposed to the full onslaught of the Atlantic as she left Barra Head to starboard.

Scott Jablonsky and his wife Marie had a cabin on the upper starboard deck. He was born in the city of Charleston and for thirty out of the fifty-nine years of his life he practised as a medical doctor. Approaching, as he was, his sixtieth birthday, Marie decided to treat him to a nice long cruise, her logic being that because he worked very hard and almost never took proper holidays, the only way to get him away from his routine and the dreaded telephone was to get him on a ship and get him out into the middle of some ocean, whilst at the same time being totally pampered and yet still able to swim, play some ball games, go for walks, and have general exercise when he wanted it.

When she looked at this 'cold to warm' cruise she thought about the contrast between his almost total exposure to 'air conditioning' and the cold bracingly pure north Atlantic air. She was sure he would really like the part of the cruise where the ship slowed right down somewhere, miles west of Ireland, to watch whales and dolphins for several hours, and thereafter relaxing as the ship then journeyed south to the warm islands of the Azores. When she had first presented him with this, he couldn't contain his delight. He told her that that particular idea would never have entered his head, despite the fact that he spent a good part of every week telling other people to relax, go to the beach, and other such nuggets of doctorly advice.

They were at dinner in one of the main dining halls of the ship when the first officer announced that the ship would be passing Barra Head at 0800 in the morning, and advising the passengers that this was also a potential area for sighting cetaceans of all sorts, although at the same time covering himself by saying that the main event in terms of the profusion of these animals would be when the ship slowed right down for several hours in the Porcupine Bank.

'Oh,' said Scott to his wife, 'I'll definitely be up to see that. How about you?'

Barra Head

Scott and Marie decided to leave breakfast until after the ship speeded up again and passed Barra Head. They decided first to go out on deck and watch for any whales or dolphins that might be about.

'I dunno 'bout you, honey,' said Marie, but I'm just way too full after that meal last night.'

'That's alright,' her husband replied. 'An hour or two of that sea air will tweak your appetite once again.'

A lot of the cruise liner's passengers elected to come up on deck on the starboard side, no doubt thinking that the best place to see the animals would be between the ship and the myriad of islands before Barra Head.

Two hours later Scott Jablonsky turned to a fellow passenger standing next to him at the rail and said:

'For my money the whales are having a bad day at the office, whadd'ya think?'

Doug Chambers replied:

'I guess they did tell us that this place was going to be just a maybe.'

Scott laughed.

'They also said that the Porcupine Bank was going to be good. I hope they are more right about that one. Anyway, I think that we'll give it another ten minutes and then go in for a well earned breakfast. Say, would you two like to join us?' asked Scott, referring to Doug and the woman who he now had his arm around.

'Sure, that'd be great!'

The two couples made formal introductions, and within ten minutes were sitting cosily at a window table in the dining room.

Doug Chambers was a Vietnam veteran who had retired from the army with the rank of major. His wife Loretta had also served in Vietnam as an army nurse, which was where they first met. They now lived in Charlottesville, Virginia.

At 1145 the *American Princess* finally cleared Barra Head light coming onto a course of two three zero, which would take the ship in a straight line towards the northern end of the Porcupine Bank, a shallow area of water in the Atlantic, approximately the size of the county of Wexford. It is situated 180 miles west of Galway. It is so called because it is a bank which is only 148 metres deep; however all around it are depths ranging from 600 to 2,800 metres. These statistics make it an excellent habitat for marine food chains.

A combination of increased light levels together with the stable and warm Gulf Stream provide a perfect environment for the growth of plankton in the area. This results in the presence there of a whole array of whales and dolphins, for nearly ten months of the year. These creatures include bottle nose and Risso's dolphins, and Atlantic white sided dolphins which are never seen inshore. Harbour porpoises, and pilot, minke and fin whales, together with their calves, are abundant here also.

As the Jablonskys and the Chambers chatted over a nice warm cooked breakfast, made even better by the fact that they were at a window seat and could look out at the cold sea, they became aware of the gentle heel of the ship, as it changed course. They also became aware of the weather having come out of the lee of Barra. Now the ship faced into the full force of the Atlantic. Although it was blowing a force seven, that in itself did not really affect the cruise liner, which in any case was equipped with massive stabilisers for the comfort of her passengers; however, the huge and long Atlantic swells caused her to roll a little.

Captain John Whiteman's task was to ensure that the ship was positioned at the Porcupine Bank for the most part during daylight hours so that passengers could view the animals. To facilitate this and to make some allowance for the weather, he decided to bring the liner's speed back to thirteen knots. At this speed the liner would arrive there at approximately 1145 the following morning.

LE *Eithne*

Commander Mike Ford was working on some paperwork in his day cabin when his mobile phone rang. He looked at the number and immediately recognised it as that of his brother, Cormac, who lived near Oranmore. Mike had sent him a text message late the night before, wondering if by any chance he would be going out to Rossaveal to visit their parents some time over the weekend.

'Cormac, how are you getting on?' enquired Mike.

'Great, great, Mike, how are you? *Eithne* must be in at the moment, is she?'

'Yeah, we got in with the tide late last night.'

'How long are you in for? Myself and Gemma are getting an Indian tonight, would you like to join us?'

'That'd be great Cormac. How is Gemma anyway?'

'Sure she's still living with me, isn't that all that matters? Listen, are you looking to go out to Rossaveal today?'

'Yeah,' said Mike, 'how does that square with you?'

'Let me see … it's twenty to ten now, I can pick you up at the ship in twenty minutes if that's okay with you?'

'That suits me fine, see you then.'

Twenty minutes later, almost to the minute, Mike opened the door of Cormac's car and jumped in, while at the same time giving his brother a friendly dig in the arm.

'Hey, Mucky,' he said, calling Cormac by his childhood nickname, 'good to see ya.'

They shook hands and drove out of the docks area, towards Salthill.

'I suppose I can't really call you Mucky anymore now, can I? I'll have to call you professor from now on. Hey, congratulations and well done, you deserve it.'

Cormac had been made professor in the Department of Marine Studies in NUI Galway three weeks ago, and Mike hadn't met him since.

'God, you've done well,' said Mike. 'Did we ever think when we were young fellas helping on Dad's boats that both of us would end up in careers involving the sea?'

'Well,' his brother replied, 'growing up on the sea like we did didn't exactly hinder us in that regard, did it?'

Both were in fact very happy in the careers that they had chosen, and fully accepted that their upbringing probably had a huge influence on their choices.

'How's Mom and Dad?' asked Mike.

'Pretty good,' replied Cormac, who would see their parents, Tom and Gretta, on a much more regular basis than Mike would. 'Dad's leg is still giving him a bit of trouble, but Mom is in great form and, by the way, do you know that Bernie is pregnant again?'

Bernie was Mike and Cormac's younger sister. As the brothers headed out the coast road through the villages of Barna and Spiddal they talked a bit about their respective careers and their upbringing. For Mike, certainly, there was an almost seamless transition from his upbringing to his career in the Irish navy. When he was at school, weekends and summer holidays were almost always spent working with his Dad, going from the mainland to the Aran Islands.

Although now retired, Tom Ford ran a small fleet of Galway hookers and gleoiteogs. These sturdy craft did Herculean work around Galway Bay and the Connemara coast, transporting turf, livestock, people, building materials, provisions and a myriad of other cargo items between the mainland and the Aran Islands. These boats were legendary, as were the men that sailed them. They were designed and built with the Atlantic in mind and, fully laden, could carry six tons of turf.

Tom Ford was teak tough, the result of a lifetime at sea on the gleoiteogs and hookers. He operated four of these boats and his crews stayed with him for many years, having huge respect and admiration for a man they considered a friend as well as an employer. And of course, they were also his neighbours, who played cards with him in the local pub. Tom was liked a lot in the community. Day or night, summer or winter, he always answered the call if there was an emergency on the islands and a doctor had to be brought in or a patient brought out. In fact, once back in the sixties a woman from Inis Mean prematurely gave birth on board one of his boats.

This was the environment that Mike grew up in. Although he crewed with his father quite a bit, he liked to crew with the other skippers also, hearing stories and tales about everything from the islands to building boats. At fifteen he could handle a fully rigged boat and he understood the forces of wind and tide. In fact, when he first entered the Irish naval service as a cadet, his knowledge of the sea and navigation put him seriously ahead of anybody else in his cadet class. When he was sent for further training to the British Royal Naval College in Dartmouth, some of the older salts among his instructors there were very keen to hear about his father's boats and the work they did, in particular the lifestyle and culture that surrounded the Galway hookers.

At seventeen, just as he was about to do his Leaving Certificate in school, he answered an advertisement placed in one of the Sunday papers by the Irish defence forces to become a cadet. The navy only had five positions and he was sure that he wouldn't get one. However, after a number of interviews and the completion of a selection course, to his great surprise he opened a letter one day to find he had been accepted. Having told his mother, he ran as fast as his two legs could carry him down towards the pier in Rossaveal, knowing that his father would be there. His father, who, on hearing the news was as proud as punch, said in the only words he could: 'You'll be fine, boy, just fine.'

Tom Ford then enjoyed the ribbing that some of the other crews gave Mike on hearing the news.

'Jasus lads, we'll have to salute every time he comes aboard from now on!'

'We won't, we'll have to be ready for inspection on the pier!'

Fifty minutes after leaving Galway docks, Mike and Cormac arrived at their parents' house in Rossaveal. Gretta saw the car coming up the driveway, and immediately went to the front door.

Gretta Ford was a typical Irish mother. She absolutely loved her two sons, which is not to say that she didn't love her daughter also; she did, very much in fact. The phenomenon can only be described by saying that it's kind of an Irish thing.

'Hello, Mike, hello Cormac,' she said, hugging Mike, whom she hadn't seen for five weeks.

'Look what I brought out to see you!' said Cormac.

'Hi, Mam, how are you doing?' said Mike, returning his mother's hug.

'C'mon in, the kettle is boiling,' said his mother, ushering the two boys in as if they were still children.

Inside, Tom was sitting in an armchair next to the range in the kitchen, from which a gorgeous aroma of baking scones infused the room.

'Hey Dad, good to see you,' said Mike, shaking hands with his father, who was now standing.

'How's the leg?'

'It actually feels better at the moment,' replied his father, sitting down again. 'Whatever kinda stuff Johnny Mac gave me the last time seems to be doing the trick,' referring to whatever drug or ointment their local doctor had prescribed for him.

Gretta soon had a big pot of steaming hot tea and a plate full of delicious freshly baked fruit scones on the table. For the next hour or so, they caught up with all the important bits of family and other news. When tea was over, Tom turned to Mike.

'We'll stroll down to the pier and see what's going on.'

Gretta instinctively knew that this also meant 'let's go for a pint.' It's not that they wouldn't go down to the pier. Mike and his Dad always went for a stroll down there whenever he was home. It's just that they always popped into the local pub for a drink on the way back.

'Make sure ye're back for half past one, the dinner will be ready then.'

'Don't worry, Mam, I'll have him back by then,' Mike reassured her.

There was something almost ritualistically native about the father and son, both seamen, going down to the little harbour of Rossaveal, looking at the water, checking the state of tide almost as if nature and the revolutions of the earth decided to go on a 'go slow', and seeing what boats were coming and going. A ferry service operated from here to the Aran Islands, which ensured that at certain parts of every day the pier became very busy with passengers embarking and disembarking, with various items of cargo and indeed animals being loaded and unloaded. Like all of the islands off the west coast of Ireland, and the tiny mainland harbours that they come into, the arrival of the ferry is often more of a social event than a practical one.

Mike Ford's deep connection with his father found a voice in the conversations that both men had at these times. He had great respect for Tom, both as a father and a seaman, and, likewise, Tom Ford loved to hear about Mike's life in the navy as he was very proud of his son's achievements. When he and Gretta visited Mike's home in Cork, Mike would always bring him down to the naval base or, indeed, aboard one of the ships that were alongside at the time.

'Sure, you're too comfortable altogether in these things, boy', Tom would comment, to which Mike usually replied:

'Well, Dad, somebody has to do it!'

It was during these conversations that Mike noticed that he often felt something akin to guilt about the fact that his father and mother didn't know anything about Marian, his beautiful daughter that he and Cas had put up for adoption all those years ago. As he looked out at the boats tied to the harbour wall he began to feel a sense of the lovely culture he had come from, the close and caring community in perfect harmony with nature. Then he looked at his father and thought to himself that his parents weren't getting any younger.

At that moment he resolved that he was going to talk to Cas about telling his parents and his brother and sister the next time he visited. He remembered what Mucky had said to him in the car about his sister Bernie being pregnant.

'That baby will be a part of all this,' he thought to himself, 'just like my own children are, even though they live in Cork. Marian should have been too … '

After two pints, Mike looked at his watch.

'I suppose we'd better stroll back, Dad.'

The older seaman looked at him. 'I suppose we'd better.'

Amsterdam

Twenty-four hours later, Carla Blokland was no better. She kept thinking about what her husband had said regarding her deceased mother, trying as best she could to make sense of it, but in reality getting nowhere. It frustrated her that she couldn't just pick up the phone and simply ask him why he said such a thing. The whole thing just kept going around and around in her head, and then, all of a sudden, she realised something else which frightened her even more. Frank had not mentioned one word about the tug's arrival in Bantry, which she was sure was due around this time. Usually he would talk enthusiastically about such an event, even when he was two or three days from arrival at the next harbour.

At that moment, she resolved to make contact with Frank's immediate superior, Johann Naaler, in Smit Tak. Although his direct boss, Johann and his wife were very friendly with the Bloklands. He was the senior captain with the company.

The following morning, Carla and Johann met in a coffee shop.

'Johann, I hope that you don't think I am crazy or anything like that, but I'm a little worried about Frank.'

She related the details of the conversation with her husband, and Johann was indeed surprised. Sure, Frank Blokland was his friend, but he had great respect for him as a ship's captain. It definitely seemed out of character. Carla went on to tell him that he had not even mentioned coming into Bantry, and that she was sure that he was due there. Johann explained to her that yes, he was due in there around now, but he would have to check it out.

'I hear what you are saying, Carla, but it is probably nothing. In any case, I will make contact with the ship as soon as I get back to the office.'

On his way back, Johann thought about what Carla had said, and a slight sense of unease began to come over him. Carla, on the other hand, felt a little better now that Johann was going to make contact with the tug and worried a little that she may have over-reacted. She instantly remonstrated with herself. 'No, no it's a gut feeling, you didn't get it for nothing, and if it turns out to be okay, so much the better.'

As Johann drove the fourteen kilometres back to his office, he pondered about all the logical possibilities for Frank's demeanour. From a professional point of view and in terms of the tug, nothing was wrong at this stage. There was always a bit of leeway around ships' arrival times, especially when the voyage undertaken was from the eastern Med to the south west coast of Ireland with a refuelling stop en route. Lots of factors came into play in a situation like that. Frank could have decided to stay in Algiers for twenty-four or maybe forty-eight hours. Bad weather or fog en route might force the captain to slow the ship, or even alter course with a big 'dog leg' to avoid a storm. Ships are full of mechanical objects, which sometimes cause breakdowns. Fixing these could take time.

Frank Blokland was one of Smit Tak's best captains, utterly dependable and with an impeccable career record thus far. On the other hand his comment about Carla's mother was worrying. Johann reminded himself that he himself had attended the funeral of Carla's mother six years ago. It just didn't add up. He remembered how supportive Frank had been to Carla at the time. He even took an extra four days' leave to be with her. When he arrived at his office he sent a signal to the *Swiftsure*, reassuring himself that in all probability everything was okay. At some stage in the next twenty-four hours he would receive a signal back from the tug saying that everything was going according to plan and with no cause for alarm.

Galway docks

At 1620 on Saturday afternoon the rain was beating incessantly against the windows and door hatch on the starboard side of *Eithne*'s bridge. It had started about an hour earlier and, much to the disgust of some of the crew, it was forecast to continue and get worse right into the coming week. The synoptic charts clearly showed that this was the leading edge of a large front out in the Atlantic, which was moving in from a south westerly direction.

Petty Officer John Ryan, on hearing the familiar sound of the printer spitting out another signal, tore it off and read the contents. He immediately rang Lt Cdr Jim Casey in the wardroom.

'Sir, we've just got in a signal from the naval base saying that the pump will be with us on Sunday afternoon.'

'Okay, PO, thanks for that,' replied the ship's engineering officer, who then turned to the other officers who were watching a football match on television with him at the time. 'Well, we're definitely not going anywhere 'till Tuesday morning now; that pump won't be up here until late tomorrow afternoon. I'd better ring the boss and tell him straight away.'
Jimmy Casey then immediately rang his skipper on his mobile.

'How's it going, sir? The pump is up with us tomorrow afternoon. I've already asked the OOW to contact the port guys to rearrange the tug for Tuesday morning.'

'Okay, thanks Jimmy, that's great. See you later on.'

At five thirty, Mike Ford and his brother Cormac said goodbye to their mother and father, having made an arrangement that they would meet for lunch, together with their sister Bernie, in the Great Southern hotel in Eyre Square on Monday, now that Mike wasn't sailing until Tuesday morning.

Amsterdam

Five hours after he sent the signal, Johann finally got through to Carla Blokland on her mobile phone.

'Hey, Carla, I sent a signal to *Swiftsure* about five hours ago, and we haven't received anything back yet. But to be honest, I feel that wouldn't be out of the ordinary. Anyway, if I don't hear anything in the next four hours, I'll send another one. But I'm sure everything will be okay. Either way, I'll ring you this evening.'

'Okay, Johann,' replied Carla. 'I need my mind to be put at rest about this; talk to you later.'
When Carla put down the phone, for reasons which she didn't understand, she broke down and cried. It was like she was surrendering to her worst fears. At an almost primal level she just knew that all was not right, and she was frustrated by her inability to progress the information any quicker. Two and a half hours later she rang Johann back to ask if there had been any response, and on hearing that there wasn't she calmly said to him that a different course of action was needed.

'To be honest, Carla, I've been thinking the same. I can't put my finger on it, but I feel uneasy. I think we'll call in the police. I suggest that we both meet with them as soon as possible. I'll call you back in ten minutes.' Six minutes later Johann was back on the phone to Carla,

'Okay,' he said, 'I'll pick you up in forty-five minutes. I have made an appointment.'

An hour and a half later, both of them were sitting in front of two officers, one of whom was a detective inspector. Carla spoke first, outlining the train of events as they unfolded, giving the officers a sense of the type of man her husband was and how out of character it was for him to make the remark he made regarding her mother. Then Johann, who had checked back with his office five minutes before the meeting only to be told that there was still no return signal from *Swiftsure*, communicated his feelings to the officers.

The senior officer paused for a while and then said to Carla.

'When I hear what you say, I am tempted to think that what we are dealing with here at one level is pure speculation. However, in our job, pure speculation is what often solves cases. Obviously, there is an international dimension here and so therefore we will have to involve other agencies to see if anything presents that we are unable to see at this level. I will call you in the morning.'

Carla and Johann thanked the officers and left. A discussion then continued between the officers about the case, and both of them concluded that at a gut level they felt that there was something there. One hour later the officers were on their way to a meeting with the Dutch Secret Service. As with all European countries, vital but also innocuous intelligence was shared amongst the various agencies. Internally, borders meant nothing in the fight against terrorism, drugs and other forms of criminality.

USS *Samuel B. Roberts*

The depth sounder on the bridge of the USS *Samuel B. Roberts* indicated 1,461 metres under the keel, when Lieutenant Lorraine Ellis called the captain of the ship.

‘Captain, sir, ship is now abeam Cape Finisterre, speed twenty-two knots. I am now altering course to zero one five on track Cork.’

‘Okay, Lieutenant,’ replied Captain Tom Turner, who was at that time enjoying a cup of coffee in the wardroom.

Lieutenant Ellis, the ship’s weapons officer, was the officer of the watch (OOW) at this time. As her watchkeeping scan once again went outside the bridge windows she could see the very sharp bow of the ship as it sliced through the swell, which was coming from the northwest, and noticed that green water cascaded over the foredeck every fourth or fifth wave. It was as if the ship really revelled in this sea state and her thoughts seemed to get in sync with the deck underneath her feet. She really liked her job as weapons officer aboard the USS *Samuel B. Roberts*, or the ‘Sammy B.’ as she is affectionately known by her crew.

In her mind, it was the power of these weapons which made the crew feel safer when the ship sailed near or into harm’s way. The Oliver Hazard Perry class frigate of approximately 3,600 tons had two gas turbine engines totalling 41,000 hp, and a range of 4,500 miles at 28 knots. She was armed with four McDonald Douglas harpoon guided missiles which could be homed onto a target seventy miles out at mach zero point nine. She also carried anti-submarine warfare (ASW) torpedoes. Each of these ships carried two Sikorsky SH-60R Seahawk helicopters with a speed of over one hundred knots, each equipped with three Mk-50 torpedoes plus an AGM-114R/K Hellfire missile.

In Lt Ellis’s mind, few enemies would dare tangle with this potent platform. But right now all of that could be put to one side. The ship was sailing towards Ireland, a nation which regarded the United States of America as one of its best friends and vice versa. A few days of rest and recuperation, friendly people and, of course, native Guinness would be a nice antidote to the long passage the ship was now undertaking. And on top of that, along with two other members of the crew that she knew of, she herself was of Irish origin.

Lt Lorraine Ellis, or ‘Lorrie’ as she was known to her fellow officers, let her eyes drift back to the electronic chart. Cape Finisterre was the last landmark that the ship would pass, albeit offshore, before arriving in Cork.

From there it was a straight line distance of approximately five hundred miles. All of the ship's crew were looking forward to this visit. However, unlike them, she had special reasons to look forward to the five day courtesy visit to the southern Irish harbour, prior to the Sammy B. returning to its home port in Mayport, Florida. The ship had been at sea now for over three and a half months as an escort in the carrier battle group built around the USS *Nimitz*, which was operating in the eastern Med. However, the Sammy B. had turned right at Gibraltar, while the *Nimitz* and the rest of her flotilla sailed out across the Atlantic.

Lieutenant Lorraine Anne Ellis was actually born in Ireland twenty-eight years earlier. She was given up for adoption at birth, due to circumstances which she never really understood. She was, however, adopted by a couple whose world began the day they were accepted as adoptive parents.

Joe and Marian Ellis both hailed from Belfast. Joe had a small engineering works, near the city centre, which Marian also worked in, acting as secretary and doing the books. For a year and a half after they adopted Lorraine, their lives were, for the most part, full of bliss. Of course, like everyone else in the province, there was always a background awareness of the effects of the conflict that raged there at the time, and like any other parents they were fearful, not so much for themselves, but for this beautiful bundle of joy that had come into their lives.

Joe and Marian Ellis were Catholics, which, in a city like Belfast, defined who they were, who they could work for, and where they could socialise. One day, Joe was asked to manufacture what were essentially metal security grilles, for a government contract. It was a contract he was delighted to get, as work was, for the most part, scarce because of the poor state of the Northern Ireland economy at the time. The contract meant that he had to work late most evenings, so dinner at home usually didn't start until seven thirty.

One November night, just as the family was sitting down to their evening meal in the kitchen at the back of the house, a large petrol bomb crashed through the living room window at the front, and exploded. The front room was virtually immolated and the fire quickly spread to other areas of the house. Joe managed to get his wife and one and a half-year-old daughter out the back door just in time. But by the time the fire brigade arrived, the house and all the family's worldly possessions were completely destroyed. The three of them went to live with Joe's mother, the only one of their parents still alive.

For two months Marian didn't get any sleep, worrying whether something similar was going to happen. One evening Joe came home and asked his wife and mother to sit down – he had a proposition. Seven weeks later, having sold his small business, on a bitterly cold March morning Joe, his mother, Marian and Lorraine were sitting on a British Airways 737, en route to Heathrow airport in London, from where they boarded an Air Canada flight to Toronto. The family settled there, relieved to be away from the troubles in Northern Ireland. With Joe's skills, he quickly found a job in a US-owned factory near Toronto. Within a year and a half the company had really begun to notice the extent of Joe's abilities both as a tradesman and a people person. Soon after, they offered him a position in their main manufacturing facility near Groton, Connecticut, where US defence contracts abounded in the Cold War climate of that time. The job offer meant that he and his family received full US citizenship.

Young Lorraine Ellis's first taste of school life began near New London. Growing up there as she did, just like everyone else, two things were always significant; the navy and submarines. New London is the home of submarines in the US navy. Virtually every person who serves on a submarine spends some time there training or on a course of one kind or another. One of the biggest builders of submarines, The Electric Boat Company, is based nearby. Lots of the fathers, and indeed mothers, of Lorraine's school friends were in fact navy personnel.

Growing up in this culture greatly influenced Lorraine, and she loved every minute of it. When she was fourteen, she proclaimed to Joe and Marian that she was going to be a naval officer, a proclamation which came to pass some years later when she entered the US naval academy, down the road in Annapolis. She also graduated with a degree in engineering. However, notwithstanding the submarine influence of New London, Lorraine wanted to be on surface ships.

'Surface contact ma'am, 060,' said one of the bridge lookouts.

Lorraine's eyes immediately went onto that bearing with a nearby pair of binoculars. It looked like a small container ship, probably out of St Nazaire on its way down the Portuguese coast, but in Lorraine's mind it posed no danger, nor was it in conflict with the USS *Samuel B. Roberts*.

LE *Eithne*

At 0400 on Tuesday morning the small harbour tug in Galway docks manoeuvred underneath the bow of the warship. The forward line party, who were all clad in full foul weather gear, passed the towing rope down to the tug through the starboard fairlead, so that its crew could attach it to the tug's bollard. Meanwhile, down aft, the line party positioned a number of large fenders at the very back end of the port side of the ship, so that when the tug started to pull, the aft end of *Eithne* literally pivoted to starboard safely against the quay wall.

When the tug, assisted by *Eithne*'s counter-rotating propellors, had turned the ship so that she was facing the narrow lock gates which were now open, Commander Ford ordered slow ahead. The ship eased gently out through the lock gates and within minutes her starboard side was being buffeted once again by the strong wind and rain. Ten minutes later *Eithne* was now facing squarely west into Galway Bay. The wind speed at this stage was showing twenty-seven knots or, as Mike Ford noted, the top end of a force six. The wipers on *Eithne*'s bridge were all working hard in the driving rain that was now coming straight at her.

Lt Kana, *Eithne*'s visiting officer from the New Zealand navy, was looking at the Galway Bay chart on the navigation table. He turned to the skipper.

'You'd imagine, sir, that the Aran Islands out there at the head of the bay would provide a bit more shelter from what we are experiencing now.'

'Yeah, John, a lot of people who don't know this bay would think that, but there is a twenty mile fetch from Aran to Galway, and usually most of the prevailing winds are right behind this fetch. The bay gets a bit pinched here between Black Head and Spiddal,' said Mike, pointing his finger to a point on the chart. 'And so you've got a few of the ingredients needed to make the sea bigger than what you'd imagine.'

It would be another two hours before *Eithne* reached the open ocean, passing as she would between the Eeragh Light off Inis Mor to port, and Golam Head just west of Lettermullan to starboard. Visibility at this stage was very poor and on the totally darkened bridge eyes maintained a constant scan, and the ship's radars were being continuously monitored. Lt Cdr Jamie Morrisson, who had just finished his rounds of the ship, put his head in the door of the comms room on his way to the bridge.

'Anything back from Baldonnel yet, chief?'

'No, sir,' he grinned, 'the pilots must be having breakfast!'

'Okay,' replied the XO, 'it wouldn't be funny recovering them in this visibility anyway.'

The XO then made his way to the bridge and, like all trained naval officers, as he entered his eyes scanned a few of the instruments so that his brain could instantly get orientated with the ship's heading, the actual direction of the wind as it hit the ship, and a few more details like speed and depth of water under the keel. He turned to Captain Ford.

'Sir, just finished rounds and everything is looking good. That new pump for the number two engine is operating away sweetly.'

'Very good,' replied the captain. 'Might be a good idea, Jamie, to send a signal to Baldonnel for the helicopter to position to Connemara rather than Galway airport. No point in trying to recover them in this visibility, so tell them to be standing by at Connemara airport from 0900.'

'Aye, captain.'

'Okay, Jamie, you have the ship. I'm going for breakfast; we'll organise the rendezvous with *Niamh* at 0800.'

Swiftsure

Khalid concluded that, although he had finally got used to the motion of the ocean-going tug, he would never be a seaman of any kind. His thought process was that the infidel could have their accursed ocean; he couldn't care less if he never saw another ocean again in his life. The excitement level was now building, as his long months of planning were finally about to come to fruition. The *Swiftsure* was now positioned about ten miles north and slightly to the east of the Porcupine Bank, and his plan was simple.

In this position the tug's radar would pick up the liner at a range of about twenty nautical miles. After intercepting it on the radar, they would instantly know its speed and heading. Once they had that he would order Captain Blokland to turn the *Swiftsure* to the right, staying out of visual range of the cruise ship but parallel its track for the rest of the day. He knew that the ship was going to slow down for several hours, so that its passengers could watch the whales and dolphins, but he didn't know at what point in the Porcupine Bank it would do so. Khalid also knew from intelligence that he had received that the cruise ship would continue to steam slowly for about four hours after darkness.

He wasn't certain about this though, and he would certainly prefer to attack the ship under cover of darkness, but if he had no choice he would attack in daylight. Abu had told him that if he got close enough to the ship he could successfully hit it with the RIBs at ten knots, but he would prefer if the ship's speed was down to four or five knots.

At 1350 a large contact started to blip on the tug's radar. Mohammed, who had been sitting at the radar consol for nearly two hours, was certain that this was the *American Princess*, as at this stage he had got used to the other blips on the screen which represented trawlers. None of them were as big as this. At 1400 exactly, he began to notice the massive cruise ship slowing, and within fifteen minutes her speed had established at four knots.

'My brother, the basket of berries has come to us,' said Mohammed, looking at his leader. Khalid smiled, and ordered Frank Blokland to turn the ship and maintain a parallel course to the radar contact at fifteen nautical miles' range. Khalid looked at his watch and thought to himself that it would be dark in three and a half hours, and smiled as he turned to walk out of the bridge. 'The American cruise ship will be on the bottom of the ocean in four hours' time.'

Frank Blokland now realised with horror what the intentions of his captors were, and the fact that he could do absolutely nothing about it made him shudder. Khalid called Abu and ordered him to make all the necessary final checks on the RIBs and the radio control equipment.

American Princess

The weather was scheduled to improve slightly at lunchtime, which Captain Whiteman interpreted as being slightly better visibility for his passengers and their viewing of whatever sea creatures might present. He had announced this on the ship's PA system so that the passengers could plan to go out on the decks at about 2 p.m. He had also informed them that the ship would not speed up again until 8 p.m.

From a viewing perspective nothing really happened until about 3.45, when a large group of dolphins appeared, surprisingly, on both sides of the ship, matching its speed and constantly soaring out of the water only to dive back in again. Almost as if on cue, a pod of fin whales appeared on the starboard side, much to the amazement of the passengers. Some of them even remarked that if they didn't see any more whales and dolphins after this, it would all have been well worth it. However, at various intervals after that it was as if the sea creatures had just decided to put on a show.
Pretty soon, however, the light began to fade, but the crew of the ship had assured some of the passengers that they were likely to see more of them in the area of water each side of the ship, which was lit up by the lights. It was almost as if the sea creatures were attracted more by the glow of light which extended right down both sides of the cruise liner and out to a distance of approximately thirty feet.

1710 Tuesday 22 November. *Swiftsure*

Khalid and Tarka entered the wardroom of the *Swiftsure* where Captain Frank Blokland was having his evening meal. Jan, the diminutive ship's cook, had just served dessert to his captain when he was roughly grabbed by Tarka, and bound once again to the metal chair. Tarka's knife was in his hand when he roughly pulled Jan's head back by grabbing a clump of his hair. He brought the knife straight up against Jan's throat, when Frank Blokland screamed,

'No! no! no!'

Khalid spoke next.

'We are now entering the final phase of our mission. Tarka will stay by the side of this man throughout the whole of this process. If you or any of your crew try in any way to interfere, or are not completely compliant with my orders, he will be the first to lose his head,' said Khalid, pointing at Jan. Once again Frank Blokland breathed a huge sigh of relief. He was certain that Khalid intended to make an absolute point, to terrorise the rest of his crew into total compliance.

Frank had begun to put the pieces together about eight hours earlier, and had come to the stark realisation of what his captors were about to do. A debate raged in his mind throughout the day as to whether he and perhaps some of his crew should maybe rush the terrorists in an effort to overpower them. He knew that if they were allowed to succeed, a cruise liner full of people could perhaps die, having as they would virtually no hope of rescue in this location. His conscience weighed heavily as he thought out the implications of such a move but, in the end, five terrorists, each armed with Kalashnikovs ... well, all that would achieve would be total suicide. He reasoned that, alive, there was still the possibility that they could do something. He didn't know what yet, but dead, they could do absolutely nothing.

Khalid ordered the captain to the bridge, partly because he felt that he would not be in a position to influence his crew in any way there, but also because, as he said to the captain himself:

'Captain, you will conn the ship for the next two hours. Should you fail to carry out any of my instructions, I will personally shoot you.'

In Khalid's mind, taking over an ocean-going tug using force would achieve total compliance from the crew. However, the realisation by that crew that their ship was to be used as an instrument of death for several hundred innocent people could change the dynamic somewhat.

Every light source on the *Swiftsure* had been blacked out except for one large white light on the mast, so that in the darkness of the Atlantic she was like a ghost ship on an intercept course. The officers on the *American Princess* were well used to the relatively close quarter nearness of trawlers in the area of the Porcupine Bank. After all, why was the liner moving so slowly at just four knots? For no other reason than to facilitate its passengers viewing the main predators of the fish that the trawlers were hunting. The common interest of all vessels here was in fact the food chain. The liner's OOW had in fact noticed the vessel with the strange lights.

However, as *Swiftsure* was on a parallel track to the liner and also moving quite slowly, it did not pose any collision threat. The OOW shrugged his shoulders, thinking 'Aah, lights must be broken.'

Mohammed had suggested that the tug should be brought in closer to the cruise liner, such that she would converge with it but be positioned approximately two nautical miles off the liner's port bow. That would give Abu time to steer his lethal RIBs towards their target, which, at four knots, would present, if you like, a large broadside for a considerably longer period of time.

At 1915 Khalid decided to make the strike.

'Abu.'

'Yes,' he replied to Khalid through his hand-held radio.

'Are you absolutely ready to go?'

'The first RIB is connected to the tug's crane. It can be over the side and running in two minutes.'

'Very well, my brother. Stand by.'

After what seemed like an age, the *Swiftsure*'s main engines were declutched. Although still making way, her drift was slowly arrested by the strong southwesterly winds hitting her square on the snub bow and fo'c'scle. Almost as soon as Abu saw the lights of the cruise liner in the distance, his radio ear pieces barked out an order from Khalid.

'Launch the weapons now.'

The first RIB was gently lifted over the side of the tug with Jabir aboard. As it touched the water he started the ninety horsepower outboard and immediately Abu checked its steering from the remote control in his hands. The engine swivelled from right to left and back effortlessly. Having tied the bow of the RIB to the starboard rail of the tug, Jabir climbed back aboard and stood by ready to release the painter. In the meantime, with a gun aimed at the side of his face, Piet Stam connected the second RIB to the tug's crane, and promptly lifted it over the side, leaving the crane's hook connected so that it held it alongside.

Abu noticed that the liner was now approximately a mile away and closing. He smiled as he ordered Jabir to undo the painter, and then, as he pushed the tiny power levers on his remote control, the RIB jerked forward. It was unwieldy to steer for about the first fifty or sixty metres, but then his hand–eye co-ordination improved somewhat. Abu had rigged a rear facing maglight torch on each of the RIBs, so that he could see their track through the water in ever diminishing visibility. He watched the beam as it wiggled its way through the sea, and when it came abeam the centre of the liner he gently touched the left turning lever on the controller and applied more power. The RIB was now travelling at eight knots straight towards the centre of the port side of the liner. Forty-five seconds later, the shock wave from the massive explosion was felt on the bridge of the *Swiftsure*. Frank Blokland couldn't help himself; he just cried out:

'You murdering bastards.'

In the meantime, Abu had ordered Jabir to launch the second RIB. As soon as it was in the water, Abu once again established control of it with the control box in his hands. The second RIB sped away at over seven knots and this one seemed to be much more controllable. The *American Princess* continued to close the distance which made Abu's job of steering the RIB much easier. In fact, he got a bit bolder. He turned the RIB to the left when it was almost abeam the stern of the cruise liner and guided it straight in to the port stern quarter of the ship. The second explosion succeeded in bending the liner's two prop shafts; however, it also blew the rudder clean off the ship.

There was almost a stunned silence between the captors and captives on the *Swiftsure*, but slowly the first started to rejoice, while the second recoiled in horror at what they had seen.

Khalid, as ever, was the first to speak.

'Captain, you will now steer one two zero, slow ahead.'

The still blackened out tug slowly steamed further away in the dark, heaving Atlantic ocean.

1930 *American Princess*

The first explosion blew a forty foot square hole in the port side of the ship, six feet of which was below the waterline. A secondary internal explosion occurred when one of the liner's main heavy fuel tanks blew up seconds later. Twelve of the *American Princess*'s crew who had been working near the port main engine console were killed instantly, and three others were drowned within minutes. When the fuel tank exploded, several of the watertight bulk heads surrounding the engine compartment were shattered, sending shrapnel flying around the crew's cabin quarters. Although no one was killed, there were thirty-six people injured, sixteen of them seriously.

The second explosion, when it came, caused no fatalities or injuries. However, the bent shafts caused the ship to shudder violently, which resulted in four of the passengers falling down a staircase six decks up and several other passengers slipping and falling. The fact that the rudder was blown completely off caused the ship to lose steerage immediately, and as she slowed down, she began to drift beam on to the waves, creating an increasingly uncomfortable roll.

However, the most serious problem for the ship was the thousands of gallons of water that were now flooding in through the massive gaping holes in her side and in her stern.

Surprisingly enough, the sheer size of the ship meant that the captain and the three officers who were on the bridge at the time didn't really feel the full power of the blasts, although Captain John Whiteman instinctively knew that a terrible thing had happened to the port side of his ship. He immediately ran to the port bridge wing where he would be able to look down the entire length of the side of the ship and hopefully get a sense of what had happened. The lights from the ship's side cabin windows provided enough illumination for him to see what he knew was an enormous hole, into which a lot of water was now pouring.

Immediately, he ordered all watertight bulkheads to be closed, along with sending two officers to investigate what had happened, but he was already aware of the unmistakable slight list to port. He walked, slightly uphill to the starboard side of the bridge where the ship's radio room was located.

One of the officers dispatched to assess the damage down below was on the radio to the bridge within minutes, crying.

Virtue, Vice and Honour

LE *Eithne*

Petty Officer Ryan was standing at the open door of the radio room which was located just aft of the ops room when he heard the unmistakeable opening words of an incoming transmission every seaman fears most.

Mayday, Mayday, Mayday

This is cruise ship American Princess

Mayday, Mayday, Mayday

Our position is N'53.10 W'13.40

We have suffered 2 serious explosions,

port side, presently listing 5 degrees

Casualties unknown, many injured

Repeat – our position is N'53.10 W'13.40

Sub Lt Angela Hogan, the officer of the watch (OOW), who also heard the transmission, immediately hit the ship's comms button.

Captain – Bridge

Mike Ford replied:

Bridge – Captain, go ahead.

Sir, we have just received a mayday signal from an American cruise ship approx 110 miles west of our position, sounds serious.

Okay … get the rest of ship's officers to the ops room, right now, and get Senior Chief Morgan to the bridge.

Yes, sir, right away.

As Mike Ford covered the eighty feet from the officers' mess to the bridge, several thoughts simultaneously rushed through his head.

Cruise ship … Passengers … Jesus … How many … 100 nautical miles west of us … Atlantic ocean … Winter … 5° list … Taking water … Time … How long before she sinks … Many injured?

Jamie Morrisson ran out of his day cabin, almost knocking Mike Ford over in his hurry.

'Sorry, sir.'

'Jamie, get this ship to action stations and get the helicopter standing by on the flight deck.'
'Yes, sir, right away.'

Mike Ford knew that the off watch crew members, some of whom would be asleep in their bunks, could not physically do anything about the situation right now but he also knew that, whatever was going to confront the crew of his ship, he wanted a ready, fully briefed and prepared crew. He knew enough at this point to know that people's lives now definitely depended on the actions of *Eithne* and her crew.

As soon as everybody was in the ops room, Mike read out the initial report, taken by PO Ryan, to the rest of the officers and immediately ordered a comms link to be opened with the *American Princess.* As soon as contact was established he requested to speak with the captain.

'Sir, this is Commander Mike Ford, Captain of the Irish naval ship LE *Eithne*. What is your present situation?'
Everyone in the ops room heard the cruise ship captain's response over the speaker.

'Aw, thank you, sir. This is Captain John Whiteman, we gotta pretty bad situation here. Two explosions, big! One amidships at the waterline level on the port side, and one on the port side of the stern. The hole amidships is about thirty feet in diameter and the one at the back is about the same. Knocked out our steering and damaged the port prop so right now we are beam on to the sea. We got a bad fire ragin' on the port side of the engine room amidships and we are listing about five degrees to port. We are still taking a lot of water and our pumps just can't cope at all. At this time we can confirm fifteen dead, but we got a lotta injuries, some bad. If I had to make a call on it, sir, this boat won't be on the surface in four to six hours' time, and we got eight hundred people aboard.'
Mike Ford's worst fears were confirmed.

'Okay, captain, that's copied. Can I ask you to standby for a few minutes?'

'Yes, sir,' replied a somewhat relieved Captain Whiteman that a naval vessel as against any other ship had responded. 'And thank you.'

There was about five seconds of quiet sobriety and then Mike Ford spoke.

'Okay, gentlemen, comments!'

Neil Kennedy, *Eithne's* navigation officer, who was plotting the relative position of the ship on a chart as he was listening to the mayday signal from Captain Whiteman, was first in.

'Well, sir, we're now about four and a half hours from the *American Princess*, which means she could be sunk with eight hundred people by the time we get there. And I checked before I came in ... *Niamh* is approx three hours from her, but even with her faster speed you're still looking at two and a half to three hours for her to cover the ground.'

Jamie Morrisson continued.

'Even if we could get to the *American Princess* on time, in this sea state none of these ships could risk going alongside the cruise ship to take off survivors, it would be too dangerous. That means transferring them by both our helicopter and the rigid inflatables. Too slow, way too slow ... in this weather most of 'em would die from hypothermia.'

Fl. Lt Jim Angland, who had entered the ops room two minutes earlier having ordered the helicopter deck crew to move the aircraft from the hangar deck to the flight deck, spoke next.

'Sir, the helicopter will be ready in ten minutes but, looking at the situation, even the search and rescue helicopters based on the west coast couldn't get to that ship. She's seventy miles beyond their effective fuel range.'

Mike paused for two seconds and then, in a voice that was so low its decibel level calmness even registered with him, spoke:

'Okay.'

'If we don't do something drastic right now, history will record a disaster in the Atlantic second only to the *Titanic* with two Irish naval vessels within a hundred miles of it and unable to do anything to help it.'

'That, gentlemen, is clearly not going to happen, at least not on my watch.'

'Yes, Jim, you're right ... the 61s in Sligo, Shannon and, for that matter, Waterford don't have the legs to fly to the cruise ship, but last time I looked we had a very small airport at the back of this ship, and as I see it we can position to an optimal refuelling point within an hour.'

Lt Cdr Jamie Morrisson, *Eithne*'s executive officer, was staring at the radar screen.

'Sir, have I got this right … you're going to get the 61s to fly to *Eithne*, refuel and carry on to the cruise ship, take off survivors, and bring them back to *Eithne*, refuel and/or return to the cruise ship to collect more and bring them back aboard?'

'That is precisely what I intend to do, Jamie. As on-scene commander that is the only option open to me.'

'Yes, sir, I believe it is,' replied the XO. 'I'll signal *Niamh* to stand by for the moment.'

Five minutes later the following signal left the *Eithne* by satellite uplink to the Irish marine rescue co-ordination centre (MRCC) located just off Stephen's Green in Dublin and also to naval headquarters on Haulbowline Island in Cork.

1952 22 Nov 05 N'53.07 W'12.10
Mayday received
Cruise Liner American Princess
Her position is NW
2 explosions
15 dead, many injured
Ship sinking (captain's estimate 5 hours)
70 NM beyond range of Sar 61s
Only hope of saving lives at this stage
is for Eithne *to position to optimal posn'*
to facilitate refuel of 61s en route to American Princess.
61s can rotate back to our deck with survivors
and for JP5 top up.
Deploy Top Cover asset soonest for ATC.
Need two full trauma teams to come with one of the helicopters.

Ten minutes later Commander Ford briefed Captain Whiteman of his intentions and also that he would send the ship's Dauphin helicopter together with two clearance divers out to the cruise ship to assess the damage when *Eithne* had sufficiently closed the range between the two ships.

MRCC

Colin Dowling sat on the most comfortable swivel chair in front of the array of screens in the marine rescue co-ordination centre just off Stephen's Green in Dublin. The light rain that was beginning to patter against the only window in the room had caught his attention. In his mind, that coincided with the front that was slowly pushing in from the Atlantic. His attention drifted up to the huge map of Ireland, which showed with various coloured lights the different coast guard stations, radio beacons, lighthouses and all of the search and rescue (SAR) locations around the country. Red and white coloured helicopter symbols showed with red lights in Waterford, Dublin, Sligo and Shannon airports. These were the main search and rescue bases in the country and each of them had two S61 SAR helicopters on twenty-four hour standby with crews in their ready rooms.

Blue symbols showed the lifeboat stations and different other colours denoted coastal and cliff rescue units, mountain rescue units and all of the voluntary SAR and coast guard units. Two big squares showed the air corps base in Baldonnel and Ireland's only naval base at Haulbowline Island in Cork harbour. As the duty radio operator, Colin's mind never strayed far from the radio room adjacent to the ops room. At 1955 one of the printers burst into life, spitting out a message which Colin instinctively knew was serious.

LE *Eithne*

'Turn the ship on to a course of "two nine zero" and get me all the speed you can,' Mike Ford said to the OOW.

A few moments later everyone aboard felt a slight shudder through the ship as the engines and shaft revolutions increased to maximum. At this time Mike was aware that the sea state, which he had noted in the earlier weather report, was due to get worse in a couple of hours due to an incoming Atlantic front. But he would deal with that when the time came. In the meantime his primary concern was to position the ship as quickly as possible to the optimal point. The atmosphere in the ops room was now tense as officers were detailed to make all the necessary preparations on board to facilitate what Mike Ford knew was going to be a 'one chance' rescue.

He ordered the officers' mess to be immediately converted into a close copy of an operating theatre. This wouldn't be difficult, as it had been designed into the mess when the ship was first built, the long wardroom dining table optimally positioned and designed to double as an operating table. As he thought about it, there were going to be three categories of people coming off the helicopters: people who were not injured at all, 'walking' wounded, and seriously injured. Of course there would be subcategories to each of these, for example people who were basically okay but maybe suffering from mild hypothermia or shock, or maybe seriously injured people who were either conscious or unconscious. Either way he had to develop a plan while he had the time.

The secondary problem that was about to face *Eithne*'s crew was the sheer number of people coming aboard. Eight hundred people would be a significant addition to any frigate's standard crew, not to mind the large helicopters that were simultaneously being refuelled on her flight deck. The problem wasn't so much the number of people as where to put them; spaces would have to be found below decks for everyone. Moreover, the wounded would need spaces where the ship's medics and the incoming trauma team could treat them.

'Em, sir,' said Jim Angland, 'I've just been doing some figures here. At eight hundred people divided by three helicopters, you're looking at 266 per helicopter. At a push, those 61s can pick up twenty-five people, so let's assume at a real push they can stuff thirty in, especially seeing as they might be able to juggle their fuel weight for the hop back to the ship … that means each helicopter is going to have to make nine round trips from *Eithne* to the cruise liner. That means we are looking at a total of twenty-seven landings on the deck.'

'Hang on a sec,' said Lt Cdr Jimmy Casey, *Eithne's* engineering officer. 'We'd better get the JP5 fuel pumps and hoses looked at now while we have some time. I'm not saying there's anything wrong with them – there's not – but it would do no harm to get them checked anyway.'
Jamie Morrisson then asked: 'What are we going to do with our own helicopter while all this aerial activity is going on around us? It can't stay on the flight deck.'

'Any thoughts on that, Jim?' asked Captain Ford.

'Well, sir, I was thinking … we could put it into the pattern with the 61s, and even if we only winched up three people at a time, at least it would be something. Also, that cruise liner is full of all sorts of equipment that we might need in a hurry, I'm thinking of blankets, rugs, bandages, pillows, all sorts of things. We could ferry stuff like that back to *Eithne* if we only picked up able-bodied passengers.'

'Yeah, that's a good idea,' replied *Eithne*'s skipper. 'And anyway, we may need the option of ferrying equipment across from here to the two divers.'

'Sir, I suggest that for the duration of this mission we should have a RIB deployed, maybe a couple of hundred metres behind, trailing the ship, especially when those helicopters are coming in low and slow to land and refuel on our flight deck. The sea state is forecast to get worse in the next few hours so the deck isn't going to be as flat as we would like it. I suggest a four-man crew on the RIB and we can relieve them by simply alternating the port and starboard RIBs every hour.'

Lt Gerry Stewart had spoken for the first time since the crisis began, but Mike Ford understood that. Lt Stewart was the ship's gunnery officer who also doubled as the ship's diving officer. He had a quiet disposition but was known aboard for the importance he placed on safety.

'Okay Gerry, well done. Make it happen, and for God's sake make sure that the diesel tanks in the RIBs are topped off.'

Casa Maritime Surveillance Aircraft Charlie 253

Galway airport on Ireland's west coast was one of the airports used by the air corps Casa crews for 'away' night ops training. Comdt Brian Gould had landed the aircraft call sign Charlie 253 at Galway at 1955 and the crew were enjoying a meal in the airport restaurant which doubled as a briefing for the two extra trainee radar operators who were aboard. At 2005 his mobile phone rang in his pocket. He was sure it was his wife who sometimes rang him at around that time, hoping he would be on the ground. Comdt Aidan Vallely, the aircraft's co-pilot, noted that the phone call was more one-sided than normal, followed by a slapping closed of the phone.

'Aidan, get the crew at the ready and have the aircraft's fuel tanks topped off immediately. This is no longer a training exercise.'

Within fifteen minutes Charlie 253 was speeding down Galway's westerly facing runway 'two five' into a stiff breeze. As the aircraft climbed out, and established on a course two six five magnetic, Aidan Vallely could see the lights of Galway city and could clearly make out the north shore of Galway bay intermittently lit up by the villages of Barna and Spiddal. And then Charlie 253 disappeared into the cloud face, still climbing to flight level eight zero, (8,000 ft) en route to position N'53,07 W'12.10, which he had already punched into the aircraft's inertial navigation system.

1955 SAR Base, Shannon Airport

Squally rain and wind from the developing front knocked against the window of the crew ready room in the search and rescue base which was located near the eastern end of Shannon's eleven thousand foot runway, while inside three of the duty crew were either reading newspapers or having a nap. The other, co-pilot Anne O'Donnell, was in the adjacent little kitchen finishing off a yoghurt which she had saved from earlier in the day.

The crew had come on duty at 1300 and at 1340 they had flown to the Aran Islands to conduct a winching exercise with the Kilronan lifeboat. After that the aircraft (callsign: Romeo 22) had returned to base (RTB) in Shannon where it was thoroughly washed, to make sure there were no corrosive salt deposits left on its skin, and refuelled, ready for its next mission, when and wherever that may be.

As she came through the door to the ready room the telephone rang. The others were immediately on their feet, knowing full well that when that particular phone rang they were going somewhere. Anne O'Donnell had written down details of many rescue situations, but everyone listening noticed that this was different. Firstly, it took longer and, secondly, they became aware of the incredulous expressions on her face, something that would not be normal in the helicopter search and rescue community who had witnessed the most terrifying rescue situations. As she put down the phone she calmly relayed the message to the rest of the crew.

Captain Paul O'Sullivan and the rescue crew of Helicopter Romeo 22 took about four minutes to get kitted up in their drysuits. Since almost all of their operations were over water these drysuits were absolutely essential for the crew's survival in the event that the helicopter itself had to ditch, and apart from that the winch man was regularly dunked in training operations with rigid inflatable boats and other craft, not to mention real time rescue situations which sometimes took place in extremely hazardous weather conditions.

The headset around the ears of the air traffic controller (ATC) in Shannon barked to life.

'Shannon tower, this is Romeo 22 for immediate departure on radial two seven zero with information hotel.'

'Roger Romeo 22, clear take off on heading two seven zero, QNH one zero one four and squawk two zero four zero, wind two eight five at eighteen gusting twenty six.

The tower had cleared the helicopter for an immediate lift off into the prevailing wind while giving them the sea level barometric pressure and a four digit code ... which when entered in the aircraft's transponder would enable Shannon radar control, which ranged out to fifteen degrees west, to clearly identify their position and altitude. Within five minutes similar events were taking place in the search and rescue bases in both Sligo and Waterford airports. As the Irish and British coast guard act as one in major emergencies such as this, the Irish coast guard then tasked its British counterpart to provide cover for these areas for the duration of the mission.

The White House, Washington DC

The National Security Agency (NSA) in Fort Meade, Maryland was the first American agency to hear of the explosion in the Atlantic, and within six minutes the call came through to the White House switchboard. The President was in a meeting with a deputation from the oil industry when one of the secret service agents quietly entered the room, walked to the President's side, and whispered in his ear.

Eight hundred American lives on the line ensured that the meeting in progress ended within half a minute. As the oilmen were escorted out some of them noticed the heightened state of alert that had suddenly come about which was not there when they entered an hour earlier. When the last of the visitors filed out, the President asked for immediate telephone contact to be made with the national security advisor, chairman of the joint chiefs, and the chief of naval operations (CNO).

One hour later all of the above, together with Admiral Tom Kane (C-in-C Atlantic fleet) were seated in the Oval office. General John Kowolski (chairman of the joint chiefs) spoke first.

'Mr President, sir, at this time we are still developing details so we don't know the full picture just yet, but shit, how does an ocean liner in the middle of the Atlantic suffer two explosions, almost simultaneously, which are nearly 250 feet apart in its hull?'

The President immediately looked at the senior naval officer in the room, Admiral Frank Hughes, chief of naval operations (CNO)

'Frank, any ideas on what is happening here?'

'Well, sir, data is thin on the ground just yet. Despite the current security situation around the world and with the tightening up of security in harbours and all that, I don't see how it could be a deliberate attack on American citizens, especially in that location. For God's sake, it's only 180 miles or so off the west coast of Ireland.'

The President himself, a former F15 pilot with the air national guard, then asked: 'What ships, if any, do we have in the area?'

'Sir,' said Frank, looking at Admiral Tom Kane, 'Tommy here can give us a pretty up to date answer to that question.'

'Em, yes sir,' said Admiral Kane.

'Right at this time we have nothing within two days of the incident except the USS *Samuel B. Roberts*, she's an Oliver Hazard Perry class frigate. She was a component of the carrier battle group around the *Nimitz*, which is returning from the eastern Med now. When the fleet cleared Gibraltar the Sammy B. turned right on route to Cork, in the south of Ireland, for a courtesy visit. I've sent a signal to her to close the *American Princess* soonest, but unfortunately she's still five and a half hours away even at flank speed. She's got two Seahawk SH60 helicopters aboard. Her captain will send one of them ahead to recon the situation when he gets within range.'

'Christ,' said John Kowolski.

'Are there any other ships nearby?'

'Details are still sketchy, sir, but we understand that the Irish navy have two ships in the general area. One of them is their flagship, the LE *Eithne* – she carries a helicopter – and the other is one of their patrol vessels, kinda like a small frigate, she's the LE *Niamh*.'

At that moment a buzzer sounded on the intercom on the President's desk.

'Sorry, sir, I have the director of the National Security Agency on the line, he says it's important.'

'Okay,' said the President.

'Jamie, how are you doing?'

'Fine, sir, just fine. I got some more information here that you guys there might find helpful.'

The President then pressed the loudspeaker, so that everyone in the room could hear the contents of the call. Admiral James Fischer then continued.

'Sir, I've just spoken with the flag officer of the Irish navy, Commodore Tom Garrett. He says that the position of the *American Princess* is outside the range of their land-based SAR Sikorsky 61s. However, the *Eithne*, that's their lead boat, has positioned to an optimal refuelling point so that the choppers can refuel and continue on to the liner. The captain of the *Eithne*, a guy called Ford, Commander Mike Ford, had declared himself 'on-scene commander' and his plan is to ferry survivors back to the *Eithne.* The Irish have sent a Casa maritime patrol aircraft, which has just arrived at the scene and is acting as top cover for the helicopters. They've tasked a Nimrod out of Kinloss to relieve the Casa when her fuel goes bingo. In fact, sir, they have sortied three of their 61s because of the big numbers and one of em's bringing a full trauma team out to the *Eithne* en route. In fairness, given the time constraint we are looking at, I gotta say that the Irish are getting their act together big time.'

The President winced. 'Mother of God, three helicopters … eight hundred people … middle of the Atlantic! That's a big ask.'

'The second part of the conversation, sir, is a little more worrying. Apparently, Commander Ford sent two of his crew out ahead to the liner in their Dauphin helicopter to help supervise their evacuation. One of em's a clearance diver who had a look at the damage and reported that it seemed like the explosions happened outside the skin of the ship. *Eithne* apparently has an explosives officer aboard so I think their intention is to send him out to have a look on the next helicopter.'

'Jesus, Jamie,' said Frank Hughes, 'if that diver's report is correct, we're into a whole new ball game.'

'I mean, what the fuck could possibly have made the strike? Hardly a submarine.'

'Yeah,' replied the NSA, 'I've arranged to speak with Tom Garrett again in ninety minutes, at which time we might know a bit more about what caused the damage.'

'Well done to the Irish,' said the President.

'Haven't the Brits got any boats in the area?' asked the chairman of the joint chiefs.

'I seem to remember that incident with the Canadian sub that went on fire, the *Chicoutimi*, wasn't it? They seemed to have two destroyers on the scene pretty quickly, which wasn't a million miles from where the *American Princess* is now.'

'That's true, sir,' replied Admiral Tom Kane.

'I checked that before coming to this meeting, and as luck would have it they've got no one out there just now. However, HMS *Grafton*, one of their frigates, is sailing from Plymouth within the hour. Trouble is, she's about fourteen hours away, and according to Captain Whiteman the cruiser mightn't be on the surface in five hours' time.'

'I guess everything is in the hands of Commander Ford now,' replied the CNO. 'Still, on the basis of what he has done already, if he was in the US navy, he'd be a four ring captain now. Tom, send a signal to the Sammy B. straight away, to make all speed to the datum immediately, and do what they can to assist. Even if the cruise liner is on the bottom of the ocean by the time she gets there, he could possibly forward deploy his helicopters en route.'

As Admiral Tom Kane left the room, the director of the National Security Agency, who was still holding on the other end of the line, then said to the President: 'Sir, let's just look at the information that we have at this time. Fact one, this cruise liner is holed in two places, big holes; fact two, she ain't in an iceberg zone; fact three, the only surface ships nearby seem to be just trawlers; fact four, we're not aware of any submarines in the area; and fact five, an Irish navy clearance diver is already of the opinion that the two big holes were caused by something external to the ship rather than internal. Sir, something sucks here, big time, and I need to get on it.'

2035 Waterford Helicopter Romeo 26

Two garda patrol cars pulled up outside the accident and emergency department of the Cork University hospital with their blue lights flashing and their sirens temporarily turned off. Almost immediately a full trauma team which consisted of an anaesthetist, a surgeon, and two theatre nurses made their way out through the rain and were helped into each car by the garda crews. Their equipment was then placed into the boot of each car and with sirens turned on again the two cars headed towards Cork international airport at speed. At this stage the evening traffic that usually chokes the South Link in Cork had dissipated so the patrol cars had a relatively easy time getting on to the main airport road.

Fifteen hundred feet above the village of Killeagh in east Cork the Waterford-based rescue helicopter Romeo 26 was screaming towards Cork airport at 140 knots. In a designated area on the south ramp a jet A1 tanker was standing by, waiting for the incoming helicopter to give her a final top off before her long sortie out into the Atlantic. Cork airport police had already opened and were guarding the main vehicle entrance gates which led to 'airside' so that no time would be lost in getting the trauma team boarded on the incoming helicopter.

A Southern Health Board forward emergency vehicle arrived about two minutes after the patrol cars. On board was a supply of different blood types secured in a refrigerated box. Eight minutes later the giant Sikorsky touched down but kept her engines at flight idle while she was refuelled. While this was being done, the two patrol cars swerved around the last entrance gate and were directed to a position close to the helicopter by the flight marshal. As soon as the refuelling was completed the trauma team, almost stunned by the deafening roar of Romeo 26's engines, made their way to the port door and were helped aboard by the winch operator, while the winch man stowed their equipment.

Ninety seconds later the helicopter lifted into an eight-foot hover and, having been cleared out of Cork on a westerly heading, took off into the south westerly wind and rain. Ten minutes later Cork radar control instructed the crew to call Shannon control.

LE *Eithne*

At that moment the phone rang in the ops room.

'Skipper, go ahead.'

'Sir, we have just got a signal from the naval base,' said Sub Lt Angela Hogan. 'It says that a Casa, call sign 235, will be in our overhead in forty minutes, and the three SAR helicopters are also en route. It seems the Waterford 61 picked up the trauma teams at Cork airport together with their equipment and stocks of blood.'

'Okay, that's copied,' replied the ship's captain.

At this time *Eithne*'s radio room was receiving offers of help and position reports from some of the trawlers that were operating in the area. Indeed, her radar operator, Leading Seaman Dan Kearney, reported that some of them had changed course to position closer to the ship. This would be absolutely normal in a major emergency at sea. Any vessels within the vicinity of the emergency would automatically offer their assistance to the on-scene commander.

Mike Ford looked over the shoulder of the radar operator at the screen and noted that there were seven trawlers inside a ten mile wide track between the *Eithne* and the *American Princess*. It occurred to him that if any of the helicopters had to ditch while making the round trip back to his ship the position of these trawlers could be crucial in saving lives. He immediately ordered that a request be made to the skippers of these trawlers to maintain a ten mile orbit of their present position until further notice.

Without exception all seven reported back in the affirmative within five minutes. Commander Ford then turned to the nav officer.

'Listen, Neil, plot two track lines five nautical miles apart between *Eithne* and the cruise liner, and then estimate optimal positions along both those lines, for the trawlers in the area to position to. That way, as the helicopters are moving up and down the track, to and from the ship, if anything goes wrong we have an asset, hopefully nearby, that can help out.'

Mike Ford knew that helicopters operating at the extreme edge of their endurance could be vulnerable. The rescue mission itself, when he thought about it, would probably go down as one of the riskiest ever undertaken by a naval warship. Nevertheless, in his mind he had to put all the dots in the right places to absolutely minimise the unthinkable – one of the three 61s going down, especially with twenty or thirty survivors on board. He also had to work with what he had. For sure, some more trawlers were still calling the *Eithne* and offering their assistance, and their position was being plotted in that respect. Mike Ford was steadily building up the big picture.

Tactically, one side of him wanted to keep the best asset he had, the LE *Niamh*, with her superb speed, near *Eithne,* but the other side of his brain knew that the best place for *Niamh* was to position to half way down the track to the liner and take up a five mile orbit when she got there. With a capability of nearly twenty-five knots at full tilt, *Niamh* and her crew would be best placed in that position to move towards a downed helicopter. Mike's logic also told him that her presence there would reassure the helicopter pilots, and if one of them had to ditch, perhaps because of losing one engine coupled with a maximum all up weight, they may just be able to limp along, closing the distance between their position and *Niamh*.

'PO Ryan, get the following signal off to *Niamh* straight away.'

Signal to *Niamh*

Position to N'53.07 W13.10

Initiate 5 mile diameter orbit on that point.

Liaise with fishing vessels to optimise positioning.

Ford

As senior officer afloat, Commander Ford had overall tactical control of the two Irish navy ships in the area.

Within forty seconds of the signal leaving *Eithne*, her radar operators reported a change of course and an increase in speed as the dot that represented the LE *Niamh* on their screen moved to where Captain Ford wanted her to be.

Lt Cdr Jamie Morrisson, *Eithne*'s executive officer, turned to his captain.

'Okay, sir, most of the spaces that we need below deck are now cleared, and the wardroom is beginning to look like a cottage hospital.'

'Good, good, Jamie, make sure the cooks have got a move on with the soup.'

'Yeah, that's covered, sir. Chief Mulligan had actually got 'em going on the soup almost as soon as this thing broke; he's also got two of the ratings organising every blanket on the ship. Also, sir, Senior Chief Morgan reports that the heli-deck is now ready for re-fuelling operations along with taking survivors aboard.'

'By the way, Jamie, I think it would be a good idea if you went to the hangar deck with a radio ten minutes before the first helicopter arrives in. Just to keep an eye on things and make sure everything runs smoothly. Everything that is going to happen back there in terms of scale is going to be bigger than anything we've done before. The bosun will be there soon, he's checking to see if the ratings quarters are ready to take some of the survivors.'

Earlier, Mike Ford had detailed Sub Lt Gerry Stewart to survey all of the available spaces on board the ship, with a view to planning where exactly to put all of the survivors. The officers agreed from the start that the large hangar deck, which housed the ship's Dauphin helicopter, would be better used as a staging area. As each helicopter came in and disembarked between twenty-five and thirty people, the plan was that an assessment would be made of the condition of each survivor, together with the possibility that he or she may have had family members with them. After that they would be allocated to different areas of the ship. These areas were many and varied in size. The officers' mess or wardroom would be essentially the ship's hospital where any primary lifesaving treatment would be given to any badly injured or burned survivors; the settees at the television end would become three or four makeshift 'accident and emergency' beds, while the long dining table near the adjoining kitchenette would become the main operating table. The suitability of this was established when the designs for the ship were first drawn up; moreover, the proximity of the wardroom to the hangar deck was also helpful.

Other areas of the ship also had advantages. The large ratings mess and eating area by itself could probably accommodate, albeit more intimately than designed, ninety to one hundred people. Also, the non-commissioned officers' mess and cabins could accommodate a similar number.

2120 Naval Base, Haulbowline Island

Commodore Tom Garrett was at that moment in a meeting with Captain Alan Parle, the CO of the naval base, and Commander Joe Lyden, head of naval intelligence.

'Gentlemen, this situation in the Atlantic appears to be much more sinister than what we're looking at. As of now, I am of the opinion that whatever happened to that cruise ship was an act of terrorism. We don't know who the perpetrators are, but our ships out there are now involved in something more than just a rescue mission. Accordingly, I want a special operations cell set up immediately on the base to assimilate all the data incoming, and to co-ordinate the overall rescue effort. Somebody somewhere, it seems, wanted a shipload of Americans sent to the bottom, and they have chosen to carry it out in Irish territorial waters. The Irish navy is now doing its best to ensure that this doesn't happen and, given the proximity of *Eithne* and *Niamh*, I'd be more than interested to find out who that somebody is. Just before I came into this meeting, I spoke with the chief of staff, and the only external will be his naval representative in GHQ. Also, Chief Superintendent Barney Fitzgerald is on his way down to the base as we speak. Even though the Irish coast guard have designated Mike Ford as the on-scene commander of a rescue mission, this whole incident has now moved into the territory of the Maritime Security Act.'

'Sir, about half an hour ago I actually spoke to Barney Fitzgerald's number two. It seems the Dutch police have been on to them with concerns about some sort of ocean-going tug and its skipper.'

FOCNS. and Captain Alan Parle immediately looked up at the slightly younger intelligence officer. Alan Parle was first in: 'Jesus Christ,' he said, looking at Commodore Garrett, 'that has to be our tug, you know, the one that is coming from the eastern Med to Bantry Bay, what the fuck is going on?'

At that moment the buzzer went off in Tom Garrett's office.

'Sir, Chief Superintendent Fitzgerald is here now.'

'Okay, send him in.'

Lt Cdr Clare Collins, the commodore's personal staff officer, then escorted the chief superintendent down the hall to his office.

Tom Garrett and Barney Fitzgerald had actually known each other for about three years. Both of them were members of the Defence Security Committee (DSC), which met on a regular basis.

'Barney, come on in, welcome,' said Tom, shaking hands with the senior Garda officer. 'How are you keeping? This is Captain Alan Parle, he's in charge of the base and dockyard here.' Both men shook hands and then the commodore continued: 'And I believe you know Joe.'

'Yes, how are you Joe?' replied Barney, not directly divulging how he knew him. Years working in the intelligence community had taught him to be circumspect.

For the next half hour or so the four men discussed the information that they had to hand.

Within an hour of the meeting, the special operations cell was fully set up in the naval base communications centre (comcen). All base leave was cancelled for the next five days. Before Commodore Garrett had left his office to go to the first meeting, he had ordered that a signal be sent to LE *Emer*, which was on patrol forty-eight miles north of Malin Head in Donegal, ordering her to suspend patrol duties and to position immediately to Galway Bay. A further signal was sent to *Niamh*'s sister ship, LE *Roisin*, which was at that moment alongside the oil wharf in the naval base, serving as duty ship. The signal read as follows.

Position asap Bantry Bay.
Prepare for possible hostile contact
including armed interdiction.
Garrett

For the most part an operations cell, or ops cell in military speak, fulfils three primary functions in a country's defence forces. The first is that it becomes the entity into which all information and intelligence surrounding a specific operation or event is funnelled. Secondly, it is a secure area within which designated personnel can be completely isolated, to plan and prosecute any actions that may be deemed necessary by the ops cell team. Thirdly, by its very nature, it maintains the absolute need for high level security and secrecy surrounding any mission that may be planned therein.

The comcen ops centre in the Haulbowline Island naval base was no different.

When the ops room command team was fully present the doors were locked and armed guards posted outside. Arrangements were made for tea, coffee and food, including sandwiches, pastries, fruit and a selection of yoghurts, to be brought in.

Tom Garrett then gave a brief appraisal of the situation.

'Gentlemen, as you know there is a certain protocol employed when the operations room is used. However, when there is a suspected act of terrorism in Irish territorial waters panning out right before our eyes, that protocol gets bumped up a bit. I have been watching this situation develop right from the start and, to be honest, an act of terrorism is precisely what I believe has occurred. Let me briefly outline the facts.

1.
A cruise liner in the north Atlantic suffers two explosions within minutes of each other, in totally different parts of the ship.
2.
Not just any old explosions ... both of them caused very specific damage. Enough to sink the ship within five or six hours.
3.
Just from preliminary observations, one of our best clearance divers thinks that the hull plating was damaged from the outside; in other words, based on the way the plating was bent, he cannot see how anything inside the ship could have caused it. Explosions like these can leave vital clues about the point of impact and so on.
4.
The only vessels in that area at that time were trawlers; we are able to ascertain that from the satellite vessel monitoring system that we employ. There wasn't even an oil rig supply vessel anywhere near the area, and
5.
We get one piece of intelligence, just one, and it concerns an ocean-going tug, which we know about anyway.
The thing is, that tug happens to be coming from the eastern Mediterranean.
Now gentlemen, the last point I want to make is this: the part of the world's oceans that we patrol hasn't had an incident like this since the U boat activity around the convoys in the Second World War. Since then we have every maritime aid known to man at our disposal ... things like satellites, reliable machinery in our ships, good coms and so on. Incidents like this just don't happen nowadays, something bad is going on out there.'
Commodore Garrett then turned to the only policeman in the room.

'Any ideas, Barney?'

'Well Tom, this incident happened more on your beat than the one I'm used to,' said the chief superintendent. 'However, before I came down here I asked my number two to go back to the Dutch for more details about the origins of the tug report. Also, on the way down to the base another signal came in from the Brits about a text message that was sent from

somewhere near Edinburgh to somewhere near Algiers a few days ago. The text simply read:
Strawberries and blackberries in the basket now. The Brits can't make any sense of it.'

Commander Lyden had his chin in his cupped hand, looking pensively at a series of nautical charts on the far wall of the ops room. He then got up, picked up a pair of dividers and started measuring distances. 'Leith,' he announced to several turned heads. 'Leith, sir, that is where the cruise liner departed from. So let's say the cruise liner had a mean speed of sixteen knots ... well sir, that puts the ship uncomfortably close to both when and where that text was sent from.'

Oil Wharf, Haulbowline Island Naval Base

A lot of activity now surrounded the LE *Roisin*, whose sister ship the LE *Niamh* was at that moment positioning itself between the *American Princess* and the LE *Eithne*.
Although *Roisin* was the duty ship and, accordingly, at the ready on the oil wharf for an immediate departure, this was different; it was not a rescue mission. The ship had been ordered to sail on a war footing. Armaments were checked and supplemented, and extra boarding equipment embarked. Lt Cdr Joe Sorensen, *Roisin*'s captain, knew about the incident out in the Porcupine Bank, but was not yet in the loop regarding the suspicions harboured by his superior officers. However, right now that didn't matter; his orders were clear and succinct ... Bantry Bay asap, hostile contact, possible armed interdiction. That was enough for him. Just about double the shore personnel needed to let go the ship were standing by to heave the lines off the bollards on the wharf, to allow *Roisin* to clear the base. Five minutes before *Roisin* sailed, a navy patrol jeep drove right up to the side of ship and four fairly rugged looking sailors got out, with kit bags and other equipment, and boarded immediately.

Line parties let go fore and aft, came the order from Lt Cdr Sorensen.
Roisin moved at a faster than normal pace as she passed Cobh. Then as she
came around the Spit Bank light, her captain ordered three quarters speed.

Swiftsure

Aboard *Swiftsure*, which was still completely blacked out, there was no sound from the crew. They had been shocked to the very core of their being at the unbelievable act of barbarity which they had witnessed. The business end of a loaded Kalashnikov ensured that they would stay that way. On the other hand, the perpetrators, no longer negatively affected by the swell, were in high spirits at their ultimate achievement. Mohammed, being his usual self, planning ahead the next few moves, waved Khalid into the skipper's cabin.

'My brother, Allah is with us on this great night.'

'Yes, Mohammed, he is,' replied Khalid. 'However, we have a few more obstacles to climb before we are clear of the infidel.'

'What can go wrong, Khalid? I have planned our escape meticulously.'
Khalid had indeed thought well of Mohammed's plan. After the strike they would quietly slip away unnoticed from the melee that would inevitably ensue in the stormy waters of the north Atlantic, and take up a south westerly heading towards the Dingle peninsula. Mohammed had ensured that enough explosives were embarked in Algiers to blow up the tug and its crew, sending it and them straight to the bottom, while leaving no evidence of any sort, when they no longer had any use for it.
He had instructed Abu to fit a two-hour timing mechanism to the explosives, such that when they left the tug five miles west of Brandon creek, having turned it onto a westerly heading with the autopilot engaged and the tug's crew securely locked up in a cabin, they could make their getaway in *Swiftsure*'s RIB. They would then come ashore in the tiny isolated inlet on the western shore of the Dingle peninsula, where Jabir

would be waiting somewhere nearby in a car. The plan then was to drive towards Dublin and hopefully assimilate into the more multicultural population that exists there, the better to make good their final escape when the hue and cry died down in the following days and weeks.

'From experience, Mohammed, I can tell you that any amount of things can go wrong.'

'Yes, I agree with you. It is not the Irish I am worried about, but the accursed Americans and their British lapdogs, who seem to be able to reach out into any part of the world.'

Mohammed paused before replying to his superior.

'Khalid, that is one of the reasons I selected the Brandon creek as the initial part of our escape. Just like the location in the Porcupine Bank where we successfully made our great strike against the Americans, it is the last place on earth they would consider looking. And anyway, I am reasonably confident that they do not even realise that, firstly, it was a terrorist attack and secondly, even if they did, that it had its origin in the Middle East, so what reason would they have to look for a connection to us?'

'Yes, Mohammed, I am sure it will be as you say.'

In the meantime, *Swiftsure* was making fifteen knots towards the Dingle peninsula, which by Mohammed's calculation would have them there in approximately nine hours.

Frank Blokland, who was at that time steering the tug, was now acutely aware that his captors had achieved their ultimate mission, which meant that at some stage in the near future they would no longer need the services of the tug's crew. A cold feeling enveloped him at the thought of what may happen; however, he replaced that feeling quickly with a need to come up with a plan, some sort of a plan. That was going to be very difficult, he thought, as he stared at the weapon in Tarka's hands, which was aimed directly at him.

At that time, Jabir was sitting in the restaurant of the Dingle Skellig hotel, enjoying a meal. He had landed in Shannon airport two days earlier and after hiring a Volvo estate car using his false passport and driving licence, and posing as a UK businessman, he slowly made his way towards the city of Limerick, and then south west towards the large town of Tralee, before driving on out through the rugged Dingle peninsula.

Casa 253

The Casa 253 maritime patrol aircraft of the Irish air corps was now fully on scene, orbiting *Eithne* at two thousand feet. The flight from Galway to the Porcupine Bank had been flown at eight thousand feet, so that the twin-engined Casa's powerful barco MPRD 9651 downward looking radar would show all contacts within a 150 mile radius. Before she left flight level eight zero, Cmd Brian Gould, the aircraft's commander, had ordered the radar operator to save an image before they descended from the higher altitude. The radar operator noticed the pattern of the vessels near *Eithne*; all of them were moving towards her. However, he noticed one vessel which was steaming away in a south westerly direction from the incident, and remarked to himself that this was not usual, as most vessels would either stand by or move closer so that they could be available to provide assistance if needed. Nevertheless, he didn't take much notice of it as Casa 253 had begun her descent into the area where *Eithne* was operating, and he was more concerned now with identifying the three Sikorsky S61s, which would be arriving soon to transfer survivors from the cruise liner to *Eithne*.

LE *Eithne*

The first helicopter to reach *Eithne*, code named Romeo 22, had touched down on the flight deck at 2120. She was quickly refuelled while staying at flight idle on the deck. Five minutes later, she lifted off and headed in the direction of the *American Princess*, with one extra passenger aboard, Lt Gerry Stewart, *Eithne*'s gunnery officer, who was also an underwater explosives expert. Commodore Garrett had signalled Mike Ford telling him that he wanted a second, more qualified, opinion on the suspicions of the clearance diver, who had earlier reported that he felt the explosions on the ship had come from an external source.

Twenty-five minutes later, Romeo 22 came into a high hover above the slanted swimming pool area of the *American Princess*. It had been guided to that position both by the radio operator on the cruise liner and a series of four orange lights which had been set up on the deck of the ship, so that the helicopter pilot would have a visual cue also of the section of the ship that he was going to lift survivors from. At this time the *American Princess* was listing at six degrees and still taking water. Even though her crew had every available pump on board working to pump out the water that was flooding into the ship through the two holes caused by the explosions, they were hopelessly inadequate. The cruise liner was doomed, and at this stage the only question that really remained was whether this rescue could succeed in getting all the survivors off before she plunged to the bottom of the ocean.

Romeo 22's winch operator put a strop around Lt Stewart, while the winch man, John O'Donovan, put the second strop around himself. Jim Carroll, the helicopter's winch operator, then pressed the lift button on his console and the two men in strops, who had been sitting with their legs dangling out the side door of the helicopter, were initially lifted about a foot upwards so that they were clear of the helicopter's deck. The winchman then gently pressed the down button and both men slowly came down onto the deck of the *American Princess*. Lt Stewart was immediately whisked away by *Eithne*'s clearance diver, Stephen Jones, while John O'Donovan arranged for two reasonably healthy looking survivors to be lifted up into the helicopter. Having secured the strops around both, he instructed them to keep their arms firmly down at their sides and to absolutely obey any instructions that the winch operator would give them as they approached the door of the helicopter. In normal rescues the winchman would accompany each survivor up on the lift into the helicopter; however time was running out for the eight hundred people aboard.

As the first two survivors to be winched off the cruise ship were dragged into the helicopter by the winchman, a scramble developed between some of the survivors waiting on the ship's deck. It was as though there was a general realisation by the passengers that the ship was indeed going to sink. Panic then broke out, resulting in a heave of people from this section who became frantic at the thought of never seeing their loved ones again. Petty Officer Tom Dunne had flown out on *Eithne*'s helicopter on the

first flight to the cruise ship. Born on a farm in County Mayo, he was built like a tank, but of more significance right now he also had a voice to go with it, and he wasn't shy about using it. He boomed out an instruction that carried over anything that the helicopters or wind could offer.
'Shut up, I want order … right now.'
This was followed by a vacuum of silence which was promptly filled in verbally by the rugged looking petty officer.

'Okay, listen up everybody, we need to get all of you people off this ship. That can only happen in an orderly way so from now on, everybody here has got to follow the instructions of the rescue personnel.'
Then he paused, waiting for a reaction. More than a few sighs could be heard from the worried survivors who seemed to accept what the navy NCO was saying. The weighted strops came down towards the liner's deck again and two more survivors were promptly winched up.

Further aft of the cruise liner which was now lying uncomfortably abeam of the sea, another winching location was set up in a reasonably open area of tilted deck. This winching area, however, was strictly for injured or elderly passengers and their partners. Romeo 24, the Sligo-based Sikorsky S61, had now established in a hover over this area. This part of the operation was always going to be much slower from a winching point of view. Firstly, a decision was made to winch two of the able-bodied partners of the injured passengers up into the helicopter so that they could assist in lifting the injured off the gurney, and placing them as comfortably as possible on the deck of the aircraft. While Romeo 22 managed to pack twenty-five people in like sardines, Romeo 24 was only able to carry fourteen due to the nature of the injuries.

Dr Scott Jablonsky and nurse Loretta Chambers were, with the assistance of their respective spouses, doing their best to treat the injured passengers, both in terms of applying some form of first aid until they arrived on *Eithne* and also transporting them from whatever part of the ship they were in to the winching area. This was not easy, in particular trying to cope with the list of the ship; however, they also had the assistance of quite a few other passengers. For the most part their main tasks were applying sling supports and providing blankets to keep them warm; however, there were quite a few seriously injured people also.

The sea water which was flooding into the ship precluded the *American Princess*'s crew from entering the area, and accordingly they were not certain of the number of crew casualties at this stage, but they estimated about fourteen having accounted for everybody else. The explosion that occurred midships, however, had penetrated into several passenger compartments, killing eight of the passengers instantly and leaving another thirty with severe to horrific injuries. Unfortunately, even though the ship was travelling very slowly when the explosion occurred, quite a few of the passengers who had seen their fill of whales and dolphins had retired to their cabins to get ready for dinner.

As Scott Jablonsky trudged through the wreckage of these cabins he remarked to himself that it was a relief to have a nurse with field experience of Vietnam beside him, someone who wasn't going to be shocked in the same way that an ordinary person would by what each cabin presented. Part of the difficulty for the Charleston-based doctor was the transportation of these casualties from whatever part of the ship they were in to the winching area, and then having to transfer them onto the winching gurney to be lifted up into the helicopter. He knew instinctively that some wouldn't even make the first part of this journey. Up on deck Romeo 25 had just arrived overhead, having been vectored into position by the air corps Casa 253, two thousand feet above. Romeo 25. The Waterford-based Sikorsky had briefly touched down on *Eithne*'s flight deck to disembark the two trauma teams, together with their equipment, before joining in the now three-ship pattern to and from the cruise liner.

LE *Roisin*

As *Roisin* smashed her way into the heavy seas five miles south of the Old Head of Kinsale at twenty-one knots, her captain, Lt Cdr Joe Sorensen, peered to his right at the light that flashed at a frequency of every ten seconds to warn mariners away from this famous headland. His ship, he knew, was going into harm's way, but he also knew that his navy had trained both himself and his crew to a very high standard.

The Irish navy was taking no chances with this mission. The flag officer, himself a former special forces officer, had decided that *Roisin*'s boarding party should include as many sailors who had had experience and weapons training with the Irish Army rangers as he could get his hands on. The Irish Army rangers are the special forces component of the Irish defence forces. They train with other military forces around the world, including the SAS and the Swedish and German special forces units. Their mission is primarily to deal with hijackings, hostage rescue and providing security for foreign dignitaries visiting the state, and any other terrorist activities that may arise. They operate at a very high level of readiness and theirs is a life of ceaseless training to the highest standards. Defence force personnel from any of the three services can be accepted onto a selection course, which is held annually. This course lasts for four weeks and the students must be able to cope with a lot of physical and psychological pressures. The course also includes weapons handling, mountain navigation, survival skills and many other aspects of special forces training. Although only less than 1 per cent of them are invited to do further training in the special forces basic skills course, the other 99 per cent bring valuable experience back to their own commands, and the navy was no exception.

Tom Garrett wanted as many of these as he could muster in the short time available. In addition to the four who had boarded *Roisin* just prior to sailing, five more had since been assembled from other ships and from base personnel. These five were now in the NCO's mess enjoying a very nice meal, albeit at 2215. While they waited for the AW139 Agusta Westland medium lift helicopter that had just lifted off from the air corps base in Baldonnel, en route to the naval base to pick them up and take them out to *Roisin*, the base commander had ordered the duty cook to prepare an energy sustaining meal of steak, scrambled eggs, salads and fries, exactly what was needed to meet the high energy demands of the next five to six hours.

At 2315 the AW139 helicopter landed on the square with the help of the base duty officer who, acting as ground marshal, guided the helicopter in to the landing area. After the aircraft touched down, her commander kept her at flight idle while the five special forces-trained navy personnel were strapped in, together with the small amount of equipment they were bringing with them. Ten minutes after landing, the helicopter then lifted off into the wet, windy and extremely black night sky, taking up a south westerly heading.

Ops Cell

Chief Superintendent Barney Fitzgerald was handed the phone by Joe Lyden.

'Sir, it's your man,' said Joe Lyden.

The chief superintendent took the phone and curtly answered.

'Fitzgerald.' He paused ... 'okay ... okay, thanks for that.'

He then wrote down a telephone number which had obviously been given to him by the caller, before putting down the receiver and then turning to the others in the room.

'Seems like the police chief in Rotterdam wants a word in my ear. I think he may have intelligence that he wants to share only with me.'

Tom Garrett was pensive when he heard this. After a moment, he turned to the chief superintendent.

'Barney, it seems like they have some intelligence that they want only you to hear, but just before you ring, bear in mind that the tug is in fact Dutch flagged, in effect Dutch state property, with a Dutch crew aboard. I feel that we are going to have to get diplomatic permission to board her, especially seeing as she is outside our twelve mile limit.'

'Well let's see what he has to say,' said Barney as he picked up the receiver and dialled the number. The call lasted about seven or eight minutes and for the most part the chief superintendent was replying with 'I see' and 'okay' as he furiously wrote down details while listening to the voice on the other end of the line. He then proceeded to tell the other members of the ops cell what he heard.

'Well, gentlemen, the Dutch policeman it seems had a good reason for wanting to talk to me directly. The intelligence he gave me is not something he wanted to fall into the hands of the media any time soon. Apparently, Carla Blokland, who is the wife of the *Swiftsure*'s captain, Frank Blokland, received a call from him within the last three days. The call for the most part was normal enough if not shorter than usual. It seems that the lasts words spoken by Captain Blokland were the usual pleasantries and goodbyes from a husband to a wife, and apparently finished with 'give my regards to your mother'. The trouble is, Carla Blokland's mother died six years ago, so the opinion of the police chief in Holland is that either Captain Blokland has suffered some form of neurological disorder, or this is his way of getting a coded message out that there was a problem on the tug.

Carla first voiced her concerns to Captain Johann Naaler, who is the senior training captain for Smit Tak, the company which owns the *Swiftsure*. According to him, Frank Blokland comes with an excellent record and is not given to any sudden memory losses. Captain Naaler sent a number of signals to the tug and, having not received a reply for twelve hours, decided to accompany Carla Blokland to the police authorities in Amsterdam. He also confirmed that the *Swiftsure*'s last port of call was Algiers, where she took on fuel and departed on schedule. The *Swiftsure*'s orders at that point were to sail directly to southern Ireland.'

Commodore Garrett immediately turned to the navy's football-loving intelligence officer, Commander Joe Lyden.

'How does this new intelligence support the data that we already have, Joe?'

Joe Lyden paused briefly while he gathered the sequential nature of the facts he already had.

'Well, sir, let's put everything we know on the table now. The *Swiftsure* seems to have done everything right, up to and including her departure from Algiers which, by the way, was the destination point of the text message which originated in Leith in Scotland, from where the cruise liner departed. For my money that's a pretty strong connection between the tug and the liner to start with. This might seem far-fetched, sir, but my theory at this point is that somehow or other the *Swiftsure* was taken over in, or near to, Algiers. Let's face it, if we assume that the tug was responsible for the sinking of the cruise liner it would be in the interests of the terrorists or whoever to control how they would embark whatever explosive devices they used. In other words, I don't think the tug could have been taken over at sea, and even if it was, how would you cross deck the equipment needed to carry out this attack? I'm not saying it would be impossible, but it's highly improbable.'

Captain Alan Parle, the CO of the naval base and dockyard, came in at that point.

'From the way I see it, it seems like a big leap of faith to assume that the terrorists, or whoever they are, planned an operation which originated from Algiers and that terminated a couple of hundred miles off the west coast of Ireland four or five days later. However, the presence of that text message is too much of a coincidence to discount the theory. Also, I know we are waiting on *Eithne*'s explosives officer to confirm whether the cruise liner's plating was hit from outside or within, but my money would be on the word of the clearance diver. So, if we advance the theory from there and assume that the liner was hit from an external source, the next question is what could possibly have hit it with enough force to blow two thirty-foot holes in its side? We know there are no submarines or warships out there other than our own, and the Casa in *Eithne*'s overhead has confirmed that the only other vessels in the area are trawlers ... the only other vessel that should be in the general area is the tug, and Barney's intel it seems has made a connection with that tug. All things considered, I concur with Joe's point of view.'

AW139 Helicopter

The fifteen-seater helicopter, powered by her two Pratt & Whitney PT6C turboshaft engines, took off on an initial course which took her directly over the town of Carrigaline at an altitude of fifteen hundred feet. This was necessary to stay below the extended centreline of runway 'one seven' in Cork airport. Having passed through that, her captain brought her to an altitude of 2,500 feet for the rest of the twenty-five minute flight to her rendevous point with *Roisin*, which was now positioned ten nautical miles south of the Fasnet Rock, and had slowed to a speed of fifteen knots in anticipation of the helicopter's arrival.

In the back of the air corps helicopter the five sailors, kitted out in jet black drysuits, were preparing the ropes to rappel down to *Roisin*'s afterdeck. A short while later the helicopter began to match its speed with

Roisin as it came up behind her. The combination of the forward speed of the helicopter, together with the twenty-two knot wind that she was faced into, provided a more than adequate fifty-five knot air speed for the manoeuvre.

After the crew chief opened the starboard sliding door, the sailors lowered their equipment bags first, the better to get a sense of the wind effect for when they themselves were being lowered down. Seven minutes later, the five were on *Roisin*'s after deck and the helicopter turned right towards Cork airport to refuel prior to returning to Baldonnel.

USS *Samuel B. Roberts*

The 453-foot frigate was now slicing through heavy seas at twenty-six knots on a course of three zero zero. Her crew of seventeen officers and 190 enlisted personnel had moved from a relaxed attitude to a deadly earnestness that characterised one level below action stations. Her captain, Commander Tom Turner, a wily Texan, had fifteen minutes earlier received a flash traffic message from Admiral Tom Kane, the commander-in-chief Atlantic fleet, ordering him to proceed immediately at best speed towards the sinking American cruise liner in the Porcupine Bank. The signal also suggested that he liaise with Commander Mike Ford, captain of the Irish naval frigate, *Eithne*, who was the on-scene commander. The Sammy B. was in fact just eighty-two nautical miles south of her intended destination, Cork harbour, when the signal was received.

Commander Turner's nav officer confirmed to his now impatient captain that even at best speed they were seven and a half hours away from the scene. The captain peered out the windows of the semi triangular shaped bridge into the blackness and the persistent spray, which necessitated the wipers to be fully on. He knew that his ship would probably not make it to the area in time to be of any direct help to the rescue operation that was now unfolding; however, he had two SH-60 Seahawk helicopters down aft. One of these could close the *Eithne* within two hours. He immediately ordered a signal to be sent to Commander Ford that went as follows.

USS Samuel B. Roberts closing at best speed. Estimate eight hours. Suggest forward deploy one SH-60 to help with rescue op. Also can send paramedics and liaison officer.

Turner. Cdr USN

Within seconds the signal had travelled up into space to an orbiting US satellite and straight down to *Eithne*'s comms room. Thirty seconds later it was handed to Cdr Ford, who like most naval officers was not known for his lack of brevity, immediately ordered what was a pretty terse reply.

Affirm. Deploy all soonest.

Ford. Cdr INS

Back on the *Samuel B. Roberts*, Commander Turner had anticipated the reply and accordingly had ordered that one of the SH-60s be readied immediately. He chose to send Lt Lorraine Ellis as his liaison officer to the LE *Eithne* for no other reason than he knew that she had Irish roots. Fifteen minutes later, with Lt Ellis and the paramedics aboard, the helicopter lifted from the flight deck of the frigate and took up a heading of three one zero degrees magnetic.

LE *Eithne*

The Irish coast guard had tasked a Nimrod reconnaissance aircraft from RAF Kinloss to sortie to the Porcupine Bank. This would be quite normal, despite the earlier deployment of the Case 253 from Baldonnel, but right now the men in the ops cell in the Haulbowline Island naval base wanted as many aerial assets as they could get their hands on.

For sure, the primary operation here was the rescue of nearly eight hundred passengers from the stricken cruise liner *American Princess*; however, there was also a crew of five innocent people being held hostage aboard a tug who, in the opinion of Commodore Garrett, may shortly have outlived their usefulness to their captors.

Sub Lt Hogan turned to her skipper.

'Sir, we have a Nimrod in our overhead now, Casa 253 is chopping (change of operational control) with her as we speak.'

'Okay, Angela, signal Haulbowline with that please.'

When Commodore Garrett received this signal he immediately sent an encrypted message to the crew of Casa 253 to position on the tug *Swiftsure* and shadow her until further notice.

Back on *Eithne* the three S61 rescue helicopters were working well in the pattern now, ferrying the cruise liner's survivors back to her deck. However, incessant driving rain and a heaving deck made conditions much more difficult for the survivors as they made their way from the helicopters to the hangar deck. It was particularly difficult for those cases coming in on stretchers. Soon, *Eithne*'s crew became aware of how crowded the ship had become although the ever enthusiastic Chief Mulligan and most of the supplies division aboard made many of the visitors feel a whole lot better by simply producing a mug of hot thick vegetable soup for them.

In the wardroom, however, things were a little different. This room now resembled the accident and emergency department of a major hospital. Most of the cruise liner's passengers who arrived aboard *Eithne* on stretchers were taken straight in there. The two medical teams were working flat out treating a variety of wounds, most of which had resulted from shrapnel damage, but many were in fact suffering from broken limbs and shock. However, they were coping, despite the fact that the 'floor' underneath them was constantly moving, periodically inducing a horrible nauseous feeling. Nevertheless, so far two people, an elderly couple in fact, had died despite the best efforts of the trauma teams. One of the trauma surgeons had suggested to Lt John Kana that is might be a good idea to check if there were any chaplains or priests aboard amongst the more able bodied of the *American Princess*'s passengers.

Meanwhile, forty metres astern of *Eithne,* Leading Seaman David Moynihan watched from his Jaguar as each of the search and rescue helicopters made their approach. He marvelled at the apparent techniques used by their pilots to set them down onto a deck that was pitching and rolling in the still worsening sea conditions.

LE *Roisin*

As soon as the ship's new crew members and their equipment were secure inside *Roisin*'s hull, Captain Joe Sorensen ordered a complete blackout, with the exception of his steaming lights, which he changed to make the ship appear like a trawler. All of the ship's upper deck portholes were blanked out completely so that, to any other ships within visual range, *Roisin* now presented as a large fishing trawler steaming out to the rich fishing grounds near the Atlantic continental shelf.

Inside the ship, however, there was a hive of activity. The entire boarding party including the RIBs' coxwains and bowmen were now assembled in the wardroom for a briefing. With the ship now in the hands of the XO, Lt Cdr Sorensen made his way to the wardroom. As he walked in all of the boarding party stood up.

'At ease, gentlemen. As most of you now know we are about to conduct an armed boarding … for real. We have reason to believe that an ocean-going tug, which is now en route from the Porcupine Bank to an area which we suspect is just outside Brandon Creek on the Dingle peninsula, has been taken over by terrorists who appear to be responsible for the attack on the *American Princess*. Intelligence suggests that the tug's own crew may still be alive but probably not for long. We suspect that the terrorists' intentions are to close to within five or ten miles of the coast and, prior to disembarking the tug, presumably on a RIB, set her on a westerly course on autopilot, with a time delay fuse attached to explosives which will go bang sometime soon after that. Needless to say, the crew will probably be bound and locked up in some cabin or other; that is, if they are still alive.'

Lt Cdr Sorensen continued.

'Right now we are rigged as a large ocean-going trawler underway towards the fishing grounds, and on our present course we will pass the tug at about seven miles off our starboard side in about three hours' time.

We have no idea what weapons these people will be packing but, given that they are of middle-eastern origin, we can possibly expect Kalashnikovs and probably knives. I intend to sail right past them knowing that they will both see us on the tug's radar and hopefully get a visual on our lights so that they can simply write us off as a passing trawler. I am going to maintain course and speed for at least ten miles further which I think will be enough to convince them to take their eyes off the radar and write us off as insignificant. At twelve miles range we will launch Jaguars one and two. The crew of each will consist of coxwain and bowman, both of whom will be armed with 9mm Heckler & Koch USPs, and a boarding party of five who will be armed with Heckler & Koch submachine guns and 9mm USPs also.'

The entire boarding party continued to listen intently to *Roisin*'s captain. The boarding officer and several of the others were taking down notes as he spoke.

'Your orders are to locate, intercept, identify and secure crew and any hostages. Your rules of engagement (ROEs) are per defence force regulations. Complete radio silence will be observed until our objective is secured. We expect the RIBs to run in at twenty-five knots, giving us an intercept time of thirty minutes. Any questions?'

'Yes, sir,' replied Lt Tony Kelly, the boarding officer,

'Do we have any idea, sir, of the profile of the tug, particularly the arse end?'

'Yeah, we're expecting it to come through from Haulbowline within the next thirty minutes,' replied the skipper, 'so you'll be able to study it before you go. The nav is putting together a sea state, cloud cover and moon phase report, but I think it is safe to say that you will be operating in total blackness.'

At that moment the telephone rang in *Roisin*'s wardroom.

'Sir, it's the XO, says it's urgent,' reported the nearest member of the boarding party who picked up the phone.

'Sorensen,' said the captain tersely.

'Sir, we have a radar contact bearing one three five, speed twenty-five knots. He's coming right up our ass so fast that pretty soon he's going to really compromise our plans.' If he gets inside the tug's radar range ... '

'Fuck,' said Commander Sorensen.

'It must be that Perry class frigate that was paying us a visit, probably heard about the incident in the Porcupine Bank on its way to Cork and diverted. Set up a secure line to the ops cell immediately, I'm on my way.'

'Yes, sir,' replied the XO.

Ten minutes later aboard the USS *Samuel B. Roberts* a petty officer first class rushed into the combat information centre (CIC).

'Sir, flash traffic from Fort Meade.'

In naval parlance 'flash' represented the absolute highest priority message. The signal simply read:

Alter course NOW onto 250 for 40nm.
Then resume towards datum.
Kane. Adm (Cinclant)

The Sammy B.'s captain was at first a bit perplexed but he nevertheless issued the order instantly.

'Course, turn two five zero right now.'

'Turn two five zero, aye sir,' came the reply, followed a minute and a half later by:

'Ship steady on two five zero sir.'

Captain Tom Turner turned to his XO and spoke in a heavy Texan drawl.

'The good ol' admiral must know somethin' that we don't. My money says the Irish must have a little sideshow goin' on here and they don't want us interferin'. I'd give you dollars to doughnuts they found the people responsible for whackin' that cruise liner.'

LE *Eithne*

Nimrod 35, Nimrod 35, this is helicopter Seahawk One, Seahawk One, fifteen DME, request clearance to land Eithne *and then rejoin SAR pattern.*

Seahawk One, Seahawk One, that's copied. Contact Eithne *on one one niner decimal niner*, came the reply from the large British maritime patrol aircraft.

The SH60 Seahawk from the USS *Samuel B. Roberts* was now just fifteen nautical miles behind *Eithne* and had sought clearance to land on her flight deck to disembark Lt Lorraine Ellis and two medical orderlies.

LE Eithne, *LE* Eithne, *this is helicopter Seahawk One, Seahawk One, request clearance to land.*

Seahawk One, Seahawk One, check endurance, Eithne?

My endurance is ninety minutes, Seahawk One.

Okay Seahawk One, clear to land pax, then immediate departure, contact Nimrod 35 for joining instructions to pattern.

Seahawk One, copy.

Seahawk One, which was then hovering just outboard of the port side of the ship, began to slip sideways until she was right in front of the bum line on *Eithne*'s flight deck. She then slowly tilted her nose upwards to slow down the aircraft, and in a deft but almost slamming manoeuvre, the pilot placed the 9,500 kg helicopter right in the circle on *Eithne*'s flight deck. He kept her at flight idle while the crew chief opened the starboard sliding door, and three drysuit-clad figures quickly made their way towards *Eithne*'s flight hangar. Waiting there for them was Lt John Kana. All four smartly saluted and, after introducing themselves, the two American paramedics were dropped off at the wardroom and Lt Kana escorted Lt Ellis along the corridor and up the steps to the deck where *Eithne*'s ops room was situated.

Inside, Mike Ford was looking at the tactical plot with Sub Lt Neil Kennedy when Lt Kana came in to the red lighted room.

'Em, excuse me, sir, this is Lt Lorraine Ellis.'

Commander Ford looked up and around to see the American lieutenant quickly come to attention and smartly salute *Eithne*'s CO. He then extended his hand, welcoming her aboard.

'Lt Ellis, welcome aboard. As you probably noticed on your way up, things are a bit busy here at the moment, and are likely to be for some time to come yet. Lt Kana will take you to your quarters where you can get out of that drysuit. You can come back here when you are ready. I'll brief you then on the situation as it is. Actually, John,' said Commander Ford, turning to Lt Kana, 'when the lieutenant is ready, it might be a better idea to take her on a tour of the ship first, showing her all activities that are on-going at the moment, and maybe grab a cup of coffee on the way.'

'Yes, sir,' replied John Kana.

'Thank you very much, sir,' said the US navy officer as she turned and left the room with Lt Kana.

As he touched his forehead with his hand, Mike Ford returned to the tactical plot that he had been working on, shaking his head.

'I know, sir,' said Sub Lt Kennedy, grinning at his skipper, 'she's gorgeous, isn't she?'

'I can see where you're coming from, Neil … it's just that her face seems familiar somehow or other,' replied the slightly puzzled captain.

John Kana brought the liaison officer to the cabin which had been assigned to her for the duration of her stay aboard. Once inside she stepped out of the drysuit that she was wearing. She emerged back into the corridor wearing US navy fatigues with the epaulettes of a lieutenant together with a baseball cap with the insignia of the USS *Samuel B. Roberts*. John Kana brought her to the bridge first where he introduced her to *Eithne*'s executive officer, Lt Cdr Jamie Morrisson, and also the OOW. In his unique New Zealand accent, he said to the XO:

'Jees, sir, that takes some beating, doesn't it? A New Zealand lieutenant introducing an American lieutenant to the XO on an Irish navy ship.'

Jamie Morrisson smiled.

'Yeah, John, under different circumstances we could have a party, but you're right, it is unusual.'

Lorraine Ellis smiled at the XO's remark and already felt at ease on board. The two then toured the rest of the ship, with John Kana giving her a running commentary on what was going on. When they entered the dining area, quite a few of the cruise liner's passengers immediately noticed the stars and stripes on the shoulder of the American naval officer, which raised a cheer from many. A few asked how she had got aboard, and she promptly explained that the *Samuel B. Roberts* had been about a hundred miles south of Cork when they were diverted up here.

Soon after that Lt Kana brought her to the flight deck again just as Romeo 22, the Shannon-based search and rescue helicopter, was about to land with another group of stretcher-laden casualties. Lt Ellis watched as seamen rushed out into the teeming rain to carry them in as soon as possible while Romeo 22 was being refuelled for the third time. She watched then as the giant Sea King lifted off the deck and was surprised to notice that the next helicopter being vectored in to land was in fact her own ship's SH-60 Seahawk with another group of survivors.

As the casualties went past her she noticed in some of them the wounds that they had taken, one in particular with a bloodied bandage applied round her head and obviously in a lot of pain. Another man had a piece of timber strapped to his leg to act as a splint. John Kana then brought her to the wardroom and pulled back the curtain that was across the open door and for the first time she got a sense of what had really unfolded. Apart from the two paramedics that had accompanied her to *Eithne*, who were now clad in white paper coveralls and wearing latex gloves, the trauma teams were so busy that none of them even bothered to look up to see who was there.

At that moment, Lt Ellis realised the full import of what had happened and it hit her like a punch in the stomach. Right in front of her were, up to a few hours ago anyway, happy American holidaymakers who, for the most part, had given a large part of their lives in service to their country. These same American lives were now forever changed due to the severity of their physical injuries, not to mention the possible psychological scars that might affect them in the future.

'How could anyone do this to innocent human beings?' she thought as she took in the scene before her. And then as if to depressingly reinforce it she noticed one of the surgeons shake his head at a colleague, indicating the hopelessness of the patient whose life they were trying in vain to save. Although she served on a US navy frigate which acted as an escort for a nuclear powered aircraft carrier in the Gulf theatre, she had never, as such, come face to face with such carnage. Nothing could have prepared her for the revulsion and shock that she experienced in that moment, and to her it was ironic that this occurred, not in one of the world's trouble spots in the Middle East, but in the ocean off the west coast of Ireland, the country of her birth.

Swiftsure

Frank Blokland was now quite worried. He realised that his ship was sailing at full speed towards some point on the Irish mainland, which probably meant that the usefulness of his ship, and more importantly its crew, could only now be measured in terms of hours. He reasoned in his mind that anyone who had the capacity to carry out the enormous crime that these people had just perpetrated wouldn't even blink at the thought of killing five more people, once they had served their purpose. He was pretty sure that the more evidence these people could eliminate the better it would be for them. Captain Blokland also noticed that Abu, the one who had put together the explosives underneath the RIBs, had been below deck somewhere for a couple of hours, which made him feel quite suspicious.

Abu in fact was working in the engine room with ear defenders over his head. He had surveyed the entire engine room and had concluded that the best location to place the explosives was right under where the engine cooling water intakes met with the hull. Two large explosions in this area, he concluded, would probably sink the ship in minutes. Being as they were amidships, he figured that the explosions would probably break the back of the ship instantly.

He also chose these two locations so that Frans de Vries, *Swiftsure*'s engineer who had to regularly come down to the engine room to oversee the efficient running of the two engines, would not see the deadly array of his work. Not that Abu cared now anyway; in his mind they would be off the tug in another few hours and, if necessary, Khalid could probably shoot the tug crew just as easily. Still, this is the way his leader wanted it so that's the way he was going to do it.

He carefully wired up the explosives to the timing mechanism, which would be set just before he and his accomplices left the tug for the ten mile RIB ride into Brandon Creek. When he was finished he moved forward first, and then towards the stern, opening every hatch that he could find at the engine room deck level, making sure that if the explosions didn't quite perform to his expectations, the ship would nevertheless flood down quite quickly and sink anyway.

Abu then made his way up to the bridge where he smiled at Khalid. No words were spoken, but Khalid instinctively knew that he had done his job well. Khalid then looked at the ship's clock which was showing 2255, and thought to himself:

'Just a little less than four more hours and we will be off this ship.'

For some reason he felt that he and the others would be far safer once they were on what seemed like a barren rocky outcrop on the south west of Ireland rather than on the sea. It was as if he had a pathological fear of the Americans or perhaps even the British who would maybe swoop down from the skies in helicopters like they did in Iraq and indeed like the Israelis did in Palestine. Mohammed peered out into the blackness, scanning for any lights that would signify other vessels in the area, but saw none.

'Why would anybody come out in this weather anyway?' he asked himself.

After that he moved over to the tug's radar, which had an effective range of fourteen miles, although in the prevailing conditions it was really only good out to eighteen. He noticed a dot just coming on to the bottom of the radar screen, away off to the south east, and at first became somewhat concerned at what he saw. He kept on looking until the dot started to move; he wanted to be certain of his facts before reporting to his leader.

'Khalid, we have a contact on the radar and it seems to be coming straight for us.'

Khalid moved straight away towards the screen and agreed with Mohammed. At that point, Captain Blokland looked at the screen, and to his experienced eye, he noticed that the ship was in fact not coming towards them but was on a parallel reciprocal course, heading north west. Khalid looked at him, almost urging the tug captain's opinion.

'That ship is not coming towards us,' said Frank Blokland,

'On its present course it will pass away to the south of us. It's on a reciprocal course, probably a large trawler heading out to the fishing grounds to the west of here.'

Khalid and Mohammed's eyes were glued to the screen as they slowly began to realise that what Captain Blokland had said was in fact right. A slight sense of relief began to come over them, when Abu addressed the tug's captain:

'How do we know it's a trawler?'

Frank Blokland replied

'What else could it be out here? In another ten minutes you will know that it is definitely a fishing trawler.'

'How? asked Khalid.

'Because at out closing speeds we will be coming within visual range of him. A trawler has a very distinctive set of lights on its masts so you will be able to see them.'

'What are these lights?' asked Khalid.

Frank Blokland went to a drawer and brought out a book and showed his chief captor what the lights would look like. Khalid took the book and went towards the starboard bridge windows and waited, book in hand, for the ship to come into visual range.

For the first time since his crew and ship were taken over in the port of Algiers, Frank Blokland began to notice that his captors, and especially Khalid, seemed a little less comfortable. He noticed how Khalid was glued to the bridge window almost urging the distant ship to come closer, sooner than it would, and also how every so often his head and eyes would scan the skies as if he were looking at stars, of which there were none. Just total blackness made even worse by driving rain and walls of spray that were now smashing over the bridge every fifth or sixth wave.

Cork

Catherine Ford arrived home from work at approximately 7 p.m. Although finished since 5.30 she had to do some shopping and collect a few items from the drycleaners on her way home. When she got in the door, she was surprised by the lovely smell of food, which emanated from the kitchen.

'Oh good, I don't have to cook,' she thought as she made her way to the kitchen with her shopping.

'Hi Mom,' beamed Emma, 'I've cooked you dinner, it's your favourite, chicken stir fry and rice.'

'Excellent, thanks love. Just what I need after a hard day at work; we had fourteen cases today, twas tough going. Anyway, what did you get up to today?'

'I got about five hours' study done because I'd like to come to Galway with you tomorrow to see the Grandmas and Grandad, and I know I won't get any done up there.'

'Yeah, no problem, but I thought you were getting your hair done?'

'Yeah, but do you know what I've done? I've booked that hairdresser in Shop Street, the one that Marian raves about,' referring to her first cousin from Galway. 'And by the way, Mom, I'm thinking of cutting it short, what do you think?'

'Are you sure?' replied Cas. 'That's a big step.'

'Well, I've been thinking about it for a while and, anyway, short hair will be easier to keep.'

'I'm sure it will be gorgeous on you love, and anyway, the great thing about hair is that it will always grow again if you aren't happy with it!'

'Yeah, I suppose you're right. By the way, what time are we heading off in the morning?'

'I'd like to get going straight after the traffic at 9.00, can you be up and ready for then?'

'Mother, I get up everyday in Dublin for college long before that!' remonstrated Emma, as she raised her eyes to heaven in mock exasperation.

Cas really enjoyed the meal prepared for her by Emma, but especially the opportunity to chat with her, mother to daughter, and catch up with the news. Being a mother, Cas was naturally inquisitive about Emma's new relationship and how things were going.

Later on, when Emma had gone out with her friend for the evening, Cas, who was by herself in the house, had time to reflect on things. She knew that Mike wouldn't be back off patrol for at least another week and the great thing about it was that she was in a job which she shared with another girl which gave her two or three days off each week. This week she worked Monday and Tuesday while Mary Martin, her job-sharing partner, worked Wednesday, Thursday and Friday. To Cas's great delight, it meant that she had a full five days off before she had to go to work again. This made it easy then to visit her mother in Caherlistrane for a couple of days, after which she would go out to Mike's mother and father in Rossaveal for a night before she headed back to Cork. This whole process had been more difficult when the children were younger, but now it was much easier.

LE *Roisin*

Down below, the hard men of the Irish navy were busy preparing for their mission. All of their weapons had to be meticulously cleaned and lightly oiled. Some had begun to apply black camouflage paste around their eyes and hands. All jewellery and loose change had been removed from the pockets of garments they would be wearing under their black drysuits, the better to maintain the crucial element of stealth which, if compromised, could cost someone his or her life. Quite a few of the team were also qualified navy divers, and accordingly had sharpened their underwater knives ... just in case.

Although the atmosphere was a little tense, each of the team had a steel-like determination and knew exactly what they were facing. However, they also knew that each one of them had gone through the toughest and most uncompromising training. Although all were experts in seamanship, surface and underwater navigation, weapons and close quarter combat, each of them also had the mental capacity to go into harm's way. And going into harm's way did not just mean taking on the perpetrators of the sinking of the *American Princess*. It also meant travelling for twelve miles in 6.5 metre rigid inflatable boats across one of the most inhospitable stretches of open ocean in the world. Huge waves, intense driving rain in total darkness and without radio contact with their mother ship ... but to the armed boarding team all of this was perversely their protector also.

Back up in the wardroom where the briefing took place, Lt Kelly and Lt Cdr Sorensen, together with Chief Ray O'Donnell, the second in command (2IC) for the mission, were going over the final details. Lt Kelly would command Jaguar One and Chief O'Donnell would command Jaguar Two. Both RIBs would approach each side of the stern of the *Swiftsure*. At this stage each of the three men now had a copy of the tug's profile and were delighted to see that, like most tugs, she had a low free board aft, but nevertheless, enough height for the RIB to sneak in under, hopefully without being seen. Chief O'Donnell figured that the teams would probably be okay with the height for boarding, especially with the RIB's coxwain judiciously riding up and down the stern wave. Nevertheless it was decided that each RIB would carry what was essentially a miniature version of a Jacob's ladder with a grapnel hook attached to the top of it.

Cdr Sorensen was looking at the latest sea state report, which in one sense was a wasted exercise because looking out of his own ship gave him a pretty good idea anyway. The two Jaguars would be approaching the tug with the seas behind them, which in fact meant that because *Swiftsure* was going with the weather, there shouldn't be too much of a vertical movement in her stern. And that would be good.

Ops Cell

At this stage Commodore Tom Garrett was doing the naval equivalent of pacing the floor. He knew that Lt Kelly's team was going to be in action within the next hour, while at the same time he knew, from the reports coming in from *Eithne*, that from now on things were going to be more difficult. At this stage the three helicopters, plus the addition of the Sammy B.'s Seahawk, had in fact taken over five hundred people across to *Eithne*, but the worrying thing was that Mike Ford had received reports from Captain John Whiteman that not alone was the cruise liner's list increasing but she was also beginning to go down more by the stern. Tom Garrett knew that this was not a good development. The more water that got into the ship the more the weight of that water would become a critical factor in the amount of time she would actually stay afloat. Things were now becoming a race against time.

Almost with a telepathic undertone another signal came into the Ops Cell from *Eithne*.

Am detailing two 61s to pickup
only able-bodied pax for winching to Niamh.
This will half the distance for the helis
and Eithne can concentrate on receiving wounded
Ford. Cdr.

Niamh's captain, Lt Cdr Charlie Keane, received a slight variation of the same signal and immediately ordered the ship to be turned into wind so that the helicopters could hover safely over her stern area. Several of her crew wearing foul weather and high visibility gear, together with life jackets, made a 'V' shaped cordon in towards the diving stores area door so that as the cruise liner's passengers were winched down and had the strops taken off them, they wouldn't become entangled in any of the stern gear on the afterdeck. The 'V' shaped cordon of sailors ensured that the survivors would be quickly and safely hustled inside *Niamh*'s hull. This was important as *Niamh* was now uncomfortably pitching and rolling in the heavy seas.

Soon the first of the 61s appeared overhead and started the slow process of winching down passengers two at a time. For the most part this was working well; however, two of the passengers in the second helicopter, who were being let down in a double strop, got the fright of their lives. Just as they were about ten feet above the deck, a momentary severe squall caught the fuselage of the aircraft, lifting it upwards and sideways away from *Niamh*'s pitching deck.

This resulted in the two hapless individuals being carried along underneath, as the helicopter initiated an orbit to re-position back to *Niamh*. The deafening noise of both the helicopter and the driving wind and rain, just thirty feet above the totally black, cold and now quite stormy ocean, certainly concentrated their minds. The 61 completed a full orbit before finally arriving back over *Niamh*'s afterdeck.

When they were eventually de-stropped onboard *Niamh*, the bosun, who had to shout to be heard above the deafening noise of wind and aircraft, candidly told them:

'At least ye've got a good story to tell your grandchildren!'

The Minister for Defence was the first political figure to be in the know from a very early stage. The chief of staff and his naval representative had provided him with an up-to-date account of proceedings on a regular basis. Michael Boland was regarded as an excellent Minister for Defence. A former army officer, he knew the ins and outs of the Irish defence forces and had provided funds for badly needed new equipment across the three services. Tom Garrett in particular was quite happy. Two new ships were

now on order for the navy, with an option of two more in the next two years. These new ships were fundamentally much larger than any of the existing fleet, due to the multi role tasking which would be required of them.
On Tom Garrett's watch Irish naval ships had sailed to all corners of the earth, essentially flying the flag and supporting trade missions. Irish people, coming as they were from the most westerly country in Europe, had always represented the country in a very good light abroad. Missionaries, athletes, musicians and above all peacekeeping soldiers had ensured that her reputation was always held in high regard.
Now, Ireland's small but professionally dedicated navy was once again representing the country in a way that few other platforms could achieve. Ireland had, after all, produced a few key people in the development of some of the world's bigger navies. John Holland, from County Clare, was the father of submarines in the US navy, while Admiral Brown, from County Mayo, was the founder of the Argentine navy. In addition, Commodore John Barry who came from Tacumshin parish in County Wexford, the son of a poor tenant farmer who was evicted by his British landlord, is rightfully regarded as the father of the United States navy (USN). And so when modern Irish naval ships sailed to these countries, there was, if you like, a bigger dimension to their presence.

Minister Boland had put the Taoiseach into the loop within ten minutes of receiving the news of the attack in the Atlantic. Because of the navy's suspicions that this in fact had been a terrorist action with a perpetrator in its midst, a total news blackout had been imposed for the moment. The Taoiseach himself had received a call from the US President expressing his grateful appreciation for the Irish navy in their efforts to save the lives of nearly eight hundred Americans who had come into harm's way.

Back in the ops cell the secure telephone rang and was answered by Commander Lyden, who turned immediately to commodore Garrett.

'Sir, the Taoiseach is about to come on the line.'

Tom Garrett took the phone

'Garrett.'

'Just one moment, commodore,' replied a senior civil servant. Then,

'Hello, Tom, you're pretty busy down there I'd say.'

'Yes, sir, so far everything is running smoothly. The trouble is we don't know if we have enough time to get the rest of the people off the cruise liner before she sinks.'

'We're going to have to go public with this soon, Tom,' said the Taoiseach.

'Yes, sir, I know. You're right, but if we could have another hour, it would really suit us. I'm aware that we will have to activate a major emergency plan as soon as possible but that would give the game away too soon and accordingly mess up our plans. In any case, sir, we will actually have plenty of time, because the first of the survivors won't be coming ashore for several hours yet. And Mike Ford out on *Eithne* is compiling a list of the casualties and their injuries, which will give us a good heads up on how we disperse them throughout the country relative to their injuries, and in that regard we are working up the logistics so that everything will be in place well before any survivors reach dry land. But unfortunately, sir, there's a lot more injured people than we first anticipated.'

'Okay, Tom, you're doing great, keep up the good work,' said the Taoiseach.

'Thank you, sir.'

The Taoiseach had in fact been briefed by the chief of staff about the armed boarding operation which was about to commence shortly. However, he didn't make any reference to it even though he was on a secure line.

Galway

At 0055 a Garda squad car quietly pulled up outside a bungalow in the western end of Salthill. The two policemen knocked on the door and after about five minutes it was cautiously opened by a slightly dishevelled and worried looking middle aged man.

'Hi, sorry for getting you out of bed, sir, but are you Martin O'Shea?' asked one of the officers.

'Yeah, what's the problem?' replied the tired looking air traffic controller.

'We need you to come to the airport as soon as possible.'

'Why, what's up?' asked Martin.

'Well, right now we can't give you too much information, but the airport needs to be opened as soon as possible, it's some sort of emergency. Can you get dressed as quickly as possible, sir, and we'll escort you to the airport.'

'Okay, sure, come on in out of the cold, and I'll be with you in five minutes.'

Galway airport is situated to the east of the city. It is a small regional airport and as such doesn't remain open through the night, but tonight was going to be different. Martin O'Shea had difficulty keeping up with the squad car as it escorted him through the streets of Galway and out towards Carnmore. As he drove he racked his brain, wondering what in the name of God could be going on and was even more confused when on arrival at the airport he was met by the airport manager who was in the company of a number of Gardai and detectives.

'Hi Martin,' said the airport manager.

'What's going on, Bill?'

'I'm a bit like you, I haven't got a clue, and no one seems to want to tell me. Anyway you'd better get up to the tower as soon as possible and check all the approach and runway lights. One of those guys there is a detective superintendent; he says we'll know exactly what's going on within the next half hour or so.'

'Okay, that's good enough for me,' replied the air traffic control man as he made his way to the base of the control tower. When he got there he saw a small detachment of armed soldiers, obviously from Renmore barracks in Galway, drive out onto the now lit up apron, the headlights of their jeeps highlighting the driving rain.

Dingle

When Jabir had finished his meal in the Dingle Skellig hotel he cautiously looked around the restaurant tables. All of the faces he saw seemed to be engrossed in jovial conversation or laughter. Everyone seemed so happy, except one couple in the corner who seemed to be quite tense.

'No need to worry about them,' he thought, 'and all the others seem to be caught up in their conversations.'

Jabir was wearing a very smart casual outfit, expensive looking shoes, fawn trousers and a sweater with a golf logo on it, and draped over the back of his chair was a heavy three quarter length leather jacket. His scan of the room over, he got up and slowly walked towards the door of the restaurant and the last thing he noticed was the tense couple, whose hands were now joined together on the table, eyes locked solidly on each other.

'They must have made up,' he thought as he left the hotel, going towards his car. A few moments later, when she was certain that Jabir wasn't going to return to the restaurant, perhaps to pick up something that he may have forgotten, Detective Garda Maria Douglas unclasped both her hands and her gaze from Detective Sergeant Eamon Morrissey. She quickly uploaded a text into her mobile and pressed the send button. Her message was received almost instantly by one of two armed plain clothes detectives waiting in an unmarked car in the rear most part of the hotel car park.

Swiftsure

At first Khalid found it difficult to believe the picture he was seeing out of the starboard bridge window was the same as the radar screen he was looking at. He was convinced that the vessel he was looking at was coming straight at the *Swiftsure*. Night time at sea can have that effect, especially on someone who is not used to it. However, slowly his eyes started to notice that Frank Blokland and the radar were indeed right. The ship in the distance was now opening up a space which was getting slowly bigger and more to the south of them, and as Khalid followed it through every nautical mile he became visibly more relaxed, as he slowly realised that this ship wasn't a threat to them at all.

'Well, captain, you are right after all. I bow to your superior knowledge,' said Khalid while handing the binoculars to the *Swiftsure*'s captain. Frank Blokland took the glasses and trained them on the ship which was now almost abeam of *Swiftsure* at a range of less than eight miles moving in the opposite direction. As the captain watched the passing ship his experienced eye recognised the lights of a large fishing trawler ... but not the hull. Visibility was very poor, but he nevertheless kept his eye on the ship, which to his mind did not seem right. He noticed that as the ship came up to the peak of a swell there was something different about the hull shape, and there was something else, that was just not describing the picture he should be seeing.

'Yes,' he thought, 'I've got it. The only lights showing are the mast head lights of a trawler operating at night, but there are no bridge lights or deck lights. Why is that? What is going on?' He focused again on the blackness of the hull, which he couldn't see very clearly, but he could make out its shape. These were not the lines of a trawler, he thought! And what is that hump between the fo'c'sle and the bow?

Instinct told his experienced mind that there was definitely something wrong with the picture he was looking at. Captain Blokland's mind was racing now. How could a large super trawler look so wrong ... at this very time ... in this very place. What is going on? The dilemma in his mind revolved around taking in the picture as it was being portrayed or acknowledging what was.

Khalid noticed him looking at the passing ship for quite a while, and immediately concluded that the tug's skipper was probably contrasting the positions of its crew with his own.

Frank Blokland slowly put the binoculars down on the ledge that ran around the inside of the bridge windows. He allowed his thoughts to scramble around the little bits of information that his mind had just processed. Having looked at it through the high powered binoculars, he thought to himself that it was ironic that he had, in the first instance, convinced his kidnappers that the vessel was indeed a trawler, while on the other hand he would have great difficulty now in convincing an experienced mariner that it was, in fact, such a vessel. For once, he was delighted that the bridge on his ship was kept almost totally dark at night to maintain the crew's night vision. He didn't want Khalid to notice that he was thinking so furiously.

Slowly, the lights of the passing ship faded into the darkness and, soon after that, Frank noticed that everyone's attention had now returned to the front windows of the bridge. It was as if the whole incident of the passing ship was now dismissed and forgotten about. As if to affirm his thoughts he watched Khalid move over towards the radar again and, on noticing that there were no other contacts in any of the radar quadrants forward of the tug, Khalid turned to Mohammed.

'No further contacts to worry about.'

What Khalid could not have known was that a warship belonging to his deadliest enemy was slicing through the water, slightly out of the tug's radar range, on a course of two seven zero, at nearly twenty-eight knots, only thirty-nine nautical miles from where he stood.

He knew even less about the other ship, and the even deadlier intentions of its crew, who belonged to a country that he would never have called his enemy, and which was now lurking twelve miles astern of him.

Captain Blokland went back to the controls of *Swiftsure* as she steamed on towards the craggy south western Dingle peninsula. As he did, he quietly flicked a switch which turned off the after deck illumination lights of *Swiftsure*, without anybody noticing.

LE *Roisin*

Eight and a half thousand feet above the *Swiftsure*, Casa 253 had now established itself in a slowly evolving orbit. Its radar operator could see everything that was going on in that part of the Atlantic for miles, including the *Eithne*, the *Niamh,* and the now crippled *American Princess*, plus contacts for each of the helicopters which were furiously working the pattern, in a race against time to get all the survivors off the American cruise liner.

However, he was only interested in one ship, an ocean-going tug which he noted was on a heading of one three zero magnetic with a speed of approximately fourteen knots.

Down in *Roisin*'s comcen the radio operator received another encrypted report from the aircraft high above the ship. The message passed was the same as the previous one fifteen minutes earlier.

Target still moving on one three zero.

Speed fourteen knots.

Casa 253.

The radio operator immediately called the captain.

Sir, message from Casa 253.

As before

Lt Cdr Sorensen, on hearing the message, turned to the ship's radar operator.

'Range to target?'

The radar operator was back almost immediately.

'Eleven point four nautical miles, sir.'

Roisin's captain went to the ship's main PA system.

Boarding parties close up, fifteen minutes.

He then turned to the ship's coxwain.

'Cox, starboard steer three six zero, speed two.'

'Starboard steer three six zero, speed two, aye sir.'

Down below the boarding crew started to make the final preparations and checks. Each man paired off with another and meticulously checked each other's equipment and gear, drysuit zip closures, body armour, velcro closures, weapons and a myriad of other small but very important details. Each member of the team carried a Heckler & Koch MP5 9mm sub machine gun, together with a H&K USP 9mm hand gun strapped to their thigh. They also had a Harris encrypted high frequency comms set. Their Nomex drysuits were in fact fire retardant, goretex breathable immersion suits, and underneath the ballistic helmet was a Nomex fire retardant hood which covered the whole face with an exception of a slit for the eyes.

After each of the team was fully checked they made their way towards the RIB decks where they noted that each of the Jaguars was now fitted with a mounted general purpose machine gun (GPMG). This would be useful should the need arise to strafe the tug. The starboard RIB, which was now on the lee side of the ship, was launched first, and as soon as the bowman released the bow rope attached to the ship's boom, Jaguar One peeled away in a semi circle around *Roisin*'s stern.

At that point *Roisin*'s XO ordered the ship to come back around to provide a lee for the launching of Jaguar Two.

'Port steer one eight zero.'

'Port steer one eight zero, aye sir.'

Roisin came around into the weather with her bow climbing onto a large wave and then falling off it with an enormous amount of spray as she took on the best that the weather was throwing at her.

'Ship is steady on one eight zero, sir.'

'Very good,' replied the XO.

Within a minute the second RIB was in the water and was soon abeam Jaguar One. Neither of the RIBs displayed any lights, nor did they make any communication with *Roisin*. They just slid away into the dark foreboding night making twenty-two knots over the unforgiving waves. Once clear of the ship the two coxwains opened the distance between the boats, just for safety, while the boarding officer scanned the GPS indicated heading which would bring them right up behind the *Swiftsure*.

As the RIBs closed the distance towards the ocean-going tug, each member of the team reflected on what was about to happen, which in fact was a good thing, as it distracted them from the horrible sea state they were having to deal with. Jaguar Two's coxwain saw the white stern light of *Swiftsure* first and immediately signalled his opposite number on Jaguar One. Both RIBs then reduced speed by a couple of knots as the large stern area of the tug began to open up.

Lt Kelly ordered the coxwain of his own RIB to slow right down to five knots when they were about fifty metres behind *Swiftsure*, while at the same time signalling the coxwain of the other to do likewise. This gave the entire team a chance to scan the after deck of the large tug with their night vision binoculars. For the most part they weren't looking for anything in particular, but they certainly didn't want to see any of the tug's crew or their captors strolling around the after deck, perhaps smoking a cigarette. The crews of both Jaguar One and Jaguar Two shifted perceptibly their positions in the RIBs, almost like a pride of hungry lions in the final phase of stalking a prey.

Tony Kelly knew in his heart of hearts that it would be very unlikely for the team to find somebody strolling about the tug's afterdeck in this weather, but training and experience told him also that you never ever took a chance. You always checked ... and then cross checked. He pressed the chest-mounted button on the team's specially encrypted comms, which was worn as an ear and mouth piece by everybody.

'Jaguar Two.'

'Jaguar Two, go ahead.'

'Well, chief, how's it looking to you?' he half whispered into the tiny mike that was less than an inch from his mouth.

'Yeah, sir, everything looks pretty normal to me, I'm not seeing anybody outside.'

At five knots the two RIBs were just rolling down into the valleys and climbing the peaks of the waves, which meant that they were losing sight of the *Swiftsure* momentarily every fourth or fifth wave. Lt Kelly pressed the PTT button again.

'Okay, chief, at exactly two minutes from now we go as per the plan.'

'Roger. Copy, sir, that's two minutes.'

What Lt Kelly didn't know was that, right at that moment aboard *Swiftsure*, Jan, the ship's cook, who had earlier brought four meals up to the wardroom behind and below the bridge for each of the captors, was now collecting the plates and cutlery and bringing them back to the galley.

Swiftsure

Khalid had come to the conclusion earlier that it probably would be better for them to get food inside themselves before they left the tug, as he wasn't sure when they would be able to eat again once they landed on the Dingle peninsula, and anyway, they were all hungry at this stage, mainly because they hadn't eaten since before the strike.
The reality was that when Khalid had seen the white stern light of the 'trawler' finally disappear over the horizon, travelling in the opposite direction, he felt certain that they had successfully accomplished their mission. He did not regard the 'disposal' of the tug's crew to be a threat in any way, and in any case, all of the arrangements for that were already set up and in place.
In his mind he could now finally relax, and that's exactly what he did. Sitting down in one of the comfortable wardroom armchairs, he watched as Jan handed each of them plates filled with rice and lamb, before putting a bowl of sliced fruit on the small table. Tarka, Abu and Mohammed were each carrying large semi automatic weapons. However, when the food came, they simply either slung the weapons over their shoulders by the strap or laid them down at their side as they hungrily started into their meal. When Mohammed was finished he went back up to the tug's bridge to keep an eye on the captain.

Frans de Vries, the tug's engineer, was at that time in his cabin catching up on some much needed sleep. Half an hour earlier he had conducted a routine check of the engines and was now sound asleep. Captain Frank Blokland and Piet Stam, the first officer, were both on the bridge, the latter working on IMRAY chart C55 under the red glow of the chart table light.

Jaguar One

Fifty metres astern of *Swiftsure*, Tony Kelly gave the order to go. Jaguar One took off like an even more scalded cat to cover the distance in a straight line as soon as possible towards the starboard afterdeck, while

Jaguar Two immediately turned right and made a square base approach to the same side of the ship, leaving enough time for Jaguar One's crew to board and the RIB to then fall back. The coxwain of Jaguar One slowed the throttles slightly as the RIB mounted the big wake which was coming out from under the starboard quarter of *Swiftsure*. It was extremely difficult, but he had to get it just right, as this was arguably the second most dangerous part of the operation.

It wasn't for the faint hearted to come alongside an ocean-going tug in a rubber boat a fraction of its size, especially that close to its propellers, in this appalling weather. However, this, more than anything else, together with constant training and huge professionalism, constituted one of the unique strengths of the Irish navy.

LS Peter Delaney, Jaguar One's coxwain, expertly brought the RIB alongside the tug, and in seconds the five members of Lt Kelly's team were up and over the gunwhales and straight away established in a crouched position, weapons aimed at every possible area forward of the tug's afterdeck that could be a threat. Almost before the last man was over the side onto the tug LS Delaney throttled back and allowed the RIB to fall back into the darkness of the night, while his bowman kept the mounted GPMG constantly trained on *Swiftsure*'s side decks.

At that moment, Jaguar Two moved into the exact same side, and repeated the exercise almost precisely. Chief O'Donnell and his team were aboard and covering even more possible threats with their weapons.

Good armed boarding doctrine dictated that the entire team board one side of a vessel only, instead of both. This was so that all of their weapons would be trained outwards from themselves in one direction, to deal with a threat, whereas if the team was split in two, one on each side, points of aim could be in conflict.

Lt Kelly and Chief O'Donnell had studied the *Swiftsure*'s layout plans thoroughly back on *Roisin*. However, they were surprised to notice that a main hatch from the accommodation area out to the afterdeck had been left open. They had expected to have to force their way inside the hull of the ship somehow or other. What they didn't know was that Abu had deliberately left some hatches open, including this one, thinking that the

Swiftsure would sink quicker after the explosion he had planned. This immediately changed the assault plan of the team.
'Sir, this gives us another option,' said the burly Chief O'Donnell. 'I think we should split the team into three, what do you think?'
Lt Kelly thought about it and could see the advantages. He knew that the same rules would apply when they eventually burst onto the bridge as when they had boarded by one side of the stern; that is, they could only go in one side for fear of cross fire resulting in a 'blue on blue', so the first team would assault the bridge. The second team would enter the accommodation block of the tug and secure that on their way up towards the wardroom, and the third team, consisting of just two, would cover the starboard side of the bridge, not daring to go in, but to make sure none of the perpetrators tried to make their way out.
'That sounds good, chief,' he replied. 'You take three and make your way towards the port side of the bridge, I'll take another three and we'll move up through the accommodation block towards the wardroom, and the other two can cover the starboard side of the bridge.'
'PO Jones, PO Doherty and LS Manning, you'll be with me, PO Hackett and LS Cuddy, you two cover the starboard side of the bridge and the rest of you will be with Chief O'Donnell,' Lt Kelly continued.
'Chief, work your way up towards the bridge, and as agreed, hold back until I get to the rear door of the wardroom, which will probably take a bit longer because we'll have to secure seven cabins en route. When we've achieved that objective, we'll both co-ordinate the attack. You two guys hold back from the starboard side of the bridge, we don't want any rounds going out the bridge windows towards ye. Just keep the bridge door covered in case anyone inside tries to come out of it. Any questions?'
For the most part, shaking heads gave the team leader the answer he wanted.
'Okay, let's do it.'
Each of the three teams then covertly moved off. Lt Kelly was first to enter the rear hatch, his weapon at eye level scanning the narrow red lit corridor which had cabin doors each side of it. On seeing a hand signal from him, PO Jones and LS Manning moved on ahead of him. PO Doherty then moved up behind the lieutenant and placed his right hand on the circular

knob of the first door, turning it quietly. Two of the team entered the room and on finding that there was no one there, they backtracked out, closing and locking the door behind them.
This manoeuvre was slowly and painstakingly repeated for the next four cabins. When they entered the sixth, they discovered a bearded man blissfully snoring in the bunk. Without turning on the light and with two semi automatics aimed at his head, PO Doherty prodded him awake with the butt of his weapon. Frans de Vries, who had only been asleep for about half an hour, was not really pleased at being woken. His first thought was that the weapon that prodded him belonged to one of his captors. However, as he came out of his sleeping state, he got the shock of his life. He thought to himself, how the hell did these people get aboard? He didn't' hear any helicopter and also the tug was making fourteen knots, how could anyone board at that speed.
'Who are you?' he asked.
'The question is,' replied Lt Kelly, 'who are you?' while at the same time bringing his weapon ever closer to the man's face, as if there were no other weapons trained on him.
'My name is Frans de Vries, I am the engineer of the *Swiftsure*.'
On hearing the peculiarly Dutch accented English when the man spoke, Lt Kelly eased back his weapon a little.
'I'm Lt Kelly from the Irish navy, maybe you can tell us what's going on?'
'The *Swiftsure* was taken over by four terrorists who are responsible for blowing up a cruise liner a few hours ago.'
'And besides you, how many other crew members are there?'
'Four,' replied the engineer, 'but you'd better be careful. Each of the terrorists is armed with an AK 47.'
'Have you any idea what they'd be doing around now?' asked the lieutenant.
'Well, I know that Jan, that's our cook, he's the real small guy, was preparing a meal for them before I went to the bunk.'
'Hmm, that could be helpful. Okay, stand by,' said the lieutenant.
Lieutenant Kelly then pressed the PTT button of the team's comms set and quietly spoke into his mouth piece.

'Okay guys, we've got five crew, and four tangos. One of the crew we've found in his bunk, each of the tangos has an AK 47 and the guy down here tells us that they've just finished a meal.'
From outside the port side of the ship, which was in the lee of the weather, Chief O'Donnell replied.
'That's copied, sir. If they've just had a meal there's a good possibility that they will be at the very least sitting down, possibly even a bit sleepy.'
'My thoughts entirely, chief,' replied Lt Kelly. 'PO Hackett, you got that too?'
'Yes, sir, we heard all that, sounds good.'
'Okay, stand by everyone for a moment.'
'Are you the only one in the bunk?' Lt Kelly asked the *Swiftsure*'s engineer.
'No, our deckhand, Johann, is asleep in the next cabin up. The middle eastern guys only take naps during the day on the couches in the wardroom, and like I said, Jan has been busy cooking a meal and the captain and first officer are on the bridge. In fact, if you turn left at the end of this corridor, you'll find the galley; if Jan is in there that's another one of us out of the way, and I'm almost certain that Captain Blokland and Piet Stam will be on the bridge.'
'Okay,' said the lieutenant. 'You stay here and don't make a sound, no matter what happens. Unfortunately, our doctrine dictates that I handcuff you to the bunk. I'm happy that you are who you say you are, but you gotta understand, I can't take a chance either.'
'Chief, hold your position for another while, we might just find that the cook is in the galley before we make the assault and the engineer thinks that the other crew members will definitely be on the bridge.'
'Waiting for your signal, sir,' came the reply.
The team then slowly and quietly made their way up the corridor, their weapons covering every possible point of threat. Johann was similarly awoken and handcuffed to his bunk, and also ordered to stay quiet. They had already closed the rear hatch and locked it from inside to make sure that no surprises were going to sneak up behind them from that quarter.
Once again, the door to the galley was quietly opened and the eyes behind two aimed weapon sights saw a low-sized man with his back turned cleaning a worktop. Lt Kelly made a 'pssst' sound while simultaneously putting his index finger over his mouth urging silence as Jan turned around

and froze on the spot. The shock he got was the result of the cumulative experience of weapons being menacingly aimed at him, being roughly tied to a chair, being absolutely certain that his throat was going to be slit from ear to ear and now being confronted by more armed men who in his mind looked like something out of *Star Wars* and were also, he thought, going to shoot him. His only impulse was to nod his head in agreement with the lieutenant's request as he leaned backwards against the worktop feeling a little faint.

'We're from the Irish navy. Where is the captain and the first officer?' Lt Kelly whispered.

'I was up there five minutes ago, and both of them are on the bridge, but so is Mohammed,' said the very frightened looking cook.

'Is he carrying a weapon?' asked Lt Kelly.

'Yes,' said Jan.

Lt Kelly thought about the advantages that he had at this stage. One, the team had successfully boarded the tug without being seen. Two, they now knew the number of crew members and the number of terrorists. Three, they had one more valuable piece of intel before they finally committed, which was that the terrorists would be the only people carrying weapons, or have weapons near them. Four, each of the terrorists has just finished a large meal.

Galway Airport

Martin O'Shea was now sitting at his console in the tower, having been briefed by the senior Garda officer about the arrival of six air corps aircraft. He was told that these aircraft were part of a response to a major emergency that had developed in the Atlantic and also that they would be arriving without flight plans filed.

Commodore Garrett's hand was still at work here. He didn't want this operation to go public until the armed boarding had been completed and the tug secured, and that was that. He was not about to have the operation compromised in any way.

Even though Martin O'Shea didn't have any flight plans, he did have radar, and pretty soon he began to see tiny squares appearing on it, moving in a westerly direction towards Galway. Ten minutes later his headset came to life.

Galway approach, Casa 256.

Casa 256, this is Galway approach, go ahead.

Casa 256 is abeam Ballinasloe at 4,500 feet, we will be landing in seven minutes.

Galway approach, Casa 256, you're identified on radar and you're number one for landing, runway 'two six', runway surface wet, visibility nine, nine, nine, nine, wind is two nine zero at twenty-seven knots, gusting forty-one, report on finals.

Galway approach, roger copy, report finals, Casa 256.

After the last transmission, Martin turned on the heater in the small control tower. Outside, squally driving rain was hammering against the large panes of glass.

'Thanks be to God that I'm not out in that,' he thought. A few minutes later, the commander of Casa 256 pressed the PTT button.

Galway approach, Casa 256 is now visual on long finals.

Casa 256, you're clear to land, runway 'two six', wind is now two seven five at twenty-nine, gusting forty knots.

Casa 256, clear to land.

The maritime patrol aircraft of the Irish air corps was weathercocked in a sideways configuration as she bled away the last bit of height before her captain put in a bootful of right rudder to straighten her out and touch down on Galway's wet and windy runway. After rolling out she turned and slowly made her way towards the terminal. At intervals of approximately ten to fifteen minutes a succession of six more aircraft arrived after the Casa – two Beechcraft Kingairs, one Learjet 45 and three EC135 helicopters configured in the air ambulance role. As each aircraft was shut down, their fuel tanks were topped off. All of the crews made their way to the small terminal building which was looking pretty crowded with Gardai, army personnel and flight crews now gathered there, awaiting the imminent arrival of a senior naval officer from Cork.
As soon as the AW139 arrived in Cork airport after transferring the extra boarding party members out to *Roisin*, her commander received a message from the tower to shut down and stand by in the Cork terminal to await further orders. Captain Alan Parle, who up until now had been part of the planning team in the ops cell in Haulbowline Island, was on his way to the airport in a navy staff car. As soon as he arrived and met the helicopter crew he informed them that they were now going to Galway instead of Baldonnel.
Fifty minutes later the AW139 landed in Galway airport and taxied as close as it could get to the terminal building. After promptly making his way towards the door of the terminal out of the wind and rain the navy captain was handed a welcome cup of coffee when he stepped inside. He knew that quite a few of the personnel he was about to address didn't know the full extent of what had occurred in the Atlantic.
Chief Superintendent Madigan did, however, and immediately shook hands and welcomed him.
'Welcome to Galway, Alan.'

'Thanks, Sean,' replied the senior naval officer. 'By the way, Barney Fitzgerald sends his regards.'

The two men walked towards a single small table with two chairs behind it, which had hastily been set up for the briefing. And then Captain Parle spoke.

'Good evening, everyone, or should I say "good morning". As some of you know, there is a major rescue mission ongoing in the Atlantic as we speak. Specifically, an American cruise ship with eight hundred passengers aboard, called the *American Princess*, has been holed in two places as a result of what we believe were two large explosions, one in the stern and one amidships. As of latest reports, we understand there are now over thirty people dead and perhaps up to 150 wounded, with varying degrees of injuries ranging from very severe to slight. On-scene are LE *Eithne* and LE *Niamh. Eithne* is using her flight deck to bridge the gap that exists as a result of the lack of endurance of the helicopters. She's also acting as a refuelling station for them. At this point in time, *Eithne* has approximately four to five hundred survivors aboard, while *Niamh* is now taking the more able bodied.

Right now we have three Sikorsky S61s together with a Seahawk SH60 from an American frigate which is approaching the area rotating survivors back to *Eithne*'s deck. One of the 61s is now transferring the more able bodied back to *Niamh* because we fear that the liner won't be on the surface for much longer. In short, we are dong our very best to get as many people off that ship as we possibly can before she sinks, and when that happens, *Eithne* and *Niamh* will be making best speed towards Galway. When the cruise liner sinks, and it's only a matter of time before she does, the three 61s will be tasked to bring ashore the more seriously injured ahead of the ships. One or two of these may be able to land in Galway regional hospital and the others will probably have to disembark casualties here in the airport. It is inevitable that, due to the number and nature of the serious injuries, other hospitals around the country will have to take some of the load. That is why we are positioning fixed and rotary wing aircraft here as soon as possible.

Eithne's captain, Commander Mike Ford, is doing his best to keep us informed about the casualty numbers and the type of injuries. It is envisaged that the 61s, with crews relieved, will return back out to the incoming *Eithne* and bring more of the serious casualties on ahead. Then when the two ships arrive in Galway docks, a fleet of ambulances will take the rest of the survivors to other hospitals in Galway to be checked out. Inevitably, due to sheer numbers, quite a few will have to be flown to other hospitals around the country.

So, as of now, we're playing a waiting game here, but the important thing is, we're ready. We have no idea what the medics are going to come up with, so logistically we can only plan for the rest of the day as and when the information comes in.

To sum up, all of the aircrews will be stationed here for the day and on immediate standby. There is already an armed detachment from Renmore keeping an eye on things out on the apron and there will be another detachment out here at approximately 0700 to help with stretchers and with walking wounded coming off the helicopters. Also, our expectation is that some of the wounded, who will have initially arrived into the Galway regional, will be sent out here in ambulances for onward air transfer to perhaps Cork or Dublin.

It goes without saying that Chief Superintendent Madigan and his men will be active around the airport for the duration also. I will be the commanding officer for the Galway part of this operation and I intend to set up a base here in the airport. So, are there any questions?'

'Sir, is it known who or what caused the explosions on the cruise liner?' asked one of the listeners.

'Well, at this stage, we're working on a theory but I'd prefer not to say anything for a few hours.'

'Oh, okay sir.'

'Alright then, I'll be in town for the next hour with Chief Superintendent Madigan.'

Within five minutes Captain Parle was sitting in the back of an unmarked squad car with the chief superintendent. They immediately made their way to the Dock Road area of Galway city to evaluate the logistics of getting several hundred cruise liner passengers off the two ships and transferring them to hospitals.

0130 Wednesday 23 November, Ops Cell

At 0135 the phone rang in the ops cell.

'Commander Lyden.'

'Hello, sir, is it okay to bring the food up now?'

'Excellent, excellent, we're kind of hungry over here right now.'

The duty chef and the PO steward in the officers' mess carried between them on trays a large basket of piping hot sausages, enough sandwiches to keep the ops cell occupants going until breakfast, and a couple of large pots of tea and coffee, which was what Commander Lyden had ordered earlier. When the door was opened and the chef walked in, Commodore Garrett was first to smell the freshly baked scones that were an extra on the tray, which resulted in a smile developing on his face. The chef quietly announced:

'I just thought that I'd throw a few scones in the oven for ye, sir, seeing as how we had the time.'

Commander Lyden then quipped:

'PO, that was a possible promotion bearing piece of initiative!'

That comment had the immediate effect of lightening the tense atmosphere that had prevailed in the ops cell all evening, but especially since they had received the signal from *Roisin* that the armed boarding team had gone in. Tom Garrett in particular was waiting anxiously to hear that the boarding had gone well, but at the same time he was also fearful. This was an enemy that was different, an enemy who would resort to any measures to complete their mission, and would, in Commodore Garrett's mind, be prepared to die in the process, taking as many casualties as they could with them.

At that point, however, he privately remonstrated with himself.

'We've hand picked the best people for the job. Each one of them is superbly fit, and all of them are kitted out with the most up-to-date equipment available. More than that, they have received the best training also. Would I like to tangle with my boys? Definitely not!' he concluded.

As they munched through the sausages and sandwiches the phone rang again. This time it was Captain Alan Parle in Galway. Commander Lyden immediately put him on to the flag officer.

'Garrett.'

'Good morning, sir'

'Hi Alan, how are you getting on up there in Galway?'

'Pretty good at the moment, sir. All of the aircraft are now on the ramp, which is so small it can barely hold them. The weather here is pretty crap and it's forecast to continue, but it won't interfere with flight operations. I've had a meeting with Superintendent Madigan and he's laid out a plan for when *Eithne* and *Niamh* come along side in Galway docks. In short, the Guards are going to close several streets around the docks area, including that road out by Loughatalia as a route towards the airport. They are also going to temporarily close a couple of roads towards the Galway regional hospital.'

'Any news from Renmore?' asked Tom Garrett.

'Yes actually, they've provided a unit to secure the airfield and I was talking to Colonel Loughnane who said that he will have another unit on standby for when the helicopters arrive to act as stretcher bearers and help the wounded out of the helicopters.'

'That sounds good.'

'By the way, sir, I've decided to keep the AW139 here in Galway. Colonel Loughnane has arranged accommodation for the pilots in the officers' mess in Renmore. You never know what might come up in the morning.'

'Okay, good idea,' said Tom Garrett.

'Any news yet on the boarding, sir?'

'No, nothing yet. They launched from *Roisin* for the run-in about half an hour ago, but we're not really expecting to hear anything for at least the next half hour. Anyway Alan, keep in touch.'

'Okay, sir, talk soon.'

Commander Garrett put down the phone and immediately began to put copious amounts of butter and raspberry jam on one of the still warm scones. Barney Fitzgerald was doing likewise, while Joe Lyden topped up the cups of coffee around the table. The discussion ensued for the most

part around the state of affairs at that particular time, when Barney Fitzgerald received a text on his mobile.
Subject in situ at creek, ERU standing by covertly.
'That's good,' said the senior policeman. 'The emergency response unit guys have our pickup man in his car down in Brandon Creek; they're all ready to make a move when we give them the go-ahead.'
'Excellent,' said the flag officer.
The collaboration between Tom Garrett and Barney Fitzgerald ensured that everything would happen at the right time. It would be easy now to order the ERU to pick up the suspect down in the Dingle peninsula, but that could compromise the armed boarding operation if there was an ongoing communication between him and the captors on the *Swiftsure*. Barney Fitzgerald was not about to let that happen.
'Dare I say it,' said the intelligence officer, 'everything seems to be in place now, we've just got to wait.'

LE *Eithne*

The entire crew of *Eithne* were now working flat out. Never before had so much been asked of them. Up on the bridge the executive officer, Lt Cdr Jamie Morrisson, was co-ordinating every movement of the ship, which was difficult because, on the one hand, he had to always have her pointed fifteen degrees off the wind and maintain a speed of ten knots so that the helicopters could land on her flight deck. However, on the other hand, he also had to maintain station, at least to within a five mile square box, in the designated area. This meant that every twenty minutes he had to turn the ship and return to that point.
In the ops room Commander Ford was busy co-ordinating the overall mission with Sub Lt Kennedy and Lt Lorraine Ellis from the USS *Samuel B. Roberts.*
Most of the rest of the crew were in one way or another attending to the needs of the cruise liner's survivors, whether it was the flight deck crew handling the incoming aircraft or the stewards and cooks looking after their comfort in the ship's limited spaces.
All the while the trauma team and the medics were stretched beyond their limits where the injured were concerned. The surgeon had told Commander

Ford an hour earlier that quite a few of them would have to be in, as he put it, real hospitals within the next few hours if they were to stand any chance of surviving. From Mike Ford's point of view, this was going to be a difficult call no matter what way he looked at it. He could send one of the 61s back to Galway with six or maybe seven of the most serious casualties but then how many more people could he get off the *American Princess* in the time it would take to load those casualties aboard the aircraft, fly them ashore and wait for the aircraft to return to the pattern. Difficult though it was, there was always only going to be one option, and that didn't involve any of the aircraft securing from their present station. His highest responsibility was to save as many lives as he could.

The situation on the liner was, if anything, getting worse. The list had increased in the last hour, which made winching operations off her deck more difficult, especially for the navy personnel and the liner's crew who were helping the ship's passengers get into the helicopter strops. The angle of the now very wet and slippery deck was making it extremely difficult for the passengers to get around. Most of them had to hold on to anything they could get their hands on, just to stay in the one place. The real danger presented when they had to let go to move towards the strops.

Romeo 22 was the next helicopter to arrive overhead the *American Princess.* Captain Paul O'Sullivan, her very experienced commander, found that holding her in a stable hover over the ship was proving increasingly difficult. With the huge cruise liner beam on to the sea and rolling, he had to contend with not just the strong and unsteady wind but also the effect of the unstable air rising up the windward side of the ship. Having nowhere to go, it came upwards causing a maelstrom of dirty air just where the helicopter needed to be.

Each of the helicopters were now loading the maximum number of passengers they could fit into their fuselage, and then some more. The only question that occupied anybody's mind right now was time. How much time was left before this huge ship slid beneath the surface forever, taking any souls that were still aboard with her?

Paul O'Sullivan tried to put this question out of his mind as he eased Romeo 22's cyclic forward and a tad to the right after Jim Carroll, her winch operator had closed the starboard sliding door. The large medium lift aircraft banked around nearly 160 degrees before establishing on a course back to *Niamh.*

Anne O'Donnell saw it first. Romeo 22's able first officer noticed the slight orange flicker on the warning light panel indicating the possibility of metal particles in the oil near the tail rotor drive shaft.
Tail rotor chip detector light, called the helicopter's co-pilot.

Oh Jesus, that's really going to spoil the day now,' responded the aircraft's captain.
The chip detector light comes on when a tiny piece of metal, present in the oil in the tail rotor gearing, creates a circuit which alerts the pilots to the possibility that metal fragmentation of some degree has occurred.
It might be just a tiny stray piece of metal. Let's burn it and see what happens,' said the captain hopefully.

Two minutes later the red light came on again, only this time it was not a flicker; it was bright red, as multiple particles of metal were now present in the oil chamber. Then, without further warning, one of the planetary gears attached to the tail rotor drive shaft disintegrated, causing the engines to overspeed due to a lack of resistance. When this happens the helicopter and its passengers are just one step away from being doomed, and Paul O'Sullivan took that step immediately. He slammed the collective to the floor while at the same time easing forward on the cyclic of the aircraft, establishing it in autorotation. He then pressed the lever to inflate the two float sponsons which were located just above the helicopter's main gear. Anne O'Donnell simultaneously pressed the PTT button on the cyclic that she was holding.
Mayday. Mayday. Mayday.
This is Romeo 22. Romeo 22.
Our position is N'53.1 W13.35. Thirty one aboard.
We are autorotating to the surface
and need immediate assistance.
Over.

Every ship and aircraft in the vicinity received the message loud and clear and every one of them knew that a helicopter autorotating down to this sea state in the total darkness of the night stood a very slim chance of survival. From fifteen hundred feet, which was the altitude he was flying at, he knew that he would be in the water inside two minutes. He asked the first officer to brief the other two crew members, who already knew anyway, and also the passengers. Paul O'Sullivan's mind raced as he thought about what was imminently going to happen. Would she float for a little while or would they land 'side on' to a wave and be immediately knocked over, which would almost certainly reduce their chances of a possible egress to nil. The helicopter was coming down now at almost 1,800 feet per minute. He was able to see the mountainous surface of the sea with the help of the aircraft's search light which he had trained to light up an area just outside the door next to the command seat.

At about twenty feet from the water he flared the aircraft using the residual inertia left in the rotor blades to cushion the landing as best he could while at the same time, in his mind, invoking a helping hand from his Dad who had passed away five years earlier.

The helicopter slammed violently into the side of a large wave, but miraculously did not disintegrate immediately.

LE *Eithne*

Commander Ford's ship was too far back to help in the rescue of any possible survivors from Romeo 22. LE *Eithne* was crucial to this entire operation, for one reason and one reason only. Her flight deck! The three other medium lift helicopters were still operating away in the pattern, each rescuing twenty-five or thirty more people off the stricken cruise ship, on every trip bringing them back to the safety of *Eithne*, and now *Niamh* also. However, *Niamh* was much closer to where Romeo 22 went down and Mike Ford ordered her to go to the scene at best speed. He also made contact with the RAF Nimrod, asking its air traffic controller to vector all of the remaining pattern helicopters back to *Eithne*'s flight deck.

Two thousand feet above, the mission commander aboard the RAF Nimrod aircraft tasked Romeo 25 to immediately go to the spot where Romeo 22

went in, while at the same time getting the other pilots to take survivors back to *Eithne*'s flight deck.
Back up in *Eithne*'s ops room, it suddenly occurred to Mike Ford that the incoming US frigate had in fact two SH60 helicopters embarked. He called Lt Ellis over to the console.
'Lorraine, am I right in assuming that you have two helicopters aboard the Sammy B.?'
'Yes, sir, we do. However, I know that our standard operational procedure (SOP) doesn't allow us to launch a second one unless the first one has come to grief in some way.'
'Well, Lorraine, as on-scene commander that other helicopter is an asset that right now I have a lot of use for.'
'I know, sir, I can see that perfectly well. If I could go to the comms room and talk to the Sammy B. on the HF.'
'Now would be a good time, Lorraine,' said the captain.
'Leave it to me, sir.'
Within five minutes, Lt Lorraine Ellis was talking via a satellite encrypted line from the LE *Eithne* to the executive officer of the USS *Samuel B. Roberts*, which at that time was making absolute best speed towards the *American Princess*, but nevertheless was still approximately three and a half hours out. She told him about Romeo 22 going in and Commander Mike Ford's request for the second SH60 to be deployed immediately.
'God damn Lorraine, you know our SOPs don't allow us to do that unless our own helicopter goes in, but to be honest with you, I'd okay it if it was me. Hang on a moment and I'll talk to the boss.'
Lorraine waited while the XO talked to Commander Tom Turner, the Sammy B.'s captain. Within two minutes he was back on the high frequency line.
'Lorraine, the boss has ordered the second SH60 to be launched immediately.'
'That's great. Thank you. sir.'
Lorraine made her way back down to the ship's ops room and reported to Commander Ford that the second helicopter would be with them soonest.

Ops Cell

As the occupants of the ops cell sat back and relaxed after their meal, it was clear that the tension around the whole mission had reduced somewhat. Everything seemed to be going to plan, even though the flag officer was definitely not going to be happy until he heard from, as he put it, his 'boys' in the armed boarding team. However, having been there himself quite a few years earlier, he was quietly confident that everything would go according to plan.

As if to reinforce this feeling, Barney Fitzgerald's mobile rang once again, and when he had finished the call, he announced that the Dutch police had picked up two men of middle eastern origin, who had been seen loitering for the last forty-eight hours not far from the home of Frank and Carla Blokland in Ferdinand Bolstraat in Amsterdam.

Commander Joe Lyden thought about this.

'You know, sir, when you think about those two guys picked up in Amsterdam outside the house of Captain Blokland, no doubt watching his wife and child, it's easy to see how the terrorists took over the *Swiftsure*.'

'What are you saying, Joe?' asked Tom Garrett.

'Well, sir, just think about it. I'm not saying it would be difficult to take over an ocean-going tug – all you need is a few men armed with semi automatics and you could achieve your aim in double quick time – but if you needed the crew of the tug to operate her while you carried out whatever it is you were going to do, you'd also have to think about maintaining control of them for the duration of the mission. And let's face it, any crew held hostage or kidnapped in a situation like that would be constantly looking for ways to either overcome their captors or, in some way or other, get out of the situation they were in. The captors would certainly have an awareness that they would probably try anyway. So, what better way to maintain control of them than to take over the ship and then present Captain Blokland with photographs of his wife and child ... game over. Any notions that the tug's crew might have of trying to overcome the terrorists at that stage get dampened down pretty quickly.'

Barney Fitzgerald nodded in agreement.
'Tom, I have to say, I agree with Joe's analysis. It seems to me that whoever planned this knew that they were going to be at sea for some time. If I was them, I'd be thinking to myself that the tug's crew are the experienced seamen, they know their ship, they know the ways of the sea etc. It's quite possible that the terrorists could perceive this as a vulnerability in their plan in terms of maintaining control over the crew, unless one of them is a master mariner or something like that, and from what we know already I'd be inclined to discount that possibility.'
Right at that moment a flash traffic signal came in from Commander Mike Ford on *Eithne*, which completely shook the senior officers in the Haulbowline Island ops centre.

Romeo 22 down
Posn between American Princess *and* Niamh
Estimate 31 pax aboard
Niamh *making best speed to datum*
Ford Cdr.

Joe Lyden's face said it all.
'Oh fuck, no,' he uttered, looking at the other members of the ops cell team, 'one of the 61s has gone in.'
Commodore Garrett let out a similar but more refined expletive.
'That's really going to put us back now,' said the navy boss. 'Apart from the possible loss of thirty or so lives, we're also down 25 per cent of our airlift capability.'
Ten minutes later the ops room received another signal from Captain Ford.

Second SH60 aboard USS Sammy B.
being deployed at this time
Ford Cdr.

Stealth, Steel and Deliverance

Swiftsure

Abu, Mohammed and Tarka were all sitting down in the comfortable armchairs of the *Swiftsure*'s wardroom while Khalid was on the bridge. Each of them had eaten an extraordinary large meal knowing that next time they ate properly could be twenty-four hours or more later. Khalid figured that they may have to lie low even on dry land for a day or so, and in that regard he had ordered Abu to bring a bag of food with them. This would be okay for snacking on, but it would not have constituted a main meal.

The large meal, coupled with a dessert of fruit and ice cream, had induced an almost sleepy tiredness in them as their bodies fought to digest it. In simple terms, the three in the wardroom were quite happy to sit in their armchairs, savouring the relaxation, while at the same time having their weapons quite close by. Khalid, on the other hand, had taken his turn to be on the bridge guarding the ship's captain and first officer. Subconsciously he no longer saw the tug's crew as being a threat to his mission. As far as he was concerned, they were now totally subdued, especially knowing the effects that the photographs he had produced of Captain Blokland's wife and child would have on the whole crew. They wouldn't dare try anything and, anyway, they were guarded twenty-four hours of every day, the exception being when only one at a time was allowed to go to the bunk for a sleep. In other words, Khalid thought that their capacity to plan any resistance at this stage was virtually nonexistent.

This, coupled with the conviction in his mind that they were alone in the desolate ocean off Ireland's west coast, caused him to relax and let down his guard slightly.

Lt Kelly, on the other hand, was right on top of his game. Right outside the single door that separated the wardroom from the corridor moved four stealthy figures. They were so close that they could hear the terrorists talking, but couldn't understand a word they were saying. Lt Kelly then silently slipped back into the galley and pressed his comms button again.

'Chief.'

'Yes, sir.'

'We're almost ready to go, double check watches now.'

'Yes, sir. Nine, ten, eleven, twelve,' said Chief O'Donnell.

'Concur,' said the lieutenant. 'We go on zero zero.'
'Zero zero it is. Out,' said the big chief.
In the thirty or so seconds left to elapse, both Chief O'Donnell and Lt Kelly each took a thunderflash out of their drysuit pockets. Lt Kelly's number two gingerly placed one of his hands on the handle of the wardroom door while Chief O'Donnell's number two did exactly the same with the starboard bridge door handle.
Both of their watches, which had earlier been synchronised aboard *Roisin*, slowly ticked, as each of the men counted off the seconds in his head ... 'fifty-seven, fifty-eight, fifty-nine, zero zero.'
Within half a second of each other, both of the doors were opened approximately twenty centimetres, and the two thunderflashes were thrown in along the floor almost instantaneously. Before the doors were fully closed again two enormous explosion-like noises caused both areas to vibrate severely. The combination of the extreme noise and the vibration resulted in everybody inside becoming completely disorientated and confused.
In that moment, the superbly fit navy special forces burst into each room with a violence that was stunning in its expediency. All safeties were off on their weapons and the collective teams instinctively had a weapon aimed at the chests of every person in the wardroom and on the bridge.
For about two seconds of suspended animation, nobody moved. The process of getting over the shock of the thunderflashes and the realisation of the now new reality seemed to occupy the minds of the four captors. The clarity that slowly began to come back for each of them was, quite simply, a further realisation that, if only a finger moved, they would die instantly in a hail of bullets.

Slowly and shockingly, Khalid's mind was wrenched from its position of relaxation. 'How could this be? How could these people have got aboard this ship? Who are they?' In a split second, an anger welled up in him, borne of the realisation that his escape had failed, and worse, he would never roam the countries of Europe and North Africa again. In the next second he thought about the fact that there was nowhere that he could call home; he could never stay in any country for too long for fear of being caught. This would be his nemesis. To him, being caught meant one of two

things – either being killed or left to rot in a jail of the infidel for the rest of his life. There was no way Khalid was going to endure this.
His astutely sharp mind, which had carried him to this stage of his life, once again instantly presented him with the reality of the situation. He now faced his ultimate dilemma – move and die, or face the rest of his life locked up. He chose the former. His two hands reached down to cover the twenty centimetres to his right-hand side towards the armed semi-automatic that was resting on the edge of the sofa. His fingers never touched the weapon; he died instantly as six nine millimetre rounds found their mark.

The effect of this on the others was numbing; they hardly dared to breathe as they froze in their seats. Lt Kelly's team then moved quickly to disarm each of them. Back up on the bridge, Captain Blokland and Piet Stam also had weapons aimed at them. In the eyes of Lt Kelly and Chief O'Donnell, everyone on this ship was a threat until they were absolutely identified as not being so. Accordingly, all five were roughly pushed face down on the floor and handcuffed. They were then fully searched for any other weapons including small hand guns or knives, and all of their shoes were taken off. The tug's captain and first officer experienced the ferocity of the assault to the extent that both of them independently concluded that to say anything at this stage might result in instant death. Discretion therefore moved them to go along with everything, and when the time was right all would be okay.
Chief O'Donnell was first to speak.
'Which of you is Captain Blokland?'
'I am,' said the figure lying face down on the floor on the far side of the bridge console.
'Who is the first officer?'
'I am,' reported Piet Stam.
Chief O'Donnell said nothing but went down the three steps to the wardroom to visually check what he had orally heard through his earpiece from Lt Kelly – that the wardroom was secure. Both men looked at one another.
'All secure, check,' said the chief.
'All secure, check,' replied the lieutenant.

Chief O'Donnell immediately ordered Mohammed to be brought down to the wardroom where he was positioned alongside Abu, Jabir and Tarka. All four were then promptly gagged with duct tape to prevent communication between them. Lt Kelly then went to the bridge and ordered the handcuffs to be removed from the tug's captain and first officer. When the tug's skipper stood up, he shook hands with Lt Kelly.
'I am Lt Tony Kelly from the Irish naval ship LE *Roisin*. Sorry about the handcuffs, but I'm sure you will understand, we take no chances, captain.'
Frank Blokland nodded his head in both acknowledgment and relief that he and his crew's ordeal was finally over.
'Thank you, sir,' he said to the navy lieutenant. 'I really appreciate you and your team's efforts. I saw what appeared to be a large trawler going the opposite way earlier, I presume that was you.'
'Yes, captain, in fact it was. However, we can talk more about that in a while; we have a lot to check before we can call this vessel secure. By the way, your other three colleagues are safely locked into one of the cabins in the corridor.'
Lt Kelly then ordered PO Hackett, who was an engine room artificer (ERA), to take three others with him and thoroughly search the ship, starting with the engine room, looking for any devices that may have been planted.
It didn't take long for the four members of the assault team, two of whom were explosives experts, to find Abu's handiwork. After all, they were navy personnel, they would know instinctively the best or, more appositely, the most vulnerable places on a ship to place such devices. And equally it only took them about six minutes to make the crudely put together devices safe.
On hearing this, the lieutenant turned to Frank Blokland. 'Will you come with me to your radio room?'
'Yes, lieutenant,' said the tug's captain.

LE *Roisin*

Five minutes later Lt Cdr Sorensen heard the words he had been waiting for.
'Sir, the *Swiftsure* and its crew are now secure. We have three people in custody and there is one casualty.'

'Well done, Tony, good work. We'll de-brief later,' said the ecstatic captain who immediately sent a signal to the ops cell in Haulbowline Island and also to Mike Ford, the on-scene commander in the Atlantic.
Commander Sorensen ordered the ship to move at best speed towards *Swiftsure* to close the distance between it and the RIBs. As *Roisin* surged forward, going with the weather, her able captain was thinking about the best way of dealing with this situation now in terms of landing the terrorists. Normally, in a situation like this, they would have been cross decked to the naval ship which would be more secure. However, with the prevailing weather conditions he decided that the best way forward was to escort the *Swiftsure* directly to the Haulbowline naval base in Cork. He would leave the assault team aboard *Swiftsure* to guard the prisoners until they could be handed over to the civil authorities. He called up Lt Kelly, outlining the plan and stressing an immediate departure from the area. Less than five minutes later *Swiftsure*'s engines were operating at maximum revolutions as she steamed on a south easterly heading towards the Fastnet Rock. In the meantime *Roisin* and her RIBs closed the distance to each other and were promptly recovered aboard. It didn't take long then for *Roisin* to catch up with the Dutch ocean-going tug where she matched its speed and set a course for Cork harbour.

Romeo 22

Captain Paul O'Sullivan's heart skipped a beat. Against all the odds, he had managed to flare the helicopter so perfectly that it landed, or more appositely, slammed, into the side of an oncoming wave. It didn't matter though, he thought. 'It's down.'
'Jesus, Anne,' he said to his co-pilot, 'I think we're floating and upright. Go back there and help out with the pax and make sure the life raft is at the ready.'
As Anne O'Donnell pulled back the curtain between the cockpit and the aft cabin, she was devastated by the utter chaos that met her eyes. The impact of the landing had thrown survivors all over the place but, more especially, on top of one another. The winch operator signalled to her that he had the helicopter's life raft now unsecured from its stowed position and ready to deploy. The three helicopter crew present in the long aft cabin knew that

they had to regain order from the blind panic that had now developed among the survivors. Winch Operator Jim Carroll, and Winch Man John O'Donovan began to force their way down through the group, essentially trying to calm individuals and also getting everybody into an upright position. Anne O'Donnell turned on the emergency internal lighting, which helped the situation somewhat, and then began gathering and checking flares, strobe lights and a number of 'grab' bags. While all this was going on, Paul O'Sullivan watched in horror as the helicopter slid up over the peak of the next wave and coasted down the opposite side into the valley that formed before the next wave came along.

His absolute concern at this stage was to get the rotors to stop rotating safely, but this was dangerous, because slowing rotor blades can make a helicopter quite unstable, especially in the dire situation they were in.

The next wave, however, made his concerns quite redundant. It appeared to be much steeper than the previous one and in the half a second that the helicopter was sliding down the first one, Paul O'Sullivan knew that this was it. As the helicopter was sliding down towards the next wave, it couldn't get enough buoyancy under its bow before the five rotors slammed into the oncoming wave, instantly shearing them off at the root of the rotor head with a sickening metal to metal sound. One of the rotors flew backwards and, narrowly missing the top of the main fuselage, literally cut the entire tail section off the rear of the helicopter, exposing a large hole that was only a foot above the water line.

Anne O'Donnell immediately stuck her head back inside the cockpit.

'Skipper, that's it, she's holed at the back, we've gotta get out now.'

Almost reinforcing the message, the next wave stove in one of the plexi glass windows at the front of the aircraft and Paul O'Sullivan was immediately on his feet. Strangely enough, the atmosphere aboard was now quiet, not just in terms of the jarring noise, which had now ceased, but also the quietness that had come over the survivors.

The two pilots now knew that the situation was hopeless; they had to launch the life rafts and do their best to get the twenty-seven survivors into them. The helicopter's crew would, for the most part, be alright; each of them was wearing a drysuit which increased their survivability tenfold. However, the twenty-seven survivors had only life jackets, which were fitted

with whistles and strobe lights, and each of them now had to immerse into the icy water before they could be dragged into the life raft.
'They're going to die if this thing sinks, we gotta get them out right now,' said the captain, knowing that in doing so, the risk of more than a few of them dying from hypothermia was nearly as great.
Two minutes later the first large life raft began to slowly inflate and take form. However, the second seemed to just fractionally open with a loud hiss of air escaping to the atmosphere. It then promptly sank. The first one was tethered to the door of the helicopter to be cut free when the last man was out. Jim Carroll then jumped into the water and swam towards it. He then pulled down the rope steps that would aid people to climb into it, and promptly hauled himself in. At that point, First Officer Anne O'Donnell jumped into the water so that she could help any of the survivors who would inevitably get into difficulty making their way across to the life raft.
Captain Paul O'Sullivan and Winch Man John O'Donovan brought each of the survivors to the door of the aircraft and, prior to helping them out into the water, pulled the toggle that would inflate their life jackets, and switched on the attached strobe lights. As he did so he urged all the others back in the queue to remain calm as more and more water began to flood into the fuselage. With only seven left to get out, the helicopter began to lurch sideways as more and more water began to pour into it. Paul O'Sullivan immediately ordered each of them to turn on their strobe lights and, with one hand on the life jacket toggle, to jump into the water and pull it. He then cut the thin line that was attached to the door. As the last two survivors stepped out of the helicopter, it turned completely over onto its side, and began quickly filling with water, which was now flooding in the open doorway, with the two crew members inside.
Both of them knew that their only chance of escaping now was to put into practice their superb sea survival training. Knowing what was about to happen, they both held on as tightly as they could to hard points inside the helicopter that would give them a reference to the door as the ocean flooded in. Then each of them calmly took in a deep breath, which they began to dribble out very slowly. The helicopter then began to sink and as it slipped beneath the waves and filled completely, John O'Donovan swam out the open door, still bleeding out the air in his lungs as slowly as he

possibly could. When his body was completely outside, he held on to the sinking aircraft to help his skipper out. At that point they were fifteen feet below the surface and they locked on to each other's opposite arms before they pulled the toggles on their life jackets.
The surreal calm of the underwater environment quickly gave way to the violently turbulent sea state as the two burst on to the surface.

Dingle Peninsula

Jabir was not as comfortable as he thought he would be in a right hand drive car, especially a Volvo estate. He had always been used to driving cars with the steering wheel on the left. His apprehension heightened every time a car came towards him in the opposite direction. In fact he almost pulled in and stopped, such were the roads on the way out to Dingle from Tralee. As he left the Dingle Skelligs hotel nothing looked out of place, just one or two people going about their business. He drove very slowly through the town's narrow streets and on past the harbour area where the trawlers tied up, and beyond that the marina. Outside the town he consulted his map again to check directions towards Brandon Creek. As he drove on two things hit him simultaneously. The first was that he was now driving in the dark, and the second was that the roads had got even narrower. On top of all that, the weather had deteriorated over the last couple of hours, with heavy showers being replaced by constant rain. At this point he was straining to see out through the windscreen of the car as the wipers were working at full speed.
He began to think, 'how could any sane man live in these conditions and the cold, that's another thing. Yes, the deserts of North Africa could become so cold at night, but this is a different cold, it's damp and it's wet and it seeps right into my bones.' As his thoughts drifted he began to long for the warm radiant heat of home, but for the moment he'd settle for just getting off the Dingle Peninsula once he had picked up his brothers.
Jabir turned onto the road towards Ballyferriter as he headed westwards, always driving slowly to make sure he could catch the various signposts, most of which were written in Irish. Eventually he saw the sign for Brandon Creek and drove down the narrow road that led to this tiny, but perfectly formed, cove. The creek itself was no more than thirty metres wide and at

most a quarter of a mile long. It opened straight in from the Atlantic, turning left for the last hundred metres or so; in fact the end of the pier characterised the bend in the creek. Thirty metres back from the pier was a slipway for launching small boats, RIBs and the occasional currach. The creek finally came into view when he arrived at the far side of it. Turning right, he slowly made his way down the hill around the 'U' shaped road and straight onto the pier. What he didn't know at that time was that twenty members of the Garda's heavily armed emergency response unit had taken up covert positions all around the cove, and he was also being tailed by detectives from Tralee Garda station.

The possible deductions and theories which had earlier emanated from the ops cell in Haulbowline Island made sure that Garda detectives did a lot of checking of flights into Galway, Shannon, Kerry and Cork airports. They also checked cars which had been hired in the last twelve hours, and before long they had identified a likely suspect who was travelling towards Tralee. When they noticed that he was heading out the Dingle peninsula they were sure they had their man.

At first he saw the launching slip and parked the car near it. He decided to get out and have a look around but the cold and wind changed his mind, and he promptly got back into the warmth of the car. Khalid's instructions had been absolutely clear; he was to drive to the very end of the pier and wait there in the car until he received a text message from Khalid instructing him to turn on the headlights of the car to guide the RIB towards the creek. Jabir inched the car forward over the last thirty metres to the end of the pier. However, because he was driving so slowly, and as he was not used to the manual gear shift, the car stalled. Jabir immediately turned the key to the off position and placed his foot on the accelerator. He then turned on the engine again, forgetting that the car was already in first gear, and not realising how far he had the accelerator pedal depressed.

To the astonishment of the watching ERU members, the large car violently jerked forward in two movements, causing the front wheels to clear the end of the pier. The weight of the engine, coupled with the small amount of forward momentum still present, sent the car headlong into fifteen feet of water.

Jabir didn't stand a chance; the heavy car went down by the engine first and then began to fill rapidly. His first reaction was to attempt to open the electric windows, but the water had already negated any power from the battery going to them. As he realised this he frantically tried in vain to open the door, but it was to no avail; the car was now virtually submerged, and the outside pressure of the water too great. He went into a blind panic, which was made worse by the freezing cold water which entered the car slowly at first, but then filled up rapidly.

Two of the ERU members, as a precaution, were wearing drysuits given the proximity of their positions near deep water. On seeing the drama unfold before them, both ran down to the pier, handing their weapons to their colleagues who had now come out of hiding. Without hesitating, both men dived into the water in a desperate bid to rescue the car's driver. However, not having any sub aqua equipment to hand, there really was no hope. The tide was almost fully in, and the Volvo, having drifted out some as it sank, had settled in twenty-two feet of water.

Despite rescue and ambulance services being called, nothing could be done to save him.

Within two hours a large crane had made its way out from Dingle, and the car, together with its unfortunate driver, were lifted back up onto the pier where ambulance crew removed the body.

Romeo 25

The moment Romeo 22's mayday signal was received on *Niamh*'s bridge, her nav officer immediately plotted the aircraft's position on the chart.

'Sir, Romeo 22 bearing two six zero, range eighteen miles.'

Lt Cdr Charlie Keane immediately ordered the ship onto that heading; however, due to the sea state, they were only able to make sixteen knots. The ship was now heading straight into the worst of the weather, and on every second or third wave her bow would slam violently, sending shuddering reverberations through the ship, and enormous quantities of spray over her upperworks. Sometimes she would slide straight into the following wave, taking green water all over the foredeck. Charlie Keane knew that time was everything now if the helicopter survivors stood any chance at all. Through the radio nets he was aware that Romeo 25 had

also been detailed to go to the downed helicopter, but he knew she would be lucky if she managed to winch ten or fifteen of the people aboard. He had to get there as quick as possible.
He was right. Jim Carroll had launched a rocket flare when he saw his helicopter turn over on its side and sink as he watched from the life raft. As bad as the weather conditions were, there was no fog, especially at altitude, and Romeo 25's crew immediately saw the pyrotechnic as it shot into the air and slightly adjusted their heading.
As they came closer to the point of origin of the rocket flare, they began to make out numerous strobe lights in the water, as well as a slightly stronger light, which they took to be the life raft. Turning on their VHF band, they immediately opened contact with Jim Carroll who had a waterproof VHF with him in the life raft. He immediately passed on a situation report while at the same time activating an orange smoke flare.
Even with a drogue deployed, the wind and the waves had blown the life raft a little further on from where most of the survivors were languishing in the water, some unable to swim towards it due to the paralysing effects of the cold water.
Romeo 25's captain saw before him an array of strobe lights stretching out from the distinctively higher and constant light of the life raft. He estimated that the distance between the furthest strobe and the life raft to be about sixty metres and decided to start winching from that point, reasoning that these people would never make it to the life raft anyway.
Romeo 25's captain established the aircraft in a nice, reasonably stable hover, given the wind conditions over the furthest two strobes in the water. The winch man gave the usual hand signals to guide the aircraft over the casualties. Even though the pilots up front fly the helicopter, the winch operator, who has a far better view of what's going on down below, has the use of a limited authority auto hover trim, located to one side of the door. This enables him to manoeuvre the helicopter forwards, backwards, and sideways up to a maximum speed of ten knots to achieve a better position over the casualties to be lifted.
As the winch man reached the surface, he found it strange to hear a familiar voice shouting up at him.

'Forget about us two, we're crew from Romeo 22, move on to the next strobes, you can collect us later.'
'Roger, copy,' said the winch man, and proceeded to tell his own helicopter crew through his polycon portable cordless radio to move on to the next strobes. The helicopter then inched sideways, covering the thirty metres or so to the next two casualties. Finn Lawson came down on the end of the winch line quite smoothly, but then got washed over by a large wave. When it passed over him, he turned until he could see the strobes again and quickly urged winch operator Henry Leach to move him that extra two metres that he needed to get right beside them. The first thing that his trained eyes noticed was that the first casualty, a lady who appeared to be in her early sixties, was in fact dead. Under the extreme conditions that he was operating in, he checked for any movement of her eyes, but only found that they were glazed over. He then checked her companion, a man whom Finn figured to be around the same age. Although he raised his hand a little in response to Finn's words of encouragement, he could see that he was suffering from hypothermia and appeared very weak. Finn then put the strop around.
'Okay, Henry, up we go. I've got a tango four and a tango three here, I'm bringing up the tango three,' he called out, referring in search and rescue speak to one person who appears to be dead, and to the other who appears to be 'walking wounded'. When the man was brought inside the helicopter, Captain Cathal Langton said to Finn through his headset comms:
'Hey Finn, I just got a call from *Niamh*, she's not too far out and she's in the process of launching her two RIBs. Estimate on-scene in ten minutes. I think the best thing to do at this stage is to just bring up the live ones, it'll be much easier for the boys in the RIBs to look after the tango fours.'
'Roger that, skipper,' replied the winch man as he was being lowered down to the next set of strobe lights in the water.

LE *Niamh*

Lt Cdr Charlie Keane was looking at the electronic chart plotter waiting for *Niamh* to get within a ten mile range of the casualties. As the tiny circle denoting the ship closed up to the ten mile range circle, he ordered the ship to be slowed down to five knots. He had earlier ordered the two Jaguar crews to stand by in their drysuits, and within five minutes both RIBs were in the water and speeding towards the casualties' position. Each had a crew of three, the better to be able to fit more casualties into the RIB. However, each of the RIBs had also been issued with a supply of body bags.

Charlie Keane was an experienced skipper and he knew that some of the people that the RIBs would pick up would not be alive. Almost as if to authenticate is thoughts, this was verified when Captain Langton, from Romeo 25, called the ship to give them a situation report (sitrep) advising that there were tango fours in the water. As soon as *Niamh*'s two Jaguars sped away, her captain ordered the ship's speed back up to sixteen knots, which was the best speed he could achieve in these conditions. He wanted to close the distance as much as he could between him and his RIBs.

Both RIBs took about eight minutes before they were in amongst the strobe lights. Captain Langton called them up on their radio, telling them that they had in fact winched up seven of the casualties and requesting one of the RIBs to take on board only 'tango ones' and 'twos'. His plan was to get them out of the water as quickly as possible by putting the winch man into the RIB so that he could send two of them up at a time using a hi-line technique. He was acutely aware of the danger of hypothermia in the casualties and he wanted to get them into the warmth of the helicopter as soon as possible. Both of the coxwains heard this request simultaneously, and Jaguar One was designated the platform for winching the rest of the survivors up.

In the meantime, Jaguar Two sped over towards the life raft which had Jim Carroll along with only three other survivors in it. As the RIB came alongside he helped each of them to transfer across into it. Jaguar Two then moved towards the next group of strobe lights where her two crew members lifted each of the survivors out of the water and sat them as comfortably as they could on the floor of the RIB. The two RIBs continued taking people out of the water until they were all rescued. Then, pulling alongside one another, all of the people who were deemed to be fit enough to be strop lifted were transferred into Jaguar One. Sadly, a total of five of

Romeo 22's survivors had died, mostly as a result of hypothermia and shock. Jaguar Two's three crew members, together with the rescued captain and first officer of Romeo 22, set about the grim task of placing the dead in body bags, a job made much more difficult in the prevailing sea state.

In the meantime Jaguar One came around and started her approach to formate under the helicopter, and coming in under the large aircraft's five o'clock position, the RIB then pushed her way through the rotor downwash and, with great difficulty, held station just about where the winch man would be at the end of the winch line. Finn Lawson was sitting in his harness at the end of the line as Jaguar One's coxwain judiciously advanced the throttles of the RIB in an attempt to scoop him aboard near the bow as he was winched down. Once again the sea state made this difficult, but eventually Finn was aboard and the line to the helicopter was slackened. He immediately attached a much lighter line, which had a break strain of only eighty pounds, to the bottom of the main winch line, and then, moving two of the more fit looking survivors forward, who happened to be man and wife, brought the strops over their heads and underneath their arms. He then warned both of them to keep their arms tightly in by their sides while they were being winched up. When Henry Leach, Romeo 25's winch operator, received the signal, both of the casualties found themselves being lifted up out of the RIB, being aware of the deafening noise of the helicopter, together with the sensation of the wind turning them around and around as they dangled at the end of the line, and, for a brief moment, only when they looked down, the frightening vista of the storm-torn seas.

When they both arrived at the helicopter's open door, they were dragged unceremoniously inboard, and as they sat on the floor, Winch Man Leach took off the strops and moved them back a safe distance from the door. In a morale boosting intervention, he then said that he may seek their assistance in helping other people into comfortable positions in the helicopter, once they were winched aboard. The disposition of both changed instantly from one of frightened victim to enthusiastic helper.

All the while, Finn Lawson's highline was still attached to the bottom of the winch line. As Henry Leach lowered it down again Finn was able to gently pull it aboard Jaguar One to send the next two people up.

LE *Eithne*

Mike Ford was aware of the fact that most of *Eithne*'s crew had effectively been on the go since 0300 the previous night, when they had readied the ship for its exit out of the Galway docks. For sure, some of them had managed to get a couple of hours' sleep here and there; however, since the mayday signal had come in, everybody was working flat out. In fact, the ship was operating in a surreal world, acting as a small airport out in the Atlantic in pretty atrocious conditions, with helicopters landing, refuelling and taking off into the darkness of night whilst coping with strong winds and rain. In terms of safety, people had to be at their highest state of alertness. On top of all that, *Eithne* was also operating as a small surgical hospital, as well as a temporary community centre for several hundred displaced people, whose welfare was now entrusted to the care of her crew.

Lt Ellis was also proving to be more than just a liaison officer aboard during the rescue. Her natural disposition quickly endeared her to everyone aboard. They watched as she quickly adopted a 'roll up the sleeves and get stuck in' attitude in several areas of the ship where she felt that an extra pair of hands might be helpful. Chief Mulligan was amazed when he saw her helping in the galley with the chefs who were producing copious amounts of hot vegetable soup and sandwiches, and he was delighted that her easy-going manner seemed to have a morale boosting and calming effect on the *American Princess*'s passengers.

When she needed air, she just went to the flight deck and promptly fell in with the enlisted men as they brought the survivors from the helicopters to the flight hangar. In fact, Commander Ford jokingly remonstrated with her, saying that she was not quite behaving as a liaison officer from the US navy should, and what would his enlisted personnel expect from their officers in the future!

Commander Ford, however, was quite concerned about how long more the American ship would be on the surface. The last report he had was that there were still 176 people left on the liner. Romeo 25 was still involved with *Niamh* in the rescue of the downed Romeo 22 survivors. He needed to get her back in the pattern as soon as possible. Unlike the 61s, which were

capable of carrying twenty-five plus people at a time, the Seahawk SH60s could really only carry fifteen.
His other main area of concern was, how long can the aircraft operate in these conditions? One had already gone down, and he could not afford to lose another.
The situation was also a bit of a marathon for Fl Lt Jim Angland, the pilot of *Eithne*'s Dauphin helicopter, who was also winching four or maybe five of the more able-bodied survivors back to *Eithne* each time. In fact, the whole helicopter rescue part of the operation, in terms of cockpit resource management, could only continue as long as the captains and first officers shared flying duties so that each could have a break. Fifteen minutes later, a signal was received from *Niamh*.

Rescue op Romeo 22 complete
Five tango fours
Fifteen POB Romeo 25 enroute Eithne
Eleven POBs winched Niamh
Returning on station in pattern
Keane, Lt Cdr

Mike was up on *Eithne*'s bridge when that signal came in, talking to Jamie Morrisson.
'Thank God,' said Mike, 'at least Romeo 25 is back in the pattern now, and we can resume putting able-bodied survivors onto *Niamh.*'
Mike knew that time was absolutely critical now and the single most important priority that he had as on-scene commander was to get every soul off the *American Princess*.
'Listening to the patter of the pilots, this thing is really going to go down to the wire, sir,' said the XO.
Mike thought about his XO's comment and immediately called up Captain Whiteman, the skipper of the *American Princess*.
'Captain, I need you to get an exact head count as soon as possible, and I mean everyone – passengers, crew, everyone,' he stressed.
'Yes, sir,' said the liner's skipper. 'I'll be back to you in five minutes.'

While he was waiting for the count, he sent a signal to LE *Niamh* to position towards the liner at best speed and stand off enough of a distance for the helicopters to initiate a closing series of orbits, as *Niamh* slowly reduced the distance between herself and the now perilous *American Princess.*

As Commander Ford waited for the information to come back, he ordered Jamie Morrisson to make sprint runs towards the stricken ship, between helicopter landings. He wanted both ships to be as close to her as they could possibly get in what now seemed her last hours, perhaps even minutes.

'Sir, won't that compromise the helicopters when the liner finally sinks and they will once again be out of range for the flights back to Galway, with no *Eithne* in the middle to refuel them?'
'Yes, Jamie, you're right,' said the ship's captain, 'but I have to balance my primary responsibility, which at this time is to save as many lives as I possibly can, without compromising the safety of everyone involved in the rescue mission, not least the helicopter crews.'
Mike Ford then walked in to the chart room right behind *Eithne*'s bridge, signalling the XO to follow him. He then pulled out of the chart drawer a slightly larger scale chart of the area.
'Officer of the watch, call Lt Ellis to the bridge.'
'Right away, sir,' replied the captain's representative on the bridge.
'Okay, look at this,' said Mike to his XO, while at the same time plotting the last known position of the USS *Samuel B. Roberts*, as she raced towards the scene.
'We know that this was the Sammy B.'s last position, so let's work it up to the present.'
Commander Ford deftly plotted her revised approximate position at this time.
'You can see, Jamie, she's still a few hours away from the *American Princess*, with zero hope of making it before she sinks. I'm now going to ask her to turn right and make best speed to a position north of where she is … lets see, just about here,' he said, placing the tip of his pencil at a point on

the chart that would be just about perfect for the returning helicopters to refuel. 'That will free us to position closer to the liner.'
'Sir, you were looking for me,' said Lt Ellis as she popped her head around the chart room door.
'Yes, Lorraine, I was, said *Eithne*'s captain. 'I would like you to make immediate radio contact with Commander Turner and ask him to position to roughly this position,' pointing it out to her on the chart, 'so that he can refuel the inbound helicopters. We have to move towards the liner to try to save more lives, which unfortunately puts the returning helicopters at risk of going bingo fuel well before they go 'feet dry'.
'Yes, sir,' said the American lieutenant, who then turned and went towards the comms room.
Five minutes later, she was back out on the bridge.
'Sir, the Sammy B. is turning on track to that position as we speak.'
'Excellent, thank you Lorraine,' replied the now happier skipper.
'Okay, now we've got a workable plan, we don't have to worry about the returning helicopters refuelling anymore. The Sammy B. can look after that, and even if she doesn't quite reach the optimum position, they will have enough fuel to fly to wherever she is in the ocean. The only restriction will be that her two Seahawks will have to stay airborne until the two remaining 61s are refuelled and en route to Galway.'
Just then PO Ryan arrived onto the bridge with a signal from the *American Princess*.
'Sir, signal in from the *American Princess*,' said the petty officer, handing it to Commander Ford.

One three nine souls remain aboard
at this time. Also, severe plating noises
now suggest ship is about to break in two.
No possibility of using ship's lifeboats,
as all davits now compromised due to list
which has increased by two degrees.
Whiteman, Captain

As *Eithne*'s captain was taking in the enormity of the message he had just read, PO Ryan came in with another signal from *Niamh* stating that she was now ten nautical miles from the liner. Mike ordered another signal to be sent immediately back to Lt Cdr Keane.

Forward deploy both Jaguars
American Princess *soonest.*
Advise crews to stand by for
possible imminent breakup of liner
and casualties in the water.
Ford, Cdr

Ops Cell

Back in the nerve centre in Haulbowline Island, a sense of despair came over the team in the ops cell. They too had received the last signals sent from *Eithne* to the *American Princess* and *Niamh*, and a feeling of helplessness swept through the room, each man mentally willing the helicopters to get as many off as they could before it was too late. Each one of them was acutely aware of the possibility of history repeating the fate of previous ships in peril in the Atlantic – so many of the convoy crews who went to the bottom at the hands of the German U boats packs, and the mighty *Titanic*, which didn't have enough lifeboats for all her passengers and crew.
From a strategic point of view, the rescue was going well. Up to this point, over 600 people had been taken off the liner to the safety of *Eithne* and also *Niamh*. Mechanically, with the exception of Romeo 22, everything had held up pretty well. That in itself was a mighty feat given the extreme weather conditions and the way ships, aircraft and, above all, people were being pushed to the limits of their endurance. But it didn't matter; nobody out there involved in this massive operation in the cold, dark and stormy Atlantic would have traded places with anyone ashore.

These brave men and women were committed in a way that was beyond reasonable expectation. Their immense skill and courage together with

constant training at the cutting edge was the hallmark of their very being, and right now it was being tested to new limits.
Commodore Garrett was at that time working out how many helicopter lifts back to the ships would be needed to rescue the 139 souls still aboard the liner.
He knew that although the ops cell was able to provide support and intelligence to the navy's armed takeover of the *Swiftsure*, there was not a lot they could do in terms of the rescue of the liner's survivors. Mike Ford was the on-scene commander and, as such, he would make the calls. And in the mind of the professional head of the navy, he was doing 'a damn fine job'.

American Princess

The atmosphere aboard the liner was now fraught. Ten minutes earlier a horrific grinding and tearing noise that seemed to go on forever frightened to the very core everyone who was still aboard. Several small groups of people waiting to be winched off could be seen making the sign of the cross and reciting prayers loudly, while at the same time doing their best to hold on to anything they could.
Captain John Whiteman, who was still on the bridge of the ship, had to hold on tightly to the stainless steel railing that ran from one side of the bridge to the other, just inside the front windows, as he slowly made his way to have a look at the downward side of the listing ship.
His worst suspicions were confirmed when he was able to look down the side of the ship and noticed that the line stretching all the way aft was indeed broken completely, above the area where the first explosion had occurred. He knew now that her back had broken and that the only thing keeping her, albeit just about, in one piece were the additional massive longitudinal stringers that strengthened the hull area between her keel and her waterline. His ship was in the final throes of dying. It would be quick and violent and he immediately concluded that he had to get as many of the women off as he could before she snapped in two and went to her final resting place 200 metres below the surface of the stormy Atlantic.
Despite the explosions on the ship, her radio cabin and all its equipment was still functioning. Captain Whiteman opened the door and had to sit

down for a moment due to the effort expended from pulling himself back up to the other side of the bridge and aft down a corridor in which he had to lean against the bulkhead to brace himself due to the now skewed angle of the deck under his feet.

He then called up *Eithne* immediately and requested to speak with Captain Ford, who took about three seconds to position himself inside *Eithne*'s comcen.

'Captain Ford, I was really hoping that I would not have to make this call. I have to report that the *American Princess* has broken her back and is only being held together by the stringers. In this sea, only God knows when she will snap in two, perhaps half an hour, maybe five minutes. I am going to send only women and older people on the helicopters now. Everyone aboard is wearing a life jacket; however, I feel that even if they jumped into the water as the ship sinks, they would surely be sucked down with it.'

Mike Ford listened intently to his counterpart on the *American Princess*, making notes as the conversation progressed.

'Captain,' said Mike, 'the next two helicopters to reach you are the American Seahawks. They should be able to embark over thirty, perhaps thirty-five people. I know that one of the 61s is on our deck now, and she will be back to you as soon as possible. Also, *Niamh's* two RIBs will be alongside you in about five minutes. I don't really know what to say to you, but we will make every effort possible to get all the people off, I promise you that.'

'Thank you, captain,' said John Whiteman. 'You have done a magnificent job no matter what. You and I both know the ways of the sea. Every wave that hits us now weakens those stringers. The only question left is, how many waves? Either way, it has been a pleasure and an honour knowing you for such a brief period of time. Only God knows whether we will meet or not.'

Mike Ford could hear in the voice of his counterpart that his ship was not going to last long enough to get everyone off. It was as if the American captain was resigned to his fate.

Eithne, through her sprint surges between helicopters, had slowly moved to a range of ten nautical miles from the *American Princess*. She was making sixteen knots, and so would not reach her for another thirty-five minutes or so. Still, Mike figured that the helicopter's transit time had also reduced significantly, and maybe, just maybe, that small saving in time might be just enough. However, even he had to resign to the fact that ultimately it was fate. Everyone on *Eithne*'s bridge was hugely focused on their task now but, equally, every one of them was willing the *American Princess* to stay on the surface.

Eithne's FDO reported that one of the Seahawks was now making a final approach to *Eithne*'s flight deck. The helicopter had enough fuel for at least another round trip, and so as soon as she disgorged her passengers she was up and away again. Lorraine Ellis, who was back down on the flight deck with foul weather gear on, noticed that twenty-two people had come off the American helicopter, and wondered quietly to herself: 'My God, where did they fit them?' 'Never mind.' she continued, 'twenty-two is good.' Each of the critical rescue stakeholders – the ships' captains, the helicopter pilots, the RIB coxwains, in fact just about everyone involved in the mission – was now acutely aware of the building tension around whether they would have enough time or not. However, none more so than Leading Seaman Stephen Jones, *Eithne*'s clearance diver, and Petty Officer Mark Power, *Eithne*'s capable Bosun, both of whom had been the first to board the *American Princess*, to help out with the survivors. Both men worked tirelessly to make sure that another batch of survivors was always ready to be winched up. They constantly encouraged the remaining survivors to keep focused on what was happening, and even though both knew at this stage that their own lives were also in grave danger, neither was prepared to be winched off until there was no one left on the liner.

The second Seahawk was now en route to *Eithne* with nineteen aboard. The next helicopter overhead the liner was Romeo 25. Two by two, the Irish navy NCOs sent up more of the survivors, until Mark Power shouted over the din of the helicopter at LS Jones that he had counted fifteen strops. 'Jesus, that's thirty people.' replied the clearance diver.

Romeo 25's nose gently went down as she presented her rotors to the oncoming wind and slowly climbed out in a wide arc on track to *Eithne*.

There were now sixty-eight people in total left on the liner at this stage. The next helicopter overhead was *Eithne*'s Dauphin and she managed to take six. Romeo 26 followed, taking another twenty-seven.

LE *Eithne*

Both of the Seahawks were now very low on fuel and consequently were only able to bring back the much heavier loads to *Eithne*. This meant that they could not return to the liner without refuelling, short though the distance was. Commander Ford radioed both, asking if they had enough fuel to take off into a hover out to the left of *Eithne*'s flight deck while she brought in Romeo 25 to land. Both answered in the affirmative, and as soon as the second Seahawk's passengers had disembarked, she lifted easily from *Eithne*'s deck, flying sideways to a position approximately forty metres off *Eithne*'s port beam, safely out of the way of the incoming Romeo 25, which had plenty of fuel.

The last survivor to exit the side door of the giant Sikorsky S61 had hardly cleared underneath the blade tips on his way to the flight hangar when she lifted off vertically and, on clearing slightly to starboard of *Eithne*'s funnels, raced off towards the *American Princess*.

Captain Whiteman was now with the two navy NCOs and the thirty-two remaining survivors when Romeo 25 reared up, violently stopping the aircraft in the airspace twenty feet above where the group was huddled. The winching process was agonisingly slow. However, once again, two by two, PO Power and LS Jones sent the people up, counting each lift as they went. Both were astonished when they got to sixteen lifts, but at the same time they weren't complaining. Then to their absolute amazement, the strops came down again.

Captain Whiteman told the two NCOs to get into the strops and he would wait for the next helicopter; however, Leading Seaman Stephen Jones had no intention of leaving anyone behind. He literally forced the strop around the captain's shoulders until it was safely underneath his armpits, and then closed it tightly into his chest.

Twenty-five feet above, Captain Cathal Langton, Romeo 25's skipper, was anxiously looking down at what was definitely the last two people on this particular lift. The helicopter, he knew, was very close to the limits of maximum all up weight (MAW), but he could see that there was one person going to be left behind. He immediately pressed the PTT button on his cyclic.

Romeo 25 overhead American Princess
We are at MAW
One pax left on ship
Confirm nearest helicopter?

The radio message, together with its embedded question, was picked up immediately by Fl Lt Matt Connolly, who was at this time pilot in command (PIC) of Delta 234.

Roger copy, Delta 234
We are three minutes out ...

Right at that moment, the *American Princess* took about three seconds to snap completely in half in a deafening explosive-like crescendo. Cathal Langton noticed in an instant that the bow of the ship, which up to now had been elevated somewhat due to the severe flooding in the stern, smashed the short distance downwards, causing a huge wave to spread out from either side.
From the very core of his flying being, his left hand eased up the collective on the large helicopter, causing her rotors to cone slightly with the strain before she lifted straight up into the air to about eighty feet above sea level. It was crucial to make sure that the winch line would not be in conflict with any of the liner's upperworks or radio masts. Simultaneously though, the painful realisation that he had lost the last person to be rescued gave vent when he roared out.
'Fuck, fuck, we've lost the last guy.'
Winch Operator Henry Leach urgently shouted into his helmet-mounted mike from the open side door of the 61.
'No, no, no, we've got him, he's holding onto one of the strops. Get low, get low, it's the clearance diver and he's in a suit, we can drop him.'
'Roger, going down now,' replied the somewhat relieved captain.

Cathal Langton eased the helicopter about forty metres over towards the blue flashing light of one of *Niamh*'s Jaguars, all the while descending. When the helicopter was about twenty-five feet above the surface, Stephen Jones let go his grip on Mark Power's strop. Another man falling that distance would almost certainly have been seriously injured; however, his training clicked in the second his fingers let go of the strop.

With his left hand closing the nostrils of his nose, elbow tight into the side, and his right hand stretched straight above his head and feet together, he dropped like a knife into the icy waters of the north Atlantic, splitting the surface and travelling down approximately ten feet below, before slowly making his way up again. As he broke the surface, his right hand was high in the air, thumb and forefinger joined forming a circle, giving the classic 'I'm okay' diving signal to the 'top cover' RIBs.

Within two minutes he was safely aboard *Niamh*'s Jaguar Two, while Romeo 25, with her heavy load, climbed slowly away towards *Eithne.*

The RIB's crew, together with *Eithne*'s clearance diver, then witnessed, firstly, the heavily laden rear half of the liner turn spectacularly vertical in the water inside a minute, and then sink so fast that is shocked the hardened sailors. At the same time the front half of the massive ship flipped over on her side as water flooded in through the rent and torn asunder bulkheads and her outer shell. Stephen Jones even noticed several sections of lighting within the front half of the ship extinguishing. Then, in another spectacular movement, the dying front of the liner turned completely turtle, exposing her massive keel and stabilisers. No words were spoken on Jaguar Two as the *American Princess* finally gave up and her bow slipped below the unforgiving Atlantic ocean.

The normal discipline on the bridge of any warship is usually quite formal. However, everybody on *Eithne*'s bridge erupted into cheering and backslapping, such was the huge relief of tension on hearing the news that they had finally succeeded. Down on the flight deck, *Eithne*'s crew members had become almost like Liverpool football supporters whose team had won the league championship.

Just inside the flight hangar, however, Lieutenant Lorraine Ellis, USN actually cried. She was quite overcome by the tenacity and perseverance of this small navy, and the extreme efforts they had gone to in order to save so many lives – but most of all for them, because they succeeded. She turned slowly and walked towards each of the compartments on *Eithne,* shouting in to her fellow Americans. 'We did it, we did it, we got the last man out, and we're all going home now.'
The mixture of emotions experienced by all of the survivors aboard *Eithne* was tangible on hearing this news. For most of them this was the holiday of a lifetime, which had turned into their worst living nightmare. A large number of them believed that their fate was sealed on the *American Princess*, having, as they had, no expectation of being rescued. And even when rescue came, most of them believed that it wouldn't be enough to save everyone. After all, how could a few helicopters possibly airlift nearly 800 people in atrocious conditions before the liner inevitably sank?
No, there really wasn't much expectation of being rescued, but right now here they were, safe on board two Irish naval vessels. The huge feeling of relief was too much for many of them ... husbands and wives, some of whom had earlier resigned to the fact that this was the end.
Now they were hugging and kissing each other, some of them crying with tears of happiness.

As happy as Mike Ford and the crew of *Eithne* were at that moment, there was, said the captain metaphorically, still a few balls in the air. In fact, there were three helicopters airborne, orbiting the ship, which had only enough flight deck space for one to land. The two Seahawks, on hearing that the last survivor had been winched off the *American Princess,* flew directly back to the Sammy B. The dilemma was, of course, that the two surgeons who were working away in *Eithne*'s converted wardroom needed to get some of the more seriously injured passengers ashore as soon as possible. Romeo 25, under the command of Captain Cathal Langton, was first to land with the last of the liner's passengers and crew, including Captain John Whiteman.

Inside *Eithne*'s hangar deck were four stretcher-borne patients, two of whom were attached to drips. These were immediately brought out to Romeo 25 which was, at the same time, being refuelled from *Eithne*'s JP5 tanks. Five minutes later Cathal Langton lifted the aircraft into the prevailing wind. He then made a climbing left hand turn onto an easterly heading in the direction of the USS *Samuel B. Roberts* where he would touch down and top up the fuel tanks for the longer flight back to Galway.
Next to land was Romeo 26, which was similarly loaded with three stretcher cases and also seven other casualties, who in the opinion of the medics would be better served by being in a proper hospital as soon as possible. As soon as she refuelled she took off, also in the direction of the American frigate.
Flight Lt Matt Connelly then turned to Jim Angland.
'We've got a nice big flight deck all to ourselves again!'
'And not before time,' replied his co-pilot. 'It's a good thing we got that 'c' check done, including the fuel boost pump, over the week-end.'
Matt Connelly then expertly banked the Dauphin around in a tight circle, coming in alongside *Eithne*'s flight deck. He then eased her sideways over the flight deck and touched down. With the aircraft still at flight idle, *Eithne*'s aircraft deck crew quickly attached chains which stretched from hooks in the deck to strong points on the helicopter's fuselage. Delta 234 was not going anywhere now. Matt Connelly just waited for exhaust gas and engine temperatures to cool before shutting down the aircraft.

FDO, bridge.
Bridge, go ahead.
Delta 234 secure on flight deck.
All flight ops ceased.
Roger FDO, that's copied.

'Okay, senior chief, starboard steer zero nine zero, speed ten,' said *Eithne*'s captain.
'Starboard steer zero nine zero, speed ten, aye, sir.'
'Very good, senior chief.'

Eithne then slowly started to turn right for almost 190 degrees until she came onto the heading ordered by the captain.

'Ship steady on zero nine zero, sir,' confirmed the senior chief when the ship was heading due east.

'At least things will be much easier for our visitors now,' said Mike, referring to the fact that *Eithne* was now running before the weather, and as such wasn't pitching and rolling as much as she had been.

'Jamie, I'm going to meet with Captain Whiteman in my day cabin for a while now.'

'Okay, sir,' said *Eithne*'s executive officer in a resigned tone, sensing that his skipper would probably have to 'be there' as it were for a while for the man whose ship sank.

It would take *Eithne* approximately ten and a half hours to get back to Galway at sixteen knots. However, at that speed she would miss the vital window for Galway's lock gates to be still open, but to her crew's relief, her speed over the ground (SOG) was in fact eighteen and a half knots due to having the weather behind her, which meant that she would be comfortably alongside before they closed.

Although *Niamh*'s superior speed would have had her in Galway first, it was decided that it would be far more desirable for *Eithne*, which was the bigger ship anyway, to be alongside the wall, the better to disembark the survivors to the ambulances and coaches which would be waiting there for her.

Niamh then took up station a thousand metres off *Eithne*'s starboard quarter for the 170 nautical miles to Galway.

USS *Samuel B. Roberts*

Commander Tom Turner himself made his way aft to the flight deck when the first of her two Seahawks landed. He wanted to talk personally to his air crews to get a picture of what had gone on further west on the Porcupine Bank. When the first aircraft was fully shut down the Sammy B.'s air technicians were onto the aircraft straight away to unbolt and fold back her massive rotor blades so she could be stowed in one of the ship's two hangar decks.

As soon as she was in and the hangar deck door shut, clearance was given to the second Seahawk to make her approach and land. The air technicians similarly expedited the shutting down and stowing away of this aircraft so that they could be ready to refuel the incoming Irish coast guard S61s which were en route to Galway. Seven minutes later Romeo 25 landed on the American ship, while Romeo 26, which had now arrived overhead, had to complete two orbits astern of the Sammy B. before the flight deck was once again clear. Tom Turner, wearing foul weather gear, watched the entire operation with his flight deck safety officer from between the two hangar decks.

'How in the name of God did the navy manage without helicopters?' he said once again in his droll Texan accent. 'These guys have done a heck of a job tonight; in fact, I wouldn't be surprised if this whole rescue operation were to go down in history as the greatest ever. Those boys drivin' them machines are heroes. Just think how many American lives they saved; they deserve to receive the highest medal there is.'

As Romeo 26 once again spooled up her rotors to 100 per cent, Captain Turner saluted the flight crew. Finally, the red and white coloured Irish coast guard helicopter lifted off the deck turning eastwards towards Galway.

When the captain returned to the ship's combat information centre (CIC) he picked up a mike and started to speak to the entire ship's company.

'As y'all know, the rescue operation is now over. We were scheduled to arrive in Cork yesterday, and it is still my intention to sail the ship there. However, before we do, I am goin' to sail the Sammy B. to the exact spot that the *American Princess* sank so that we can have some kinda short memorial service for those who died. Also, we gotta recover Lieutenant Ellis aboard. We're now on course to intercept the LE *Eithne*, which should be in about an hour and a half, and when we do, we'll send a RIB over for her. Captain out.'

Seventy minutes later, both ships slowed, and the Sammy B. launched one of her RIBs.

LE *Eithne*

Aboard *Eithne* Commander Ford was escorting Lt Ellis out to the port caley davit position. With the big seas that were rolling in from the west, *Eithne*'s crew decided that the safest way to transfer her onto the American RIB was to simply put her in one of *Eithne*'s own RIBs and lower it down into the water.

'I will never forget this experience, sir,' said Lt Ellis to Captain Ford, 'and I would like to thank you sincerely for having me aboard and, most of all, for the wonderful nature that I witnessed in everyone of *Eithne*'s crew during this difficult time.'

'Well, lieutenant, that goes two ways. One of the things I noticed about you was how you seemed to really boost morale among both the crew and the survivors. I am extremely grateful for that and for all the help you gave us in the short time you were aboard.'

'Thank you, sir,' said Lorraine.

'I believe you will be sailing to Cork now, so it's unlikely that we will meet because I'm sure *Eithne* will be in Galway for quite a few days yet,' continued the captain. 'But who knows, perhaps someday we'll meet again.'

'I think I'd like that, sir.'

Both officers then smartly saluted each other and Lorraine made her way to the port RIB. As soon as she was in, the inflatable boat was lowered down to the water.

Mike Ford watched as the RIB roughly splashed into the sea and was immediately dragged along in perfect station with *Eithne*, by the extended bow rope. The Sammy B.'s RIB then came alongside and Lorraine Ellis stepped back onto American territory.

He reflected on the short time that Lt Ellis had been aboard and was surprised to notice in himself that he was almost sorry that she was leaving the ship. 'Ah well, such are all our paths in life, twenty-four hours ago nobody on Eithne had a clue about this person, and suddenly out of the blue, something happens that changes all our lives.'

As the captain walked back to *Eithne*'s bridge, his mind now freed up from the rigours of the whole rescue operation, he recalled how when Lt Ellis first walked into *Eithne*'s ops centre that there was some vague familiarity about her. 'Never mind,' he thought to himself smiling, 'I guess quite a few people we meet in our lives seem familiar in one way or another.'

When he walked back onto the bridge and looked around at the people under his command, who had carried out their duties so professionally in the last twenty-four hours, he felt a huge pride. Yes, some lives had been lost, but a huge number had also been saved.
'Cometh the hour, cometh the crew,' he muttered quietly but happily to himself.

Cas

Catherine Ford woke at ten minutes past seven and stretched in the bed before going towards the shower. She wanted to be on the road to Galway just after nine. By leaving at that time she knew she would avoid the peak traffic in Cork and Limerick. When she went into the kitchen to put on the kettle, she noticed a voicemail on her mobile from Mary Martin, so she immediately rang her.

'Hi Mary, how are you getting on?'

'I'm fine, Cas, but what about you?'

'What do you mean, what about me, I've just had a gorgeous sleep, what could be wrong with me?'

'Did you not listen to the news this morning?'

'No, not yet, what's happened?' replied Cas, slightly worried.

'There's some sort of big rescue in the Atlantic going on at the moment, and *Eithne* is in the middle of it. Isn't that the ship that Mike is on?'

'Yeah, it is,' replied Cas. 'Do they know what happened, Mary?'

'I don't know. Some cruise liner was sinking and there were 800 people on board.'

'Oh my God,' said Cas. 'Listen, Mary, it's nearly eight. I'll turn on the news straight away, but thanks for letting me know anyway.'

Cas listened intently to what was in fact the only item on the news bulletin that morning, such was the scale of the rescue involved. The radio station

had gathered by telephone a panel of 'experts' who expounded on all the possible causes of this disaster, ranging from 'a collision with a large steel container' to 'something to do with a submarine'.
However, any apprehension that she felt lifted when she heard the newscaster say that *Eithne* was now steaming towards Galway to disembark the survivors.
'That's good,' she thought. 'I might even be able to meet up with Mike if he's not too busy, when I go to town with Emma tomorrow.'

Galway

By 8.30 in the morning Galway's major emergency plan had swung into action. One and a half hours earlier, Captain Alan Parle had addressed a meeting of the main stakeholders, including hospital and ambulance services, fire brigade, Gardai, the city manager, Health Service Executive (HSE) Galway docks staff, and a host of others.
Firstly, he gave a brief synopsis of events in the Atlantic in the last twelve hours. Then he continued with details of survivors, including numbers and injuries, etc. Finally he gave them an estimated time of arrival (ETA) for *Eithne* and *Niamh* and their docking sequence.
At 12.30 several roads around the docks area of the city began to be closed off, to facilitate the fleet of ambulances which would assemble on Dock Road prior to the ships arriving.
Chief Superintendent John Madigan had ordered Gardai to be positioned around the Newcastle Road area of the city where the hospital was situated, and the Lough Atalia Road out towards the airport. The first of the ambulances started to arrive in the city centre at about 1.15. The HSE had requested a huge fleet, which was drawn from many outlying areas including Loughrea, Ballinasloe, Tuam and Claremorris to supplement Galway city's own sizeable fleet.
Galway airport had in fact been closed from early morning, with flights being diverted to either Shannon or Knock airports. This of course was very inconvenient, because what could be described as the second most important mobilisation of the day – that of the press – was now taking place in that direction.

From when the story officially broke in the early hours of the morning, national and international news crews were frantically attempting to arrive in Galway before the ships docked. RTE and Sky News seemed to be ahead of everyone else, with RTE cancelling some of the main mid-morning radio programmes, giving listeners regular live updates interspersed with discussions with various contributors. Sky, on the other hand, was running live coverage of the preparations being made in Galway city to facilitate the incoming survivors. Needless to say, hotels in the city and outlying areas were quickly booked out. The Minister for Defence, Mr Michael Boland, announced that there would be a press briefing at one o'clock, in which he and Captain Alan Parle would address the media.

Media coverage would also alert Americans who were, as a result of being in a different time zone, now beginning to wake up to the news of another horrific terrorist attack on their fellow citizens. Along with a sense of rage amongst many of them, this also fomented a huge debate, with calls for the President to make a formal statement on events.

In Cork also, there appeared to be a surge in media activity on hearing the news that the USS *Samuel B. Roberts* was scheduled to dock in the city quays at 1700.

Cas

Catherine Ford and her daughter Emma listened with great interest to the evolving news bulletins as they drove from Cork to Caherlistrane. At 12.30, as they were driving from Oranmore to Claregalway, they were stopped at a Garda checkpoint. Passing the airport, they were able to see that the ramp was almost fully covered with aircraft, and there was also a large Garda presence at the Carnmore Road junction.

As Cas drove on, she remarked to Emma that there wouldn't be much point in trying to get into the city centre right now and hopefully things would be calmer tomorrow. Emma, on the other hand, was quite chuffed on hearing her Dad's name mentioned in almost all of the bulletins.

Just then Cas's older brother, Brendan, who had taken over the farm at home, rang her on her mobile.

'Sis, my God, I'm just after finishing the milkin',' said Brendan, referring to his morning chore of milking the cows. 'And I've been listenin' to the radio – Mike seems to be in the thick of things!'
'He is, Bren,' said Cas. 'Emma and myself have been listening to it all the way up from Cork. It sounds like they were reasonably successful, but I suppose we'll know a lot more in the afternoon after the two ships come in.'
'Ya, God, you're right,' said Brendan. 'Here, what time are ye arrivin'?'
'We're nearly there, coming through Claregalway now. How's mother, by the way?'
'Good now, good, she's lookin' forward to seein' ye. Sure look, I'll be over for the tae when ye arrive.'
'All right, Bren, looking forward to seeing you,' said Cas.

The White House, 2100 Eastern Standard Time

At 2100 EST, the President and the joint chiefs were happy to finish and go and get some sleep. For them, the last act of the rescue in the Atlantic had been enacted when they heard that the Irish naval ship, LE *Eithne,* was now sailing back to Galway. A massive atrocity had been averted in a nail-biting minute by minute sequence of events, which culminated in their receiving the signal from the Haulbowline Island naval base in Cork. However, the bottom line was they could do absolutely nothing about it, and they knew that. Admiral Frank Hughes, chief of naval operations (CNO), was the first to illuminate that fact.

'Mr President, sir, gentlemen, as the most senior officer in the United States navy, I have to state that once again the sovereignty of our great nation has been compromised by a terrorist attack on the high seas. It almost cost nearly 800 American lives, and our great navy with its global reach could do absolutely nothing about it. In short, sir, whether we like it or not, we depended completely on the courage and good will of one of the smaller navies in the world. In the fight against terrorism, we perhaps need to acknowledge in some way the supreme efforts of the Irish. Yes, there were unfortunately some lives lost, but without the courage and professionalism of this small navy, it is now obvious that we would have lost everyone. Mr President, sir, in my opinion the sailors aboard the *Eithne*, the *Niamh*, the *Roisin* and also the helicopter pilots should be acknowledged in some way by the US navy.'

'Frank,' said the President, 'about an hour ago I was having very similar thoughts. Right now I don't know the best way to go about it, but in the fullness of time, the bravery of all those good people will be acknowledged. In fact, can I ask you to think about it for a couple of days and try to work out the best way of going about it. In the meantime, gentlemen, I suggest we meet here at 0800 because this whole business is far from over.'

LE *Eithne*

At 1310 *Eithne* was abeam Black Head on the southern side of Galway Bay. Once again Fl Lt Jim Angland 'lit the fires' in the Dauphin's engines, while *Eithne* slowly turned through 180 degrees in a wide arc, again presenting her bow to the strong south westerly wind. Minutes later, Delta 234 lifted clear of the flight deck for the short flight to Renmore army barracks in Galway city.

Eithne then proceeded for the second time within a week to enter the narrow open lock gates of Galway docks, where she slowly manoeuvred with the aid of a small tug against the Dock Road wharf. Ten minutes later *Niamh* also slid through the lock gates and berthed right alongside her. There was a huge media contingent present in a specially set up media enclosure on Dock Street, which allowed them very close access to the disembarkation of the survivors from the ships. In fact, such was the interest now amongst the media that some television cameras could be seen from the windows of the Galway harbour hotel on the opposite side. As soon as the gangways were lowered, medical and ambulance personnel boarded the ship to supervise the disembarkation of the injured. Also, one of the first people to board *Eithne* was Captain Alan Parle, who immediately made his way to the bridge to congratulate Mike Ford for his great work.

The most seriously injured of the survivors were taken off on stretchers first, and taken immediately to the University hospital in Galway city. Next out were people with injuries like sprained ankles or broken arms in slings. The Galway docks authority had supplied another gangway onto *Eithne*'s large flight deck to speed up the process. This facilitated those who were able to walk off the ship to make their way towards the coaches, which would in turn take them to one or other of Galway's hospitals to have a precautionary check up. To some extent, all of the survivors who came off the two ships were suffering from shock.

Quite a few had requested to telephone their relatives in the United States, to assure them that they were safe and well. The HSE in Galway had anticipated this, and had a team of counsellors standing by with telephone facilities available.

Two hours later, when all of the survivors had left both *Eithne* and *Niamh*, the sailors began the grim task of carrying the body bags strapped to stretchers off the ship. Some of the older hands on *Eithne* found this difficult, as it reminded them of the Irish navy's involvement in the recovery of victims of the Air India disaster off the Atlantic coast of Ireland in June 1985. As Chief Mulligan remarked soberly:
'No human being should ever have to witness what we saw, or do what we had to do, to recover those mutilated bodies. Still, it had to be done, because those people had families.'

Alan Parle sat in one of the armchairs in Commander Ford's day cabin, drinking a cup of coffee with Mike. Both men were reflecting on the events of the last twenty-four hours and feeling a sense of relief that the entire operation went as well as it did.
'I really thought we were going to lose it sir, when Romeo 22 went in,' said Mike.
'Well,' said Captain Parle, 'I think we were lucky that only one helicopter went in, there is no doubt about it, but those machines and their crews were operating right at the edge of their envelope. How are the crew, Mike?'
'They're good, sir. Every one of them was magnificent … total commitment I have to say.'
'Well, Mike, whether you like it or not, your face is going to be on television screens and newspapers all around the world tomorrow. In fact, I believe that the Minister for Defence is staying in Galway overnight. There will be another press conference later this evening and I think he wants a briefing from you, before both you and him face the cameras.'

USS *Samuel B. Roberts*

Commander Turner felt a strange eeriness as he stood on the bridge right on the spot where the *American Princess* had broken in two and sank. Down in the cold Atlantic depths, he knew, were the bodies of fellow Americans, who tragically had not survived the initial explosions – passengers who were in cabins directly above the port side of the engine

room and also some of the liner's engineering crew who had been in or around the engine room at the time of the first explosion.
The feeling was made somewhat worse by the fact that some of them were veterans, people who had given their life's work in service to their country, and then, just as they were starting to enjoy retirement, robbed of life.
A short memorial service then followed, at the end of which a weighted rod with the stars and stripes attached to it was gently lowered overboard, where it sank to the ocean floor near to where the two sections of the liner now lay.
Tom Turner waited a respectful period of time and then ordered the ship onto a heading of 'one three zero' magnetic.
Just outside Cork harbour, about two miles off Myrtleville beach, the Sammy B. rendezvoused with one of the Cork harbour pilot boats, where an experienced pilot came aboard to bring her the twelve miles up to the city quays.
As she made her way slowly past Roches Point, at the mouth of the harbour, both of her Seahawk SH60 helicopters flew off the flight deck and headed directly towards the Baldonnel air base just outside Dublin to be checked over by the engineers there.
As the ship passed the Haulbowline Island naval base, Lorraine Ellis was standing outside on the port bridge wing. She knew that somewhere on that island was the ops cell that had controlled the entire rescue in the Atlantic, and also the armed boarding of the *Swiftsure*, which resulted in the capture and detention of the perpetrators of the attack on the *American Princess.*
She also knew that, in there was the *Swiftsure*, no doubt heavily guarded on a twenty-four hour basis to preserve any evidence that may be of value.

Twenty minutes later the Sammy B. slowly came along side Custom House Quay near Cork's city centre. It was quite obvious to everyone on the bridge that there was a sizeable press gathering outside the large decorative steel gates, which prevented public access to the wharf. They were there, no doubt, anxious to glean more information around events in the Atlantic.
Once the ship was secured alongside, and her gangway in position, two liaison officers from the Irish navy boarded the ship immediately to start

working out with the Sammy B.'s officers the logistics around all of the formalities, including engagements, formal visits, and so on.

However, for Lorraine Ellis this was a special moment. Now, she could finally concentrate on a mission of her own, one which she had been planning for the past few months, when she found out that the ship was going to be in Ireland for a few days. In short, to see if she could find any information whatsoever around her natural mother, who had, for some reason, given her up for adoption twenty-eight years ago.
She had felt a slight sense of guilt at wanting to find out something about the woman who had given her life. A guilt that was based around the feelings of Joe and Marian, her wonderful adoptive parents who, in fact, had always supported her efforts to find out more about her natural mother. She wondered what sort of circumstance had prevailed at that time, in the life of her natural mother, to make her want to give up her baby.
Was it an unwanted pregnancy, perhaps where she had been abandoned by the father? Was she abused in some way or other? She just didn't know, but she knew that something inside in her desperately wanted to find out. She had so many questions which were left unanswered, but the biggest ones were: What was she like as a person? Did she have other children? Did she like me?
Lorraine knew that she couldn't even begin to understand, which was one of the reasons she wanted to find any possible leads that would help her to meet with this woman – that is, of course, if she was still alive. She desperately hoped that she was.
Before eleven o'clock the following morning, she had in her possession contact details for the adoption agencies in both the Republic and Northern Ireland.

Galway, Thursday 0930

Mike Ford was now almost a household name all over the world. As the facts came out and the world began to bristle at the audaciousness of the terrorist attack in the Atlantic, contrasts were made with the Twin Towers in New York and the train bombings in both Britain and Spain.
Mike found it difficult to fathom the voracious appetite of the press, while at the same time understanding the need for people to know, and indeed comprehend, evil events as they unfolded. However, right now he was also concerned with bringing *Eithne* back to operational capability as soon as possible.
There was no doubt but that she would have to be sailed back to the naval base in Cork to have the main work carried out. Her wardroom, which had acted as an operating theatre, was now totally unserviceable, and a few other accommodation spaces also needed attention. Her entire food stock was virtually depleted, and bedding and toiletries needed to be replaced, together with, once again, topping off her JP5 fuel tanks. In short, she needed a mini refit.

At 11.50, Catherine Ford walked towards *Eithne*'s gangway. Senior Chief John Morgan, *Eithne*'s coxwain who was standing just inside the open hangar deck, saw her coming from the opposite side of Dock Road and waited at the top of the gangway to help her aboard.
'Good morning, ma'am,' he said. 'Nice to see you aboard again.'
'Good morning, senior chief,' replied Cas. 'It sounds like the crew had a pretty difficult time in the last two days.'
'Well, ma'am, I've been in the navy now for over thirty years, and I've never seen anything like this before. 'The captain's in his day cabin, ma'am, I'll take you up there,'
As they arrived at the door of Mike's day cabin, John Morgan knocked.
'Sir, Mrs Ford is here to see you.'
'Oh, thank you, senior chief,' Mike replied as he opened the door. There then ensued a short discussion between the three people at the door before the senior chief went down to his office one deck below.

'Mike, my God, how are you? It looks like you've very busy the past few days.'
'Yeah, to be honest, even though we were very lucky, we only lost one helicopter. I have to say, the crew were excellent. Hey, how are you?'
'I'm very good,' she replied. 'As you know, I was coming up to see mother yesterday anyway, not really expecting you to be back in Galway. Then I got a call when I woke yesterday morning from Mary Martin telling me the news. Oh, by the way, Emma decided to come up with me.'
'Oh, good,' said Mike. 'Where is she now?'
'Right now, she's hopefully in the final stages of having her hair cut much shorter in a hairdresser's in Shop Street. She's calling over to the ship when she's finished, which should be in the next fifteen minutes.'
Mike and Cas eagerly caught up with the previous two days' events while drinking a cup of coffee and waiting for Emma to arrive at the ship to see her Dad.
Twenty minutes later, there was another knock on the door and Mike shouted 'come in'.
As Emma came through the door saying 'Hi Dad, hi Mom', Cas exclaimed: 'Oh my God, your hair is lovely, it really suits you. What do you think, Mike?'
Mike was stunned. It was almost like a déjà vu as he looked at his daughter. She looked somewhat familiar despite her changed hairstyle. It was like she reminded him of someone, but he just couldn't think who that person was.
'My God, Emma, your hair's lovely, it really suits you,' said Mike, at the same time giving her a big hug and kiss. As he sat down again, he began to notice how tired he was.

The Taoiseach's Office

The telephone on the Taoiseach's desk rang twice before he picked it up.
'Sir, the President of the United States is on the line for you.'
'Okay, thank you,' said the Taoiseach.
'Mr President, sir, how are you?' he continued.
'Good, very good, sir, how are you?'

‘Well I’m feeling an awful lot better now that that operation in the Atlantic is over; it was touch and go for a while. And while you’re on, may I, on behalf of the Irish people, offer our condolences for those who sadly didn’t make it.’

‘Thank you,’ replied the President. ‘I think it’s safe to say that the American people now realise that this was a very close call. But for the Irish navy our country would definitely be mourning 800 lives. What they did out there, including the helicopter boys, was the finest example I’ve ever seen of courage under extremely difficult conditions. In fact, sir, your navy has set an example on the world stage. That’s why I’m ringing you. I feel that these people shouldn’t go unacknowledged. If they were in the US navy, quite a few of them would be decorated. We feel that the American people would like to honour those service men and women, so, in short sir, I would like to travel to Ireland myself in March and make the presentations. May I ask, how would you feel about that?’

‘Well, Mr President, that is very generous of you, and yes, I believe that, on the whole, this would be a very good idea. As is happens, I am just presiding over a review of our navy and the expansion of its capability. In fact, we’re just about to order three new ships, so yes, I’m sure it would tie in very well.’
‘Okay,’ replied the President, ‘our people can get working on it. Of course I’ll be looking forward to a nice pint of real Guinness with you also.’

Naval Base, Haulbowline Island, Cork, Thursday 24 November

The naval staff car came across the bridge and turned left on its way up towards the officers’ mess. When it arrived, Captain Tom Turner, USN, and Lt Lorraine Ellis, USN, got out of the car and were immediately escorted inside by the commodore’s personal staff officer (PSO), where they were greeted by the flag officer, Commodore Tom Garrett, and a large group of other officers and senior NCOs.

'Welcome,' said the commodore, shaking hands with the two American officers.
'Thank you, sir,' replied Commander Tom Turner. 'I would like to say on behalf of the American people and the US navy that we owe a huge debt of gratitude to the Irish naval service. I have become aware since we arrived in Cork that, not alone was the effort just out in the Atlantic, but also here in Cork, where I believe it was co-ordinated. Once again, sir, we thank you.'
'Well,' said the commodore, 'we did the best we could, and may I say to you, lieutenant,' looking at Lorraine Ellis, 'judging from the reports I've heard from the crew on *Eithne*, if you ever want to transfer to the Irish navy, I'm sure we'll find a place for you!'

USS *Samuel B. Roberts*, City Quays, Cork, Saturday 26 November

At 1530 the Sammy B. slipped her lines as she eased away from the Custom House wharf. She was making five knots as she passed over the famous Cork tunnel, deep below the bed of the river Lee, which she was now sailing on. Her engines would not stop now before she arrived at her home port in Mayport, Florida. As she passed the naval base in Haulbowline Island, all of her sailors lined the starboard side of the ship in salute, and then just inside Roches Point she slowed right down to allow the pilot boat to pick up the pilot. She then surged straight out the mouth of the harbour for approximately five nautical miles, before turning onto a heading of two four zero. Ten miles south of the Old Head of Kinsale, Commander Turner ordered the ship to 'red fifteen', which was fifteen degrees off the relative wind on the port side. This was to momentarily position the Sammy B. onto an optimal heading to recover her two helicopters, which had now just taken off from Cork airport, having positioned there earlier from Baldonnel.

One hundred and twenty nautical miles to the north, as the crow flies, LE *Eithne* was now out into Galway Bay. At Black Head she took up a heading of two two zero degrees, making sixteen knots on her way back to Cork. When she was abeam the village of Barna, Delta 234 slid easily outside

and above the portside of the flight deck, and eased slowly to starboard before touching down. Outside, Commander Ford noted that the weather had eased quite a bit from the early part of the week. As he looked out of the bridge window once again into the darkness of the Atlantic, he was still trying to fathom the events of the past few days.
Just then the radio on the bridge barked to life.

All stations, all stations, all stations,
This is Valentia coast guard radio, Valentia coast guard radio.
We have a fishing boat which is taking water
four miles west of Hag's Head

Commander Ford immediately picked up the radio mike.

Valentia coast guard, Valentia coast guard,
This is naval vessel LE Eithne.
We are approximately twelve miles
from that position.
We can deploy a RIB immediately with pumps.

LE Eithne, *LE* Eithne
This is Valentia coast guard radio.
Expedite immediately.
And you might report back to us,
as we believe the trawler's radio
is not functioning properly.

Valentia coast guard radio, Valentia coast guard radio.
LE Eithne
That's copied. Out.

One and a half hours later two of *Eithne*'s ERAs had pumped the water out of the trawler and found the damaged sea cock where it was coming in. They immediately carried out a temporary repair, which would easily last until a new sea cock was fitted. Having recovered the RIB, *Eithne* was once again under way towards Cork.

EPILOGUE

March 2006

Air Force One, this is Dublin control.
Descend flight level eight zero
on heading one eight zero

Yes, sir, Air Force One, roger copy.
Descend flight level eight zero
Heading one eight zero

Air Force One had now descended to the lower flight levels and would soon be making her final approach to Dublin's runway 'two eight'. On board, along with the President, were Commander Tom Turner and his family, and also Lt Lorraine Ellis, with her father and mother, Joe and Marian Ellis. The President had specifically requested that they travel with him en route to Ireland, so that Lt Ellis could give him a personal briefing of the events on the night of 22 November in the Atlantic.

The Ellis family were delighted, and decided that they would make a two-week holiday of the visit, so that they could tour around Ireland, while Commander Turner and his family would return to the United States on a scheduled flight three days later.

As the most famous 747 in the world was abeam the small town of Rush in north County Dublin, the radio came alive again.

Air Force One, you are clear to turn finals
onto runway 'two eight'
Report visual on finals.

Air Force One

Report finals

Air force One then banked to the right and the pilot manoeuvred her on to the extended distant centreline of runway 'two eight'.

Air Force One
Finals, we are now visual.

Air Force One
You are clear to land.
Wind two one zero at ten knots.

Dublin Control, Air Force One
is clear to land.
Runway 'two eight'.

The giant aircraft slowly descended with her four engines screaming ever louder, as more power was fed into them to keep the plane's air speed above the critical number. Almost ballet like, her rearmost main gear wheels touched Irish soil and she gently rolled out and turned off Dublin's westerly runway 'two eight'.

McKee Barracks, Dublin

The weather, uncharacteristically, stepped up to the mark for the medal presentation ceremony, which ensured that the event went very well indeed. It was held in McKee barracks in Dublin, which was, from a security point of view, very convenient for the US President, as he was staying at the US ambassador's residence about a mile away in the Phoenix Park. The Taoiseach and the Minister for Defence and the chief of staff, along with quite a few other dignitaries, were also in attendance. A representative body from *Eithne*, *Niamh* and *Roisin*, principally those receiving medals, had arrived in Dublin the previous evening, along with family members, even though only one of their ships was in Dublin.

In fact, at that time *Niamh* herself was involved in a humanitarian mission with NGOs off the west coast of Africa, and *Roisin* had just returned to Dublin from a patrol under the North East Atlantic Fisheries Commission (NEAFC), while *Eithne* was in refit in Cork dockyard.

There was once again a huge press presence, which also included many of the American networks.
After the ceremony, McKee barracks had laid on a most extravagant buffet, including a bar for all the guests. Security, too, at the barracks was, in effect, 'locked down', with American secret service agents mingling with the large guard detail which was drawn from the barracks itself. Overhead, armed air corps helicopters maintained an air exclusion zone around the area.

Commander Mike Ford, who was dressed in full number one naval uniform, along with his naval sword, was standing with Cas while chatting to a group of reporters when he noticed Lt Lorraine Ellis, in her US navy uniform, walking towards them with a couple, whom he presumed to be her parents. Having smartly saluted each other, introductions were made.
'Hello, sir,' said Lorraine, smiling at him. 'It's good to see you again. I would like to introduce you to my Mom and Dad. This is Joe and Marian Ellis.'
Mike shook hands warmly with Lorraine's parents and then promptly introduced the Ellis family to Cas.
'I've heard so much about you, Lorraine from Mike, it seems you were a big hit aboard *Eithne*.'
'I'm not so sure about that, ma'am,' said Lorraine modestly. 'Mind you, I will never forget that evening because my memory of it is that everyone on the ship was a big hit that night.'
'So,' asked Mike, looking at Joe, 'when did you fly in?'
'Well,' said Joe Ellis, 'it's hard to believe, but we actually arrived in Ireland on Air Force One.'
'My God!' said Cas, 'that's amazing. You flew with the President?!'
'Yeah,' laughed Joe, 'there had to have been a lapse in security somewhere!'
Marian Ellis then chimed in proudly.

'Oh, it was so lovely, the food, the service, and then the President requested Lorraine to go to his office to brief him on exactly what it was like on *Eithne* that night.'
'In fact, sir,' said Lorraine, 'Commander Turner and his wife are here too, they also flew here on Air Force One.

Over the next hour or so, Mike was called upon to partake in several interviews. In particular, the American networks were very interested in talking to him. In America, he was seen as the 'hero' of the rescue, and as such, he was now effectively a household name. He had in fact received an invitation from the US navy to speak at the US naval academy in Annapolis, which was a huge honour.
Meanwhile, Cas and the Ellises chatted away at a nice table they had found.
'So, are you flying back on Air Force One also?' asked Cas enviously.
'Unfortunately no,' laughed Marian. 'I believe the President is actually leaving tomorrow, whereas we, on the other hand, are going back in ten days' time on a scheduled flight. In fact,' she continued, 'we have hired a car, and we are going to tour around Ireland.'
'Oh, that's great,' said Cas, 'you'll enjoy that. Which direction are you going?'
'Well,' said Joe, 'we're going to Waterford tomorrow, and the following day we are making our way to Cork.'
'That's it,' said Cas, 'why don't you stay with us for an evening when you come to Cork? We'd love to have you for a night as our guests.'
Marian then protested that they would be an imposition on the Fords and didn't feel that they could accept, but Cas was quite insistent.
'Look,' she said, 'we'd love to have you, really, and we could take you to Kinsale for a meal. It's a lovely spot, you'd really like it.'
'Well, are you sure?' asked Joe. Cas cut him off immediately.
'Joe, I know that Mike and myself would be delighted to have you.'
'Well, okay,' he replied. 'Thanks very much for the invitation, and it'll be for just the one night, because we're going to Galway the following day.'
'Great,' said Cas.

Mike and Cas stayed in Dublin on the Wednesday evening, exhausted after the many press briefings and formalities of the day, before enjoying a leisurely drive back to Cork the following day. Mike commented to Cas that he felt quite comfortable in the company of the Ellises. They seemed to be really nice people, and he was looking forward to their visit on Friday. Just then his mobile rang.

'*Hi Mike, Tom Garrett here.'*

'Oh, hello sir,' replied Mike.

'Did you enjoy yesterday?' asked the flag officer. *I never caught up with you in the end, because every time I looked around for you, you seemed to be surrounded by the press.'*

'I know, sir, they were all over the place, but I have to say that I really enjoyed the day, and I feel that the medals were given to the right people.'

'Yeah,' said Tom Garrett, *'and no one more deserving than you. You know, it's nearly four months ago now, but the reality is, you did an excellent job out there.'*

'Thank you, sir,' replied Mike.

'Here, listen, I've got a bit of news that you might be interested in.'

'Oh, yes sir, what is it?' asked Mike.

'Well, I have to tell you, Mike that you are no longer a commander in the Irish navy. As and from zero nine hundred this morning, you are officially Captain Mike Ford. In fact, when you get back, there will be a signal waiting for you to that effect.'

'Oh my God, sir, that's the best news I've heard in a long time! Thank you very much for letting me know. Yes, sir, I think I will enjoy a very nice weekend now.'

'Well done, Mike. No-one deserves it more than you,' said the commodore. 'And by the way, you might have a bit of time now to learn how to play golf!'

Cas, who was driving at the time of the phone call, couldn't wait for Mike to turn off his mobile so that she could hear the obviously good news he had just received.

'Come on, come on Mike, tell me!'

'Well, let's just say, Cas, I'll have to take the top half of my uniform to the tailors to be adjusted.'

Cas screamed with delight, knowing exactly what her husband meant, but more importantly, what it meant to him.

Cork, Friday 10 March 2006

The Ellises arrived at Mike Ford's house around 4.30 in the afternoon on the second leg of their tour, which would take them from Dublin to Cork, and then on to Galway. Thereafter, of course, they would travel on to Joe and Marian's home town, Belfast.

On the way south Joe had remarked to Marian that he really appreciated the lovely gesture of hospitality by the Fords. In fact, he was looking forward to, as he put it, 'going for a nice quiet pint of creamy Guinness with Mike'.

Joe, Marian and Lorraine, who had done most of the driving, spent about an hour discussing the surreal circumstances under which they met the Fords. All that had happened in the Atlantic, the President's visit and the ceremony in Dublin. A truly amazing sequence of events that absolutely nobody could have predicted.

'Hello folks, welcome to Cork,' said Mike, giving Joe a help with their travel bags.

'Come on in, I have some tea and coffee on the go,' said Cas, telling the Ellises that, for her, there were few things in life better than a nice hot mug of tea after a long journey.

'It's nice that you could arrive a couple of hours before we go out for dinner, it will give you a chance to relax for a while.'

'Well, I don't know about Joe and Lorraine,' replied Marian Ellis, 'but I have to tell you something. In America, they don't understand the absolute joy of getting inside your front door and just relaxing with a cup of tea. I always used to love it where I grew up in Belfast and now I have most of my American neighbours indoctrinated into the habit. Mind you, it took me a couple of years,' she said, with a smile on her face.

'By the way,' said Cas, 'we've booked dinner for eight in Kinsale, which means we would need to leave here at about 7.30.'

'Perfect,' replied Joe, 'I'm looking forward to it already'.

When bags were put in bedrooms and people freshened up, the conversation resumed. Cas, Joe and Marian were chatting away earnestly

while the two naval officers were 'talking shop'. Lt Lorraine Ellis was curious about how things had panned out in the aftermath of the rescue operation and also about *Eithne*'s crew. How had they been after the incident? She was sure there would have been some effects, perhaps psychological or otherwise, after such a traumatic event.
Mike reassured her that, for the most part, everyone seemed to be okay. However, he did add that, in his experience, effects like that usually presented some time later, sometimes months or maybe years, if at all.

At 7.30 that evening, Mike drove the three Ellises and Cas down to the restaurant in Kinsale. He offered to be the non-drinking person who would drive, but he assured Joe that when they came back to the house later on he would enjoy a few draught cans with him.
'That's fine by me,' said Joe.
Cormac, James and Emma had also been invited, but the two boys had already been asked to a twenty-first party in town, and they didn't want to miss it. Emma, on the other hand, wouldn't be home in time for the start of the meal, so she told her mother that she would catch up with them in the restaurant an hour or so later.
When they were seated, the conversation revolved around the smoking ban in public places, that had been introduced a year and a half earlier in Ireland, and also the quite strict drink driving laws that were about to be enacted. Joe and Marian were very interested to hear this, as they felt that the situation where they lived in New London was not a whole lot different.
An hour later, just as they finished the main course, Emma arrived, and was seated next to Lorraine. Mike, who was sitting directly across the table, now realised, with shock, that the person who Lorraine had reminded him of, when she was brought into *Eithne*'s ops room by Lt John Kana, was, in fact, his daughter Emma. He further realised that the person whom Emma reminded him of, with her new hairstyle, was, in fact, Lorraine Ellis! This provided him with the answer to his déjà vous.
'God,' he thought to himself, not wanting to interrupt the flow of conversation that was already going on at the table, 'they are so, so alike.'
Just then, Joe Ellis turned to Mike.
'Come on Mike, will you join me outside while I have a cigar?'

‘Sure,’ said Mike, as the two men excused themselves from the table and went out to the restaurant’s outdoor smoking area.
‘I know they’ve got a smoking ban in California,’ said Joe, ‘but I guess where I’m living we’ll have to get used to smoking areas like this pretty soon.’
‘Yeah,’ said Mike, ‘they’re a fact of life here now.’
The two men chatted for a while, while Joe enjoyed his cigar, and after a while the conversation turned to the rest of the Ellises’ holiday.
‘You’ll enjoy Galway,’ said Mike, with a certain knowing authority.
‘Oh, yeah, I’m looking forward to it,’ said Joe, ‘but I have to tell you, there’s another reason why we’re going there. You see, Lorraine is adopted, and a couple of months back – in fact it started when she visited Cork on the Sammy B. – she made contact with a couple of adoption agencies, and ended up with a birth certificate from the Northern Ireland adoption board, which showed that, in fact, her mother was from Galway. She doesn’t really have any other details. To be honest, she doesn’t even know if her natural mother is still alive, but she wants to go there and see what she can find out.’

On hearing this, Mike felt his blood run cold. In the following seconds, he tried desperately to collect himself in the best way he could, as he wrestled with the possible reality now swirling around in his mind. He was saved somewhat by Cas appearing at the door, calling the two men to come back to the table as they were waiting to order dessert and coffee. On the way in, Mike excused himself on the pretext of going to the men’s room – he just needed a few minutes by himself to work out whether or not he was going mad.
He reflected on all the facts, the familiarity of Lorraine Ellis when she came aboard *Eithne*, certain mannerisms that now seemed to make a little more sense. And now seeing Lorraine and Emma side by side, it was just uncanny. Could it be? He couldn’t say for certain, but one thing he knew had stood to him through out his life thus far was his gut instinct. And Mike Ford trusted that more than anything. How was he going to handle this? He took another minute to shape his thoughts and then calmly returned to the table.

When the whole party returned to the Ford's house, the women had just one night cap before retiring to bed. When they did, Mike and Joe sat in front of the fire with a few cans, and eventually Mike knew that he had to ask the critical question.
'Joe,' he said, 'I have to ask you something. 'What is Lorraine's date of birth?'
'Oh,' said Joe, laughing, 'that's an easy one. It's the 14th of October, 1977.'
Mike Ford's logical, cool and calm persona simply deserted him in that moment. He felt like something had struck him on his chest, such was the intensity of the realisation that now hit him. He couldn't help it, tears just flowed from his eyes.
Even Joe Ellis, who had a few drinks taken, couldn't help noticing what was happening to the man in front of him.
'Jees, Mike, are you okay?'
Mike couldn't talk for a few moments, and Joe began to worry that maybe he had had a heart attack or something like that.
'What's wrong, Mike, should I call Cas?'
'No, no,' replied Mike, 'just give me a moment and I'll explain.'

Joe sat patiently waiting for Mike to collect himself again. He couldn't even begin to figure out what had happened to his host, but at the same time he was really waiting to be reassured that it wasn't a heart attack.

'Joe,' said Mike, 'I've had a really bad shock now, and I'm going to tell you about it, but I would like to just warn you in advance, that when you hear it, you may be equally shocked.'
'Jesus Christ Mike, what in the hell is it?'
'Well, Joe, I'll just cut to the chase. Back in 1977, Cas and I gave up a child for adoption, and Cas is actually from Galway.' He then paused a little to let the realisation slowly sink into Joe, before he continued.
'Oh, I get it now,' interrupted Joe. 'Me telling you about Lorraine has brought back all those memories, especially seeing as Cas is from Galway also.'

'No, Joe,' replied Mike, looking straight into Joe's eyes, 'you haven't got it yet.'
'What do you mean?' asked Joe.
'What I mean, Joe, is, I think that Cas and I are in fact Lorraine's natural parents.'
'But ... but ... ' struggled Joe, 'how do you know this for certain?'
'That's very simple,' said Mike. 'Our baby girl was born on the 14th of October 1977, and Cas is from Galway.'
'Okay,' said Joe, 'but Galway is a big place.'
'Have you seen the birth cert that Lorraine got?' asked Mike.
'Yeah,' said Joe, 'the mother's name is Catherine O'Donoghue, but it doesn't say what part of Galway she's from.'

'Hang on a minute,' said Mike, getting up from the sofa, and opening a drawer in a built-in alcove unit. 'Here, Joe, this is Lorraine's birth cert which we've kept all these years. It's the only precious memento that we have of her. He passed the piece of paper into Joe's hand.
'Oh, Jesus Christ,' Joe exclaimed as his eyes scanned the birth certificate. 'I don't believe it ... Catherine O'Donoghue ... and yes, oh dear God, we did actually change her name from Marian to Lorraine.'

There was a stunned silence as both men came to terms with this revelation. Joe was the first to speak.
'This ... this is unbelievable, Mike. I almost don't believe it's happening, yet it is, it really is, isn't it? The question is, what are we going to do?
The two men seemed then to observe a respectful silence as the enormity of the situation weaved its way right into their souls. Both men's feelings were given space in this sacred stillness.

The naval officer in Mike tried desperately to take over, in an effort to bring some kind of order to the situation, but failed miserably. Instead, images just flooded into his mind, of the day he met Cas at Plymouth airport in 1977 and she told him that she was pregnant, the day the baby was born, the short few days that Cas had with her, the heart wrenching day she handed the child to the adoption facilitator, and most of all, the cruel irony of their joy-filled wedding day, both secretly knowing that ultimately their baby could perhaps have stayed with them. The tears then flowed from Mike again as he realised that fate, which had dealt both of them a cruel hand in 1977, had once again presented itself, but this time … 'My God, who knows,' he thought to himself, 'and Joe and Marian, they have so obviously been a wonderful Mom and Dad to Lorraine.'

Joe, on the other hand, found himself experiencing a tiny sense of threat. And what about Marian? How would she feel about this? Their precious only child, who they had always supported in her efforts to find out about her natural parents … But now, being face to face with that reality, the rational side of Joe soon began to take over; he looked across at the other man in the armchair and in that moment saw and understood the wretched pain he was experiencing. He too was a father, and a good father at that, Joe thought to himself, he had only known him for a day or so, yet had come to really like and respect him.
'Mike, would you like to tell me what happened all those years ago?' Joe asked.
In a strange way, a catharsis enveloped Mike as he began to briefly recount the events in 1977, in particular the circumstances and the culture that prevailed at that time around children born outside of marriage. Joe nodded in recognition with a lot of what Mike said, recalling a similar culture where he grew up in Belfast.
The two men talked into the night, with Joe telling Mike what Lorraine was like growing up, filling him in as best he could with details of her life in school and college and also, to Mike's eager ears, her seemingly great love of all things naval. Mike almost couldn't hide an embodied sense of real pride as Joe gave him a brief history of her naval career so far, from Annapolis to the USS *Samuel B. Roberts*.
All the while, they were blissfully unaware of the three women sleeping peacefully upstairs, and the ferocious emotional punch that this new reality was going to present for them.
At 3.30 in the morning, Mike was first to click back into the reality of what lay ahead.
'Joe,' he said, 'you asked earlier on what are we going to do?'

‘Oh, God,’ said Joe, ‘I had almost forgotten about that. How are we ever going to be able to tell them? And in saying that,’ he continued, ‘I know that we have to.’
‘What we need here, Joe, is a plan, a plan that will work,’ said Mike, now reverting back to his more normal naval officer ‘can do’ mode. ‘Emotions here are going to be all over the place,’ he continued, ‘but in the scale of things, the person who I believe needs the most protection is Lorraine. Whatever way we go, we will have to be very sensitive around her. So, what I’m suggesting is that we get Marian and Cas into the decision making process as soon as possible; women are better at working out emotional things anyway.’
‘Yeah,’ said Joe, ‘but how are we going to do that? The three of us have planned to drive to Galway at nine in the morning, Lorraine is anxious to get up there.’
‘Hmmm,’ mused Mike, ‘that could be helpful. Joe, what do you think of this plan? Okay, it goes like this. You and I have been talking and I was telling you about the fabulous new workshops that have been built down in the naval base. You’ve said to me that it’s a pity that you are going so early because you’d love to see them. Then I suggest to you to leave Lorraine drive on up to Galway herself at nine o’clock and, anyway, there are buses from Cork to Galway every hour, which you and Marian could catch later. That will give us a chance to tell the women on our own. Do you think Lorraine will go with that?’

‘That’s sounds good. Mike. To be honest, I think that it’s probably the only way of going about it. Lorraine knows how much I like workshops, and I think that she’d understand.’

The two men then went to bed to try and grasp the short few hours of sleep that were available before they had to get up.
Lorraine Ellis laughed when she saw her Dad walk into the kitchen, followed a minute or two later by Mike.
‘Dad,’ she laughed in mock reproach, ‘look at the state of you. Were you drunk last night? You look like you didn’t get to bed at all!’

When Mike then walked in, she continued: 'Good morning, sir, it looks like my Dad has been leading you astray.'
Mike smiled, knowing exactly what she meant, but nevertheless protested his and indeed Joe's absolute innocence.
'Yeah right,' said Lorraine.
Marian, who had been listening to the conversation, then spoke.
'Lorraine, these two boys here have made a plan.'
'Oh,' said Lorraine.
Marian then continued. 'Well honey, it seems like your Dad heard about the new workshops in the naval base, and he's wondering if you would like to head on up to Galway yourself in the car, and he and I will follow on later on the bus; apparently they go every hour. I've packed our suitcases and put them in the car already. All we will need is our jackets, and anyway, Cas tells me that the Victoria hotel where we are staying in Galway is only about two minutes from the bus station, so you won't have to worry about picking us up.
'Okay, that sounds like a good plan,' said Lorraine, much to the huge hidden relief of Joe and Mike.

Half an hour later, the only people left in the house were Mike and Cas, and Joe and Marian.
'How long are ye going to be down in the base?' asked Cas. 'Me and Marian could go to town and look in a few shops.'
Joe looked very perplexed, which Marian put down to 'the morning after the night before'.
'Honey, we need to talk,' said Joe, as his two slightly red eyes looked up at Marian.
Cas was a little taken aback by Joe's remark, but Mike followed up straight away.
'The truth is,' he said, 'the four of us need to talk.'
Joe looked at the two women.
'Me and Mike did a lot of talking last night, and some things came up that the four of us need to talk about.'
Marian then interjected.
'Mmmm, does this have something to do with Lorraine?'

'Yes,' said Joe, 'in fact it has.'
Both women sat down at the kitchen table with a much heightened sense of interest, and Joe then continued.
'I think that it would be better if Mike told the story from the start, purely and simply because he was the first to become aware of it, and I guess I wouldn't have known it without him either.'
'Is this something bad?' asked Cas.
'Well no, it's not,' said Mike, awkwardly. 'On the contrary, it's probably something very good.'
And on that note he continued. He firstly recalled the time when Lorraine had landed on *Eithne*'s flight deck and was brought up to the ops room to meet him. He remembered noticing a familiarity about her that he couldn't quite explain. Mike then moved on to the time when Cas had come aboard in Galway followed by Emma with her new hair style. He then slowly and painstakingly recounted the rest of the story, up to and including Joe telling him out in the smoking area the previous evening that they had in fact adopted Lorraine, and that she was going to Galway where she knew her birth mother was from.
As the story continued, Catherine Ford's mind was experiencing multiple levels of shock and, in the end, she couldn't' take it any more. She put her hand up and asked Marian if there was any significance about Lorraine's upper thighs.
'Well, yes,' replied Marian, 'she has a small brown birth mark on the front of her left thigh.'
At that moment, Cas pushed back from the table and, tightly holding her hands across her chest, let out a scream that was primal in its intensity. Mike immediately leapt up and, folding his arms around her, held her as tightly as he could. Cas was now sobbing uncontrollably as twenty-eight years of withheld pain and heartache found release.
In the meantime, Marian was sitting there in a state of absolute shock, but still not knowing what was happening. She looked imploringly at her husband for an answer. Joe spoke gently.
'Honey, Mike and Cas, believe it or not, are Lorraine's natural parents.'
Marian's hands immediately flew to her mouth and, in abject shock, she tried but couldn't speak. She felt rooted to the spot. Joe then put his arms

around her, and gently guided her out of the kitchen and down the hall to the living room, which to him seemed the right thing to do. Both couples now had a chance to slowly take in the massively intrinsic nature of the new reality.

Half an hour later, Mike hesitantly opened the living room door and awkwardly asked the Ellises how they were now feeling. Marian immediately rushed towards him and hugged him tightly. 'God bless you, Mike. Is it okay if I go to Cas?, to which he nodded his head.
Marian didn't have to go far as, at that moment, Cas walked into the room and the two women embraced for what seemed like an eternity, while the two men exchanged glances that needed no words.

Victoria Hotel, Galway. Saturday

The bus arrived into Galway bus station, at the corner of Eyre Square, at 6.30 that evening. Joe and Marian covered the short two minute walk from the station to the Victoria hotel with a feeling of trepidation. Despite all of their discussions on the journey up to Galway, they couldn't anticipate their daughter's reaction to the news.
When they arrived they found that Lorraine had already checked in and had asked the hotel to reserve the room next door for her parents. When they entered the room, they found their luggage waiting for them.
'Oh, that's nice,' said Marian, when she saw the suitcases already in the room. 'I guess there's no time like the present, Joe, what do you think?'
'You're right,' Joe replied, 'now is now.'
Marian put on the small kettle in the room to make some coffee, while Joe rang his daughter's room to call her in. A minute later, Lorraine arrived into the room, and immediately her parents could see an excitement in her eyes.
'Mom, Dad, how was the trip up on the bus?'
'Good, good, very good,' they replied.
'Guess what,' Lorraine said rather excitedly, 'you just wouldn't believe the number of O'Donoghues there are in Galway. 'I'm now certain that I will be able to find somebody who knew my mother.'

Joe and Marian listened with empathy until Lorraine's flow of conversation came to a natural stop. Joe then calmly invited his daughter to sit down, which she did, looking at him questioningly.
'Lorraine, Mom and I have something important to tell you.'
Lorraine's heart immediately skipped a beat as she sensed, from the look on their faces, that there was something wrong.
Marian continued gently. 'It's about your search for your mother … '
Lorraine Ellis's face dropped, her eyes looking at the floor.
'She's dead, isn't she?'
Marian then slowly said: 'No, Lorraine, she's very much alive.'
Lorraine's eyes at once lit up. 'Tell me, how do you know?' she asked nervously.
'Your mother is alive and well, as is your father, your sister and your two brothers.'
Lorraine became incredulous,
'But … but … how do you know all this? I don't understand, how have you got this information?'
In as lovingly a way as they possibly could, Joe and Marian slowly and precisely outlined the sequence of events which brought them to this extraordinary piece of knowledge. Lorraine was now dumbfounded. Then Joe opened his wallet, took out a birth certificate, which was a copy of the one that Mike had shown him the previous evening, and handed it to her.

Catherine Ford woke early. She couldn't sleep, her eyes were hurting from the constant flow of tears, which she thought would never end. The wound was indeed raw and primal. She was hurting so much that she actually felt a physical pain in her chest. Alongside her, Mike was still asleep, even though it was 9.30 in the morning. Shortly afterwards, despite herself, she drifted off into a deep exhausted sleep.
At 10.15 the phone rang in the bedroom, harshly rousing her from her sleep. Mike stirred next to her, as he heard it too.
She slowly picked up the receiver as she struggled to wake fully. 'Hello.'
The first thing Cas heard at the other end of the line was Lorraine Ellis crying.